MONARCH

MANOR

By Maureen Leurck

Monarch Manor

Cicada Summer

Published by Kensington Publishing Corporation

MONARCH MANOR

MAUREEN LEURCK

KENSINGTON BOOKS
www.kensingtonbooks.com

KENSINGTON BOOKS are published by

Kensington Publishing Corp.
119 West 40th Street
New York, NY 10018

All Kensington titles, imprints, and distributed lines are available at special quantity discounts for bulk purchases for sales promotion, premiums, fund-raising, educational, or institutional use.

Special book excerpts or customized printings can also be created to fit specific needs. For details, write or phone the office of the Kensington Sales Manager: Kensington Publishing Corp., 119 West 40th Street, New York, NY 10018. Attn. Sales Department. Phone: 1-800-221-2647.

Kensington and the K logo Reg. U.S. Pat. & TM Off.

ISBN-13: 978-1-4967-1979-9 (ebook)
ISBN-10: 1-4967-1979-4 (ebook)
Kensington Electronic Edition: August 2019

ISBN-13: 978-1-4967-1978-2
ISBN-10: 1-4967-1978-6
First Kensington Trade Paperback Printing: August 2019

10 9 8 7 6 5 4 3 2 1

Printed in the United States of America

For Kevin and the kids

CHAPTER 1

AMELIA

May 28, 1923

Amelia felt complete when she was at Monarch Manor. She loved the butterflies that found sanctuary in the gardens, the veranda that protected the soft swish of the white wicker rocking chairs, and the summer cicadas that lulled her to sleep each night. But most of all, she loved that the estate rested on the shores of Geneva Lake. The water was a sparkling, magical beauty that pulled her near, and begged her to jump in.

Yet that night it was much colder, and darker, than ever before.

The black water swirled around her as she hit the surface. Her head went under first, followed by the rest of her body and her satin shoes. Her body had braced itself as she had gone over the edge of her father's steam yacht, the *Monarch Princesses*, but she still felt the shock of hitting the surface. She quickly brought her head above the water, gasped, and screamed.

"John! John!" She frantically splashed around, doing a furious twist and spin as she treaded water, her light pink satin shoes falling off and disappearing, far below the surface. Rain fell all around her, roughing up the surface of the lake, making it harder to see with the darkness of the night sky.

"Help!" she called again for her five-year-old son, even though she knew he couldn't hear her. Her eyes scanned the surface of the water for any sign of his blond hair.

She twisted around toward where the steam yacht still floated, and heard the distant shouts of the captain and guests still on board. The boat was strung with tiny white lights that glowed like fireflies against the water. A crack of lightning crossed the sky like a crooked branch from one of the maple trees that lined the shore, and the rain began to fall harder.

And still, no sign of her son.

In the distance, on the other side of the water, she could see Monarch Manor, lit up like one of the Chinese lanterns they had released into the air from the edge of the estate. The lanterns floated up into the cloudless blue sky as the wedding guests made silly wishes fueled by champagne, raspberry petit fours, and brandy.

"For a never-ending barrel of ale and for the Chicago Cubs to win the World Championship series once again," Randall Whittingham had said as he puffed on a cigar, which led to a chorus of laughter from the guests, dressed in their finest furs and dresses, and the most handsome tuxedoes.

"For the bride and groom to be blessed for many years," Amelia had said when it was her turn to release her lantern. She looked back and gave her sister Jane and her new husband, Edward, a warm smile. They lifted their champagne glasses in thanks, and the guests had collectively sighed.

Of course, Amelia said her own silent wish—the real wish that lay in her heart, the wish that she couldn't share with anyone. A prayer, really, more than a wish.

Please. Please let John be safe. Tonight and forever.

And from the dark water, she could see that the party still continued. The refreshment tent was decorated with twinkle lights and oak branches that wound around the support poles, providing cover to the guests below as they sipped their cocktails. A trail of lights connected the tent to the ice-cream station, where a white-gloved waiter handed out miniature sundaes in dishes shaped like her father's beloved yacht.

"John . . . John!" she weakly called into the night. All of her senses were both heightened and dulled at the same time—she could hear nothing in her ears but the rush of her own blood, but she knew if she so much as heard a whimper from him a mile away she would detect it. Her vision became a blurred sense of fairy lights peppered by the flashes of lightning, and she could smell the steam from the yacht nearby.

It grew farther and farther away from where she thrashed on the surface as the captain unsuccessfully tried to turn such a large boat around in such a short time.

She watched Monarch Manor and the yacht grow farther away as the waves pushed her toward the center of the lake, where the deepest water lay: The Narrows. Her arms burned from the effort of keeping herself above the water. The beading and crystals on the dress, hand-sewn in by her mother's seamstress in Chicago, were like tiny anchors, pulling her down toward the bottom of the black water.

She called out John's name one more time, as the clouds opened up and rain fell in dark sheets, obscuring the view of her childhood home.

CHAPTER 2

ERIN

Present Day

I never really thought about the things that people leave behind when they die. And by *things* I don't mean people or treasured family heirlooms, but the small pieces that inhabit junk drawers, like souvenir coins and old refrigerator magnets. We know those things are worthless, yet we can't seem to throw them away, so they get stashed away in a domestic purgatory, stuck somewhere in between trash and treasure. There they stay until it becomes someone else's duty to decide what we should let go.

I was never more keenly aware of this small piece of human nature than on the warm October morning when I slid a silver key into the door of my grandmother's house in Powers Lake, Wisconsin, and surveyed the enormous amount of stuff inside. Even from the front porch, I could see that she hadn't thrown away anything in the years before she died.

I took a small step inside, narrowly avoiding a six-foot-tall metal knight standing at attention in the foyer. I remember once when I visited her as a child I had asked her where she had gotten it, as I didn't imagine they were for sale at the nearby

Tobin Drugs. She had smiled and whispered, "Garage sale." Of course, at eight years old, I hadn't thought to ask *why.*

"Why, oh, why," I muttered under my breath as I slowly turned around, my eyes widening at the three china cabinets filled with porcelain figurines in the living room, and the jungle of dusty plastic plants decorating every corner of the dining room.

In the coat closet, I found boxes stacked end to end. I gingerly peeled back the flaps of the closest cardboard box, and the top nearly crumbled in my hands. Inside was a pile of wire hangers, haphazardly stacked on top of one another, knotting into a small metal sculpture that would certainly never be dismantled.

"Well, looks like I have my work cut out for me," I muttered as I fanned my face with my hand, to no avail. Even though it was autumn and the Midwest weather had already begun to listen to the whispers of winter in the early-morning hour, the warm air in the house hung motionless and stale.

I was about to pick up the box of Joan Crawford's favorite things and begin a pile for trash when I heard my mother's voice boom across the front yard.

"Erin, my love! Where the hell are you?" My mom, Mary Ellen, trudged into the house, her black boots marching across the linoleum floor with a satisfying *click clack* with every footstep. She wore ripped blue jeans, a black T-shirt, and a black leather jacket. Under her arm she carried her motorcycle helmet. She turned to close the front door and jumped when she saw the knight.

"Every time. Every. Time," she said with a sigh. She looked up at the ceiling. "Mom, I know you're laughing right now." She rolled her eyes before she walked over and gave me a tight hug.

I closed my eyes and inhaled the familiar scent of her earthy leather jacket mixed with the sweetness of her Marilyn Miglin perfume, a combination that could not have been more quintes-

sentially my mother. I had seen her at my grandmother's funeral two weeks prior, although it felt like longer. Right before
she turned eighty, my grandmother had died peacefully in her
sleep, her hair still in curlers and her housecoat hung on the
bedpost.

"Ready to work?" I said as I swept my hand around. "Grandma
definitely didn't slow down her 'collections' at any point." I hadn't
been in her house for a few years, as she preferred to visit us at our
house, ninety minutes south in Illinois. I think she was worried
my twins would break something. Which, given even the most
cursory glance around the house, was a likely scenario.

"Well, let's stop screwing around and get to it, huh?" My
mother's Wisconsin roots showed in every vowel pronuncia-
tion, and I fought back my usual urge to tease her about it.

We looked at each other and shrugged before I headed toward the coat closet and my mother went into the living room
to start tackling the cabinets stuffed with Precious Moments
figurines.

"I don't think this is what the estate sale company meant by
'valuable items,'" I said as I opened up a box of pens and a half-
used pad of paper. I flipped through the filled pages. "Apparently, Grandma was very meticulous about saving her grocery
lists." I closed the box and slid it into the hallway, into the ever-
growing pile of boxes marked *Trash*.

"Listen, hon: Just keep going. As I told you yesterday, we
need to get through everything, as hard as it might be." Her lined
face softened for a moment as she surveyed her childhood home,
but she shook her head and turned her attention back to the
porcelain figures. "Man, she never really collected this stuff
until after I moved out. And for that I'm glad. I can't imagine
growing up in a house with this many . . . eyes." She frowned at
a figure of a child holding binoculars.

"For sure. Although I shouldn't talk. I have boxes and boxes
in my basement filled with random junk, too," I said. "I'm sure
Katie will be so sad she's missing all of this." My younger sister,

Katie, had moved to New York the year before, to take a job in public relations for a major media outlet. Which meant she escaped family responsibilities exactly like this one. Unmarried, no kids—and no desire for any of the above—her life could not have been more different from mine. Even the finality of a mortgage terrified her, let alone the milestones of suburbs, school, house, twins, husband, and car payments that seemed to dominate my world.

I carefully spun around like I was a caterpillar building a cozy cocoon, unsure of what to go through next, when a chest in the corner of the dining room caught my eye. It sat under a secretary desk covered in antique eyeglasses. The metal and leather box had a healthy layer of dust on top and was guarded by a metal hinge worthy of a tetanus shot. "Open sesame," I said. Gingerly, I lifted the rusty latch up and opened the chest, praying that a family of mice hadn't somehow found a way to make it their home.

I exhaled when I saw it was empty except for a yellowed envelope full of black-and-white photos on the very bottom. I was about to pull the pictures out of the envelope when my phone's alarm went off.

"Shoot," I said as I saw the time. We had been there for over four hours, and I was due to relieve my mother-in-law, who was watching my twins after school. "I need to run," I said to my mom as I shoved the envelope under my arm. She tossed the box of old cable bills into the trash pile and we walked out on the front porch to lock the door.

"How are my favorite kiddos?" my mom said as she kicked a leg over her Harley in the driveway.

"Great. Same. Crazy," I said as I put my sunglasses on. "You should come and visit soon. They would love to see you."

She nodded. "I would love to. After we get this place ready for sale." She gave one last glance toward the house, a white ranch with black shutters and peeling paint on the siding, before she revved her engine and turned north toward East Troy, thirty minutes north in Wisconsin. She and my father had moved back to Wisconsin three years before, after my mom retired from her position as a history professor at Loyola University in Chicago, citing the need for open roads for her bike and a desire to stoke her passion for ice fishing.

I waved good-bye, and it was then that I realized I still had the envelope of black-and-white photographs in my possession. "Guess you're going on a road trip," I said as I tossed them into my passenger seat and pulled my car onto the highway for the ninety-minute trip home.

"Did you get cheese pizza, Daddy?" Charlotte asked. She followed my husband, Luke, into the kitchen, skipping behind him with her blond braids bobbing up and down like Pippi Longstocking.

"You know it," I heard Luke say from the kitchen. "Erin," he called, "bring Will in here!"

I stood in the foyer and saw Will staring out the front door at the pizza delivery guy getting back into his car. I knelt down next to Will and rubbed his back. He was getting so tall but still seemed so fragile. "Do you want some pizza, Buster Brown?" I had called him that nickname since the day he was born, five years ago. We had planned on naming him Ryan, but the instant I saw him I knew his name was Will. I always said that he chose his name, not me. Good thing he chose one we loved.

Will didn't turn to look at me. His eyes stared blankly out the window, his mind retreating to some small corner of his existence like a mouse hiding in a wall. "Do you want pizza—yes or no?" I firmly patted his back, trying to bring him back. Concrete questions were always better than open-ended ones.

He slowly turned toward me, his multicolored eyes looking through me like I was nothing but a window in between him and the wall. His sister had eyes that were a light cornflower blue, but Will's eyes changed nearly every year—sometimes gray, sometimes brown, occasionally green. His mouth twisted to the side as he lifted his fist and made the sign for "yes," while softly humming.

I smiled and grabbed his hand and led him into the tiny kitchen of our one-hundred-year-old house. Luke and I had bought the house four years earlier, when the twins were barely walking. He wasn't sure about the uneven floors or the scary basement that had a concrete floor and a plethora of wolf spiders, but I instantly fell in love with it. I loved that the wooden baseboards were wider than anything you would see in a McMansion, that the closet under the stairs was only about five feet tall, and that the moldings in the family room were hand-carved. Yet most of all, I loved the large trees that surrounded the house—nothing like the wimpy juvenile trees planted around the teardowns that peppered the neighborhood. It was small, but it was perfect. "Like our family," I remember cheerfully saying at the closing as Luke half-rolled his eyes. My assumptions at the time were that if we had a beautiful home only easy, perfect things would happen there.

In the kitchen, Charlotte was already pawing at a slice of cheese pizza. I led Will to a seat next to her, and Luke put a slice of pizza in front of him.

Will looked at the pizza and screeched in delight, clapping wildly. I meticulously cut it into tiny bites and put a fork in his hand. He threw it on the floor and started to scream, fists flying in the air in frustration. Charlotte expertly leaned away to avoid being hit as she took another bite of pizza, a sauce ring forming around her mouth.

I placed my hands over his and firmly asked, "What's wrong? Are you thirsty? Do you want water?" He warbled, and I turned toward the fridge, silently admonishing myself for not making him look at me and request the drink via a sign or gesture. *Next time,* I promised myself.

I filled Will's sippy cup with water and placed it next to Charlotte's glass and he stopped screaming. Both kids silent, I absentmindedly twirled Charlotte's braids around my finger, my mental to-do list growing exponentially longer. Besides all of the preparation for the afternoons I would be gone as I helped my mother in Powers Lake, I still had several hours of research into therapies ahead of me after the twins went to bed. Kindergarten in our district was only a half-day program, with the two and a half hours eaten up by a variety of basic needs and tasks, so anything extra, especially anything that required concentration or silence, had to be done at night.

"Mommy, stop. That's irritating," Charlotte said, and swatted my hand away.

I released her hair and smiled, wondering where she picked up that word. It seemed like every day she learned something new—a new name, a new word, a new fact about the world. It all came so easily to her, and all we had to do was try to keep up.

"So, how was the house?" Luke leaned against the kitchen counter and poured himself a beer.

"Stuffed to the gills, as expected," I said as I blotted my pizza slice with a napkin. Out of the corner of my eye I watched Will examine each piece of food, expecting him to find a flaw and refuse to eat—again—as Charlotte began to sing a song about the black spots on ladybugs.

"At least it's quiet." He put an arm around my shoulders and squeezed as his eyes flickered to the twins.

I laughed and leaned against his chest, enjoying a brief moment of safe respite. "There's that, at least."

"Think you'll find anything valuable hidden away in some closet?" he said as he released me and I relaxed back on the countertop.

"Like earplugs?" I smiled as Charlotte's song grew louder before Will screeched at her in annoyance and she stopped.

"Exactly. Hopefully a pair for me, too," he said. "Seriously, though, I'm glad you're getting a break. When's the last time you had some time to yourself?" he said.

I glanced at the twins, Charlotte separating her pizza into

piles of dough and cheese, and Will flapping his hands, and smiled. "Five years, I'd guess." Although it was likely longer than that. My pregnancy with the twins was difficult, dotted with bed rest and three solid months of contractions before I finally had them. Then, there was the difficult task of caring for two newborns who never slept at the same time. And finally, chasing after two toddlers who always seemed to run in opposite directions.

And all of that was before we found out about Will.

Done flapping, he picked up his plate and smashed it on the floor.

It was just another plate, another material thing we could easily replace, but as I swept up the jagged pieces and cut my finger, it seemed to hurt everywhere.

Luke was already in bed when I walked into the bedroom. He had on his dark-brown-rimmed glasses that reminded me of Clark Kent. He didn't look up from his phone as I collapsed next to him. His thick black hair had fallen across his forehead as he peered down at the screen. "Think you'll sleep at all tonight?" he asked.

I laughed as I surveyed the clean laundry still haphazardly thrown on the bed in crumpled piles. "Not likely."

He took off his glasses and stared at the rumpled clothing. "Look, my mom can help with all that. And I'll say it again: You should just stay up there in Wisconsin. Find a hotel. Have a real break."

I gave him a small smile and shook my head. "You know I won't do that."

Luke crossed his arms over his ratty college T-shirt with *Crowd Control* on the front—a leftover from his bouncer days in college. He was over a foot taller than me and broad chested, so the shirt had been a perfect fit when I was pregnant with the twins. I don't think he ever forgave me for accidentally washing it with a pair of pink socks, though, as the shirt now had a faint rose color. "Rosé all day," I had laughed the week before as he rolled his eyes.

"Someone else can take care of the twins for a few days. Really," he said.

I picked up an old hoodie, a leftover from my bachelorette party ten years ago with *Mrs. Marinelli* bedazzled on the back. The previous week, Charlotte had found it buried in a drawer and worn it around the house like a cape. I shoved the hoodie and the rest of the laundry off the bed. "Nope. I can't leave Will for that long."

"Okay, fine." Luke closed his eyes, while I grabbed my laptop and propped myself up in bed, notebook full of therapy and treatment notes at my elbow. I sighed and began to click through the layers of Web sites I had bookmarked the night before. Every night, after the twins were finally asleep, I stayed up late to research different therapies and interventions for Will, sorting through all the information in the hope of finding some breakthrough that would propel his life into a new, easier chapter. One where he could finally tell us what he wanted, without the frustration of signs and gestures. One where the world wasn't so terrifying and painful for him.

One where he could play, make friends. Sleep through the night. Stop wearing a diaper.

Find peace.

This routine had gone on for three years. When the twins were two, we had a gnawing suspicion that Will wasn't developing like his sister. Charlotte wasn't just precocious or an early talker, as we first reasoned. No, she was typical . . . and it became clearer with each passing milestone that Charlotte reached and Will missed that something was wrong.

When he was two and a half years old, we took him to a local developmental pediatrician, Dr. Dorner, a kindly old man who reminded me of my next-door neighbor growing up. He looked at us—I'll never forget the look in his eyes: a mixture of resignation and defeat—and said the word we were so afraid to hear: *autism.*

It was just a word, and not even a four-letter one. Yet it went off like a bomb that scattered dust into every corner of our lives, forever separating our family into Before and After.

At first, I thought of the quirky kids who go on to work for NASA or who find some new mathematical theory. Yet it was imminently clear that wasn't Will's variety of autism. *Severe,* is what the official diagnosis report from Dr. Dorner said, *impacting all skills and quality of life. He will need intensive therapy and intervention.*

So each night I devoted hours that should have been spent sleeping to finding ways to help him. And it was not a fruitless task. Each night, I found another story of a child who had this therapy or that intervention, one the parents might never have thought to try if it weren't for Internet research, and now their child was indistinguishable from their peers. There was hope; there had to be—others had climbed the autism Mount Everest and come down on the other side.

This will be us, I always thought as I read of a formerly nonverbal child giving a speech to their class or of a kid moving from a self-contained special education classroom to mainstream, without an aide. I even read about children who lost their autism diagnosis completely due to early intervention. There was a holy grail out there, as so many other parents said, and I just needed to find it. *I will find it. I will find a way to help him,* I so often told myself, as I pictured finally hearing his voice or watching him put on his shoes.

Hours later, after I read about a few more therapies (hippotherapy, tae kwon do) and sometime long after Luke started snoring, I turned off the light and fell asleep.

I dreamed of my grandmother's house. It was a memory more than a dream, from when I was around eight years old. I had asked her why she kept so many things in her house. She had smiled and placed her hands over mine, her fingernails painted her signature coral, and said, "Because it might be junk to someone else, but I love every piece, no matter how strange, and that's what makes it important. What matters to you, what you care about, what you surround yourself with, is beautiful, even if no one else sees it. That's what makes a house you. That's what makes it your home."

CHAPTER 3

AMELIA

"Wake up, wake up, my sweet boy." Amelia bent down and kissed her son John's flushed face as he slept in his bed. His long, dark eyelashes brushed against his cheeks as he stayed asleep, his lips parting in a contented sigh. In his hand he clutched his worn wooden toy horse, an ever-present nighttime companion.

She smoothed his hair off his forehead, and he turned over in protest. He was only five years old, yet already knew exactly what he did or didn't want. And sleeping through the morning was one thing he always wanted.

She laughed and moved across his expansive room, making her way over the carpeting that her mother had purchased in London during one of her many shopping trips abroad, and threw open the heavy curtains that hung on the enormous window that overlooked Geneva Lake. Light flooded into the room, beams illuminating the rocking horse in the corner that he still loved to sit on, and the trucks scattered everywhere that the maids hadn't picked up after she had waved them away the night before. They had looked at her in surprise, and even more so when she said she would be staying in John's room with him, instead of at the other end of the house away from the children's quarters.

Yet she couldn't be away from him, not today. Especially not today. There were too many dangers, too many people watching.

Her pulse quickened as she looked out the window, across the lawn, and down to the lake, where the outside was already abuzz with activity, like the monarch butterflies who quickly moved from flower to flower in the Hoppes' expansive garden. White tables were set up on the grass, workers in pristine blue uniforms were carrying stacks of chairs back and forth, and the gardeners were busy stringing twinkle lights across all the surrounding bushes.

Her sister Jane and her mother, Mary, were in the middle of the chaos, barking orders at the workers and throwing up their hands. Even from a distance, she could see that Jane was already crying, and she made a mental note to congratulate Alfred, the cook. She had said that Jane would hold out until at least lunchtime to get hysterical, but apparently he knew better. From the moment that Jane was engaged, she had decided that the wedding—of course—would be at their summer home, Monarch Manor. It was the best way to show off to society and to pretend to be the wealthiest of her friends.

Amelia forced herself to look at the steam yacht docked at the end of the piers. The deckhands scrubbed it with long brooms and soapy water that ran into the lake. The *Monarch Princesses,* named after her and her sisters, proudly bore flags bearing the monogram of Jane and Edward as the bar on deck was being stocked with the best champagne for the guests to sip as they arrived at the wedding after disembarking the train from Chicago.

From her vantage point, the yacht was proud, sturdy, unyielding. Yet she knew how unpredictable it could be. Servants were unloading the stack of presents, sent from all corners of the globe, from another steam yacht. Certainly, among those were gifts from Adare Village in Ireland, from Amelia's mother's relatives. Likely, their gifts would be the most humble. Her mother's relatives didn't have means, but they weren't poor, either.

Amelia's throat tightened as she thought of the green hills of Adare Village, a place she had visited before she was married. Her mother's relatives were so welcoming, so warm, with lined faces and cozy homes. They hugged her without hesitation, without any worry about social propriety. They were so different from what she had expected, from how she had been raised.

Her thoughts were interrupted as she heard John rustle in bed and turned. He sat up, rubbing his eyes and squinting at the sunlight.

He lazily signed, "Mother."

She walked over and held her arms out and let him collapse into her ugly white nightgown. She had accidentally packed it, and it had horrified the maids when they opened her chest. She kissed the top of his head and pulled him closer to her, enjoying the last few moments before they were sucked into the whirling dervish of the wedding day. Soon the overnight guests would arrive at the Hoppe estate—her other sister, Eleanor, and her family, cousins, aunt, uncles. And, of course, Amelia's late husband's family, the Cartwrights. They wouldn't miss a party even if they were in the sanitarium. All that food, champagne, and gossip . . . free.

She lifted John's chin toward her and signed, "Are you hungry?" She looked in his eyes, which were a deep blue, like the darkest part of the lake.

He stared at her with his thoughtful gaze, and at first she was worried she had signed the wrong question. Her sign language skills were good, although she often wished they could be perfect. She would give anything for her and John to communicate easily, rather than in clumsy hand gestures and makeshift phrases.

She wished that it could be easier for them. For him.

She signed, "Breakfast?" and his eyes lit up and he nodded,

scampering off the bed and running toward the door in his blue-and-white-striped pajamas that made him look like a serious old man, a fact that always made Amelia laugh. Her husband, Henry, had a pair that he wore almost every night before he died the year before, and dressing John in a replica made her strangely feel like he was close to them, at least at night. That maybe he was watching over them while they slept.

Amelia missed him more each day, his absence growing larger instead of smaller.

Oh, Henry. If only you were here. If only everything was different.

If only you could save us.

She followed John out of the room, and laughed as he scampered down the long wooden stairway with the intricately carved swirls and decorations. A maid jumped out of the way, her hand on her heart, before she frowned in his direction at the fingerprints now on the formerly pristine railing. He ran straight toward the kitchen, where Alfred waited for him, ready to cook any treat that he wanted. Alfred had prepared for John's arrival that weekend by collecting drawings of various foods, so John could point to what he wanted. When Alfred first showed Amelia what he had done, she couldn't stop the tears. He was the only one—hired help or family—who had thought to change anything to make it easier for them that weekend. He was one of the only people who knew just how difficult that day would be for her.

Amelia put on a silk robe, not bothering to dress up in a formal gown, as she knew her mother and sister would still be outside. Later, all the bridal attendants would don the pale pink bridesmaid dresses her sister had chosen and each pin a fur-trimmed pink hat into her hair.

Once again, the maid on the stairs jumped back, but this time it was from seeing a lady in her nightclothes walking around the house. She didn't think much of those things anymore, though. Due to her financial circumstance after Henry's death—after all the mistakes he had made right before he died—she had been forced to drastically reduce her own staff in her home in Chicago, living less like a society woman and more like a simple mother. The relief from the societal pressures was welcome, but everything else had shattered her heart until she wasn't sure what was left anymore.

As she walked toward the back wing of the house, she noticed the air still held a faint smell of cigar smoke. After dinner the night before, the men had retired to the billiard room as they always did, to drink, smoke cigars, and contemplate their good fortune. She walked through the porch-like passageway and finally took a long inhale of fresh air, before she pushed open the heavy dark oak door, where she found John on a large wooden chair, smiling and watching Alfred flip pancakes on the griddle.

"There she is!" he bellowed as she took a seat next to John. She leaned over and kissed him again, but he didn't budge, his eyes huge as he watched Alfred launch one pancake high into the air before it landed with a sizzle back on the pan. While that was cooking, he turned and pulled a carafe of pure maple syrup out of the butler's pantry and dish of butter out of the icebox.

The kitchen was a respite from the chaos happening in the service kitchen on the opposite side of the house, which was without a doubt bustling with platters of food and roasting meats in preparation for the reception that night. She could faintly hear the service elevator rumbling to life, carrying food supplies and crates from the docks up to the house.

"Pancakes for you as well?" Alfred said to Amelia without turning around.

"Of course," she said automatically. She tapped John on the shoulder and made the sign for pancakes. "Pancakes," she said out loud, and pointed to what Alfred was cooking.

He gave her a small nod of understanding, and warmth spread through her chest. Just two years before, a doctor had told Henry and her that there was no hope for John, that he could never learn to communicate, that they should find an institution for the deaf and dumb and have more, *better* children. She had thrown a medical textbook at his head on her way out of his office.

Alfred placed a pile of steaming pancakes in front of them and she dished two onto John's plate, carefully cutting up the pieces before drowning them in maple syrup. John picked up his fork and slowly chewed before a brilliant smile spread across his face and he looked from Alfred to his mother. He put his two index fingers together, signaling "more," and then pointed at the stack.

Amelia leaned over and tickled him in the ribs. "Silly boy. Finish what's on your plate first and then we'll decide if you get more," she signed. She watched as he slowly put another piece in his mouth, remembering when he couldn't feed himself, even at age three, due to what the doctors called hypotonia, which meant his muscles didn't know how to work properly on their own. But now, after all those hours spent with both of them crying, her showing him what to do with a fork and how to bring it to his mouth, he could do it.

She now dared anyone to suggest there were limits to what he could do. Especially Margaret, her mother-in-law.

"Not hungry this morning, madame?" Alfred said when Amelia didn't reach for her plate. He gave her a sympathetic look before his gaze went from her to John. She saw the questions in his eyes. All of the questions about their future and what would happen to them.

She had very few answers, and the ones she did have she could never share.

"Oh yes. Excuse me." She hurriedly put some pancakes on her plate, her mind snapping back to the present. "They're wonderful, as usual," she said in between bites.

Alfred nodded with pride and then looked out the small kitchen window and sighed. "If only all the guests tonight should be as grateful as you two."

Her heart leapt again as she thought of the party, of all the people milling about the lawn, asking questions, staring at her with sad, pitying eyes.

First her son is born deaf, and then her husband dies of tuberculosis. What a shame.

They would think those things and then go back to the party before the champagne made them forget their names and fall asleep. The next day, they would wake up with terrible headaches and then take the train back into the city to gossip about the wedding and what a fantastic party it was, but *did you see the horrid flower arrangements?*

As Alfred busied himself with pulling out linens and china for the pre-wedding afternoon tea, John and Amelia sat in silence. She reached down and grabbed his tiny hand, never wanting to let go.

The house around them vibrated with energy, but they were calm and safe in the tiny kitchen. She knew it was a moment she would remember forever. A time of peace. Peace that she knew would end soon.

CHAPTER 4

ERIN

The summer I turned fifteen, my parents took my sister, Katie, and me up to Powers Lake for a week-long visit with our grandmother. I'll never forget the moment of panic, and feelings of abandonment, as they drove away after what felt like an unceremonious drop-off on the front porch. From our teenage vantage point (Katie was thirteen), they nearly pushed us out of the car without stopping.

Katie and I shared a twin bed covered in an enormous crocheted doily and listened to our grandmother snore each night through the thin walls. She did let us eat Cocoa Krispies for breakfast each morning, and we spent every afternoon sunbathing on the green Astroturf-covered pier, listening to the pink boombox I had gotten for my birthday. We only moved to either flip the cassette tape over or momentarily jump into the lake to cool off.

After a long day at the lake, we would walk home on the gravel road, our sandals flipping and flopping as we tried to avoid any rocks sharp enough to poke through the rubber. Our grandmother would be waiting for us, wearing knit pants even in the summer heat, and make us dinner. She cooked things like sloppy joes and stuffed peppers—really, anything with ground beef and a sauce component. She seemed happy to have someone else to cook for on a regular basis, as our grandfather had died ten years before.

By the end of the week, when our parents came to pick us up, they were shocked when they had to peel us away from the pier and when we asked our mother to make us shepherd's pie for dinner.

Now I swallowed hard as I pulled up to my grandmother's house and thought of that visit and the way that everything then seemed beautiful and sparkling with excitement. About how it took so little to make us so happy and how it was so easy to feel carefree. It was a feeling I wasn't sure I could ever recapture. I was about to turn the car off and wait on the front porch for my mother when my phone buzzed with a text from her: *Got hung up at home helping your father look for his reading glasses. Will be thirty minutes late.* I sighed and sat back, cranking up the air-conditioning as the autumn sun beat down on the windshield. I glanced over at the yellowed envelope full of pictures sitting on the passenger seat. I reached for it and slid a finger under the envelope flap, feeling the remnants of sticky sealant.

I slowly pulled out a stack of black-and-white photographs. They were all different sizes, and some slid down into the space between the console and my seat. I flipped through the ones still in my hand. Most were family portraits, with the people dressed in formal garb, frowning at the camera. One photo, on the lawn in front of a grand Queen Anne mansion, had a mother, a father, and what seemed to be three daughters. I turned it over and someone had written: *Hoppe family, 1908. Monarch Manor.* The picture was too faded and grainy to make out any of their faces, as I searched for any family resemblance from what I assumed were my long-dead ancestors.

I put the photos back into the envelope and fished around in between my seat and the console for the photos that had fallen.

I extracted one, which was of a party on the lawn of what appeared to be Monarch Manor again, with white tables and women with parasols scattered around the lawn. The back read: *Afternoon Tea.* I set it aside and felt around, my fingers locating one more photo. I slowly lifted it up.

It was another family portrait on the lawn of the estate, but the quality was much better than the others. It was of the Hoppes again, although everyone was older. The back of the photo dated it as fourteen years later, in 1922. There were children and men in the photo—the husbands and children of the sisters, I assumed. The girls were perched grimly on their mothers' laps, enormous bows decorating their heads, with little saddle shoes on their feet. There was only one boy, on the lap of a woman on the end with light-colored hair that fell in ringlets around her shoulders. She held on tightly to the boy, as if he was about to scamper away, a gesture I recognized from when we tried to get Will to pose for a picture. The Mom Death Grip, as I called it.

I looked at the boy's face, and the breath escaped my lungs. My fingers trembled as I brought the picture closer to my face. He stared at the camera with Bambi eyes, round cheeks, and lips that pulled down. His ears stuck out slightly, and his mouth was parted, as though he was saying, "Cheese." His shoulders sagged and his legs were bowed toward each other, the soles of his feet together.

He looked so much like Will, he could have passed for his carbon copy.

I turned the photo over again rapidly, reading the inscription again, hoping I'd missed a name or some identifying marks. But as I first saw, it only had the date.

I looked at the mother again, who I realized looked nothing like me, for she was far, far prettier, and then back to the boy.

"Hello there. What's your name?" I whispered to him, a smile creeping over my face.

I was pulled away from the photo by the sound of tires squealing along gravel as my mother raced up the driveway and pulled her motorcycle next to my car.

"Remind me never to ask your father if he needs help with anything before I leave the house again," she said as she threw up her hands. She took a deep breath and ran a hand through her short silver hair as I climbed out of my car, photo still in my hand. "Let's get to it. Your father and I have fish-fry plans tonight." She turned and trudged toward the front door.

"Wait, I found something." I held out the photograph of Will's doppelgänger as she turned around. "Do you have any idea who this is?" I said as I pointed toward the family.

My mom rubbed her tanned face and grabbed the photo out of my hand, fast enough that I automatically reached for it again. She turned it over with a flash and then back to the front again and gave a low whistle.

She pointed to one of the little girls with the bows. "Well, that might be my grandmother, Emily. I've seen pictures of her as a child." She smiled. "Pretty neat."

"What's the story about the house? I never knew we had money in our family." I pointed to the Queen Anne in the background.

"Yup. I thought I told you this." She cocked her head to the side. "They had one of those big ol' houses on Geneva Lake. They made all their money in beer or whiskey or some kind of alcohol before Prohibition kind of put a damper on that party. And then the Depression happened, and..." She held her palms in the air.

I slowly nodded. Lake Geneva was fifteen minutes away, and I knew it had a deep history of old mansions and fancy, historic family estates. I just never imagined that someone in our family might have owned one of those grand residences.

"What about him? Do you know who he is?" I pointed to the little boy who looked so much like Will.

She peered closely at the photo, holding it two inches from her face. "Whoa." She looked from the photo to me. "Guess the family gene pool is a strong one. He looks just like our boy."

"No kidding," I said as I took the photo from her. "I'd love to know his name."

"Well, I might have an old family tree somewhere. Or"—she swept a hand toward the house—"we might find one inside. A needle in a very, very large haystack." She cracked a smile, her lined cheeks forming an accordion across her face. "Let's get to it, shall we?"

I held the photo in my hand and stared at the little boy for a few moments longer before I carefully placed it back into the envelope with the other pictures in my glove box, shielded from the sunlight.

Several hours later, we had gone through ten boxes full of old Christmas decorations. They all seemed fairly worthless, just boxes and boxes of broken ornaments, random ornament hooks, and cheap stockings with the embellishments half-missing. The find of a pair of 1950s reindeer that resembled the Claymation Rudolph cheered us momentarily, but then it was back to plastic metallic garlands and fake evergreen wreaths.

I offered to get lunch, and my mother grunted a yes. I drove down the road and pulled my car into the first sandwich shop I saw. On the way in, I paused on the sidewalk to enjoy the cool breeze off the lake. After being stuck in the rapidly warming house all morning, my hair was finally beginning to lift off the back of my sweaty neck.

I grabbed sandwiches inside the Sittin' Bull, a tiny shop with two tables and a lunch counter, conveniently forgetting that my mother had asked for extra onions on her sub, as I could only imagine what that might smell like after a couple of hours in the house. I turned to my car when a mother with twins casually walked past me. Two identical toddlers walked on either side of her, adorable boys wearing jeans, a continuous stream of chatting coming from them. I caught the mom's eye and smiled as she walked past. She flashed me back an easy grin and continued walking.

My face grew warm and I slowly lowered myself onto a nearby bench. Without consciously meaning to do so, I allowed myself to sink into my thoughts of the future: one where everything I worked toward, pushed for, prayed about, had come true.

In my mind's eye, I saw Charlotte, Will, and me walking down this street, hand in hand, the twins chattering away, holding a conversation with each other, while I window-shopped.

"Please, Mom. Please can we throw bread crumbs to the fish in the lake?" Will would ask, his eyes bright and clear.

I would roll my eyes in mock surrender. "Sure. Only for a moment, though."

"C'mon, Will! Race you to the pier!" Charlotte would say and they would shout and shriek all the way to the water as I laughed and chased after their tiny figures. In this universe, I didn't have to worry about therapy, meltdowns, or the phrase "Calm body." A world where I could hear his voice, where I didn't have to feel guilty about constantly putting Charlotte second out of survival. We could simply enjoy a beautiful fall day together.

A car horn brought me out of my fantasy and I wiped the tears from my eyes. Allowing myself to go to that place of What If brought me both joy and pain—a momentary relief from the present but an even harder fall to reality, back to a world where Will refused to take a school picture, so the dual frame I had sat empty on one end, an everyday reminder of the fact that the smallest of accomplishments still seemed so far out of our grasp.

"It's just a picture," Luke had said with a shrug before he turned back to his laptop after I had cried to him on the evening of Picture Day.

Yes, just a picture, I thought. Just *a picture.* Sometimes it was the smallest cuts, the nearly invisible paper cuts, that stung the most. Luke was practical, able to compartmentalize it all, a skill I often wished I had. Then, I wouldn't have to feel each setback so deeply that it nearly took my breath away. I wanted him to understand that everything felt like a test, one that I kept failing. A test that showed me every day how far the divide was between the mother I was and the mother Will and Charlotte deserved.

On the bench next to Powers Lake, I tried to take a deep breath and remind myself that we couldn't give up hope that someday things would be easier, that Will would be happier. That it would be a When, not a What If, yet my affirmations fell around my shoulders like dried leaves, crumbling at the slightest bit of wind. I felt as though I had to keep pushing, that I owed it to him, even though part of me whispered that it was hurting all of us much more than it was helping.

I walked in the door to my house that night only fifteen minutes after Luke had put the kids to bed. I planned on escaping Powers Lake early enough to kiss the twins good night, but I had ended up driving around nearby Geneva Lake, trying to catch a glimpse of the historic mansions to determine which had been Monarch Manor. Before I knew it, the sky was turning orange and pink. And unfortunately, I hit rush-hour traffic on the way home, making the usual ninety-minute drive a three-hour trek.

"How was work?" I asked as I sank down on the couch next to Luke.

"Good. Exhausting. The usual." He was promoted to a senior sales manager at the software company Lumitech two years ago. It was a title that meant he usually wasn't home until after bedtime each night.

"Kids tucked in?" I asked.

He nodded and muted ESPN. "They're wiped out. My mom

took them to the park, out for ice cream, and to the petting zoo after school."

I smiled. Meredith had an insurmountable level of energy, especially for a woman who was nearly seventy. "And both school drop-off and pickup went fine?" Will and Charlotte attended different schools for kindergarten. Charlotte at our home elementary school and Will at a different school ten minutes away, at the other end of the district, that housed his special education program.

Luke's eyes twinkled as he stifled a laugh. "Sure."

I rolled my eyes. "Okay, so what happened?"

I exhaled loudly as Luke told me that his mother took a different way to school than Will's familiar route. He started screaming and trying to unbuckle his car seat, kicking the window so hard Meredith thought it was going to shatter. By the time they reached school, he was hysterical and they were both drenched in sweat.

"Of course, she said, 'It was a minor tantrum, but it's fine!' after she told me the story," Luke said with a chuckle.

I could just hear Meredith saying those words in a voice about three octaves too high.

"Her time with Charlotte went well," he continued. "She volunteered in the school library as planned, and loved helping the class pick out books."

I nodded, folding my hands in my lap. My constant guilt was slightly assuaged by the thought that Charlotte got some special time with her grandmother, and vice versa.

"Look what book Charlotte chose from the library." Luke pointed to the coffee table.

"*The Velveteen Rabbit.*" I said the title as I picked up the book to look at the familiar cover. I ran a finger over the lettering. I used to read it to the twins when they were younger, sometimes what felt like a hundred times a day. I had identified with the appearance of the Skin Horse: patchy, worn, and looking not long for this world. I couldn't remember the last time I had picked the book up, but I loved that Charlotte knew, that she remembered.

"Did you guys make a lot of headway at the house?" he asked, his eyes back on his laptop.

"Some. After the Christmas decorations, we did find an old box of *McCall's* magazines from the 1950s, which was kind of cool. But I kept thinking about that little boy in the photo." I had texted Luke a picture of him with the caption: *Will? Time Traveler?*

I stopped as a mosquito landed on my knee. I swatted at it and a dot of blood appeared next to the dead insect. One of the downsides to living in such an old house was almost nonexistent foundation sealant, which led to an interesting first month in the house. I learned all about house centipedes, giant mosquitos, carpenter bees, and the nesting habits of mice. "A worthy price to pay," I remember telling Luke that first year. "I don't care what creature appears next; you will carry me out of this house in a coffin." He thought I was being dramatic, but I meant it.

I waited for Luke to ask me more about the photo or want to see it again, but his gaze remained on his computer. I wanted to reach out, touch his arm, and try to engage him, for him to share my curiosity, but I stayed quiet and trained my eyes on the television. Clearly, the picture didn't capture his interest in the way it did for me. It was an anecdote, an interesting fact, to him. But it felt much more than that to me, and I didn't have the energy to explain all of that to him—to try to convince him of what I wanted him to feel. What I thought he should feel. Instead, I kept it inside, safe and protected, importance unquestioned.

Later, I crawled into bed with Luke but found I couldn't sleep. Visions of the little boy in the photograph, and Monarch Manor, whispered across every corner of my brain, until I finally rolled over and grabbed my phone off the nightstand. It was usually used in desperation at 4:00 am when Will would wander into our bedroom. YouTube was a blessing in those wee morning hours that allowed me to get an extra hour of sleep.

This time, I didn't type in Thomas the Train or *Sesame Street* videos, but a search for the estate and the Hoppe family. A Web site pulled up a variety of grainy photos of the house from a distance, presumably taken by someone standing with their back to the lake, maybe on one of the piers. The Queen Anne structure had a turret that reached high into the sky and seemed to touch the clouds. The roof had overlapping shingles set in a fish scale pattern, and the wide front porch with furniture seemed to beckon me to *Come. Sit,* even over a hundred years later.

A small paragraph detailed the origins of the estate: *Monarch Manor was built by beer baron Conrad Hoppe, as a gift for his Irish immigrant bride, Mary. The couple had three daughters: Eleanor, Amelia, and Jane. The house hosted many parties over the years, most notably the Fourth of July Party each year. It also was home to the wedding of the youngest daughter, Jane. During the wedding reception, Amelia Hoppe Cartwright and her five-year-old disabled (deaf) son, John, drowned in a bizarre accident.*

And underneath the paragraph was a photo of Amelia and John—the same little boy who looked just like Will. In this photo, he sat on his mother's lap and his face held the hint of a smile. He was dressed in a white sailor outfit, and it gave him the appearance of a cherub. I smiled back at him and whispered, "John. So that was your name."

My eyes scanned the last two sentences again, and I brought a hand to my mouth as I allowed the information to sink in. *Disabled (deaf) son.*

He didn't just look like Will; he had struggles and challenges as well. And Amelia had to deal with some of the same things that I did, I imagined.

And they died together.

I typed in another search, trying to determine what happened and why it was labeled *bizarre,* but I came up empty.

I exhaled slowly and closed my eyes, feeling as though a hand had reached across the decades to show me the photograph, to tell me about this family. My family. I had a sense that I was being pulled into something that I wouldn't be able to resist, shown a path just waiting for my footprints. It couldn't all be a coincidence—or at least, that's what I wanted to believe. I wanted to believe there was meaning in the pictures, in reading what happened to them. I wanted to believe there was meaning in everything in my life, in everything that I experienced. That nothing was random, that there were no coincidences.

I held on to that feeling with the thinnest of ghost fingers, willing myself to grasp tighter on to Amelia and John, and to what really happened, and to rescue them from the veil of the past.

CHAPTER 5

AMELIA

"This one is a petunia," Amelia said and signed at the same time before she held out a brilliant purple flower. She leaned in close to smell it and gestured for John to do the same.

His blond head leaned toward the flower, his long, dark eye-lashes closing as he inhaled the sweet scent. A smile broke across his face as he leaned away, first looking at her and then bending down to smell the flower again.

John and Amelia had dressed after breakfast, putting on clothes that her mother would decide were appropriate enough to leave them alone, and took a morning walk down to the gardens in between the house and the piers. The gardens were John's favorite place to play when they visited the estate in the summers, and Amelia always thought it was because they were a place he could observe and take in the scenery, rather than having to exhaust himself with interactions. It was a place they could both have a break, but in a way that would appear proper to the rest of the family. It was a place where she could exhale, if only for a brief moment, before everything began in earnest.

Back toward the house, just off the stairs that led to the porch, a maid placed freshly cut blooms in the dipping well, a stone water bowl that kept the flowers fresh until they were ready to be brought inside. Amelia was about to point out the rows of pink roses near the white picket fence that bordered the garden, when they heard a scream come from the docks.

Amelia snapped her head toward the lake, where she saw her sister Jane standing on the grass, alone, pointing toward the *Monarch Princesses,* with pale pink ribbons and streamers bearing the couple's monogram, to match the color of the roses that would decorate the aisles and dinner tables.

Jane screamed again, pointing toward the yacht, and Amelia grabbed John's hand and began to walk across the yard to where her sister stood, her heart pounding. If anything was wrong with the boat, the entire evening would change. She reached Jane and grabbed her elbow to keep her from falling to the ground.

"What happened?" Amelia said as she pulled Jane upright.

Jane's eyes were wide, her cheeks flushed, and her chin trembled as she pointed toward the steam yacht. "The ribbons. Can't you see?"

Amelia looked back at the ship, the caretakers now watching Jane in confusion. Amelia shook her head and her sister began to cry. "The ribbons. The pink color is all wrong. They won't match the flowers."

Amelia exhaled, relaxing her shoulders, and shook her head. Screaming over nothing, Jane's special talent. Their older sister, Eleanor, was usually the one to deal with her. Eleanor was supposed to arrive last night from New York, but she had been delayed due to some business concern of her husband's. It seemed he always found a way to cut their visits short or start them late.

Amelia pulled her sister's shoulders toward her. "Look at me." Jane's eyes lifted, a glazed look moving over them. "The only person who will notice anything like that would be you, and I think they look wonderful. This is not what you should worry about; you should be thinking about how later today you are getting married. Now go inside and lie down, before it is time to style your hair and put on that beautiful gown."

Jane rolled her eyes and gave her sister a frown. "Of course you wouldn't notice that, Amelia. You have never noticed anything of the sort. I'm the one with the problems." She looked down at John and her gaze softened in sympathy, but she walked away before she could muster an apology.

Amelia wished, just once, that her sister would look at her, ask her how she was doing, what she felt, how she could help. That she could feel the closeness from when they were children, when their lives were whispered secrets and silly stories. Now the secrets remained unsaid and the stories untold.

Amelia looked down and saw that John's gaze was fixed on the arrival of another steam yacht carrying members of the Chicago Symphony Orchestra, who had been brought in for the wedding. She patted him on the shoulder and gave one final glance to the *Monarch Princesses,* where the workers were now busy with the decorations once more. She held her breath as it listed from side to side in the waves, the workers trying to balance on the large decks, like a seesaw tottering back and forth. She knew what he was thinking as he looked out on the water, at the way the waves lapped against the shore, at the unsteadiness of the boat.

Back toward the house, past the tennis courts, she heard the rumble of a motorcar engine coming to life in the garage, likely a staff member waiting to be driven into town for a last-minute supply. The roads around the lake were still unpredictable and nearly impassable during bad weather, but all the estates had garages and cars, despite the fact that most people traveled from the train station to their estates by yacht.

John took his eyes away from the water and pointed back toward the gardens. Amelia nodded, holding his hand as they walked across the green lawn.

"Oh, look!" Amelia said as she spotted a monarch butterfly

on a stem of milkweed. Her father had the landscape designer plant milkweed across the gardens, specifically to attract the monarch butterflies that her mother had always loved. Her mother told her how in the first spring in Chicago, after she came to America from Ireland, she saw a monarch butterfly and followed it for blocks. She was so intent on following it that she bumped straight into a man on the street, Conrad Hoppe, her future husband. Mary always said that monarch butterflies were the reason she had everything she did.

Amelia crouched down, not caring how her knees sank into the dirt, and pulled John close to her chest. She held a finger out near the butterfly, and John did the same. The monarch rested on the plant, its wings slowly opening and closing like the blinking of an eye. She was about to pull her finger away in disappointment when it lazily lifted off the branch, coming near them, before settling down on John's finger.

She made a noise of excitement but held still so as not to scare it away, and John's face lit up as he studied the orange-and-black wings on his finger. It stayed there for a moment, opening and closing its wings, before it flew away again. They watched it flit away, disappearing somewhere in the maple trees on the edge of the property.

"Remember how they start off as caterpillars?" she signed to John, and he nodded. She had pulled out a book on the lifespan of the monarch earlier that year, a book that she had from childhood.

She continued but didn't sign. "Then they build a great big house called a cocoon, where they rest, and then they emerge as a beautiful butterfly, ready to fly all over the flowers. They're free." She swallowed back the tears threatening to form.

She pulled John close to her and wished she could form a monarch cocoon around both of them, wishing that there was some way to set him free from all that limited him and they could fly away together like the butterflies, needing only their wings to escape.

It felt as though everything could be a danger, even the lake she loved so much as a child. She used to spend her summers with her fingertips trailing through the water, her skin always slick from swimming or fishing. Having John made her fearful of everything, on his behalf, and when she looked out on the water she couldn't help but think of the water in the middle and how it was so dark and so cold.

And how she wasn't sure if she could protect him from it. Especially not that night.

CHAPTER 6

ERIN

I didn't sleep much in the nights that followed my discovery about John and his accident. Each time I closed my eyes, I would dream of the accident, of John's head bobbing up and down on the surface of the lake, cold and afraid. It always morphed into Will treading water, waving his arms for me, as I desperately tried to swim to him. I never once reached him.

In the middle of the night, after the dream happened again, I shook Luke awake and told him about it.

He looked at me, rubbing his eyes slowly, before he said, "You should look into it if it's bothering you that much. Do some research. Find out more about the family."

"But how?" My mother hadn't found the aforementioned family tree in her house, and my grandmother's house wasn't sharing any more secrets. "I guess I could go to the library or something like that before I meet my mom in Powers Lake. Or I think there's a history museum in Lake Geneva. Maybe they would know something?"

He slowly nodded until it was clear I was satisfied, and then collapsed back down onto his pillow and immediately began snoring.

* * *

The bright orange OPEN sign on the Geneva Lake Museum cheered my heart as I drove up to Wisconsin the next day. Inside, a serious-looking man with gray hair and glasses stood off to the side of a display case of toys from the 1950s. At first, I thought he was in his fifties, but as I got closer, I realized he was likely my age but just had an old-fashioned air that dated him.

"How can I help you?" he said. His name tag read: GERRY.

I was suddenly nervous, and my hands flitted around as I said, "I'm looking for information about the Hoppe family, from back at the turn of the century."

His brows knitted together as a look of confusion passed across his face. "What kind of information?"

I put my purse up on the glass display case and then quickly shoved it off when I saw his look of alarm. "Well, I'm looking for information on their old estate: Monarch Manor. Apparently, the Hoppes are distant relatives. I found these pictures tucked away in an old box, and I was curious about them." I reached into my exiled handbag and pulled out the photo of the Hoppe family.

Gerry leaned forward and slowly whistled, a smile spreading across his face, one that made him finally look his age. "Oh yes. The Hoppe family. I don't think I've seen this photograph of them before." He leaned forward and hovered a finger over the photo. "And this is the family estate, which you know, I'm sure."

I nodded. "Do you have any idea where it was located around the lake? I couldn't find any information on where it was. Or . . . is?" I said, my voice raising an octave.

He nodded. "Of course." He turned and pointed to a map of Lake Geneva, with markers around the lake bearing labels of estates. Just north of Williams Bay, he pointed to a small dot.

"Monarch Manor! There it is." I leaned closer. "So it's still there?"

He gave me a half smile. "Some of it is. I'm afraid it doesn't look anything like your picture anymore. It has suffered years of neglect, and is due to be razed by the village soon. Such a shame. It likely could have been saved a few years ago, but now . . ." He shook his head slowly and frowned.

"Of course. I had hoped for different news, but that makes sense." My shoulders sagged.

"It's fortunate that anything is still there, to be quite honest. Many of the houses from that time were ravaged by fire at one point or another. Oftentimes, when a house caught fire during that era, the only goal would be to save the furniture and the architectural plans, and let the rest go."

He took a moment to study the photo with interest, before he looked up at me with his soft gray eyes. "What a treasure to have found this. Now you said you wanted some more information on the family? *Your* family?" Another giddy smile passed across his face, the decay of Monarch Manor out of his mind again, and he practically skipped off to find some archival materials when I nodded. I wondered what it would be like to love what you did that much, to get so much joy from things that other people likely found horribly boring.

He set a leather-bound book on the case in front of me with such force it made me wonder why I had to remove my purse. He opened the book and it cracked, groaning from the effort at having to share information after what was likely years of silence. He pointed to a photo of a grand Queen Anne home, with sweeping lake views and a beautiful sun porch with intricate carvings. On the front yard was a scattering of tables and chairs, all in white, with women in elaborate dresses and hats seated at each one. The photo was taken from too far away to recognize any of the faces.

"So here is your house, Monarch Manor, in 1915," he said. "This would have been one of Mary Hoppe's famous tea parties, held by the Lake Geneva Garden Club, of which she was a prominent member." He pointed to a row of terrace flowers, set just off the lakeshore. "And these were the gardens that were so loved by Mary and her daughters, designed by renowned land-scape architect Jens Jensen. And of course, they were designed to attract the monarch butterflies that gave the estate its moniker."

"It's just beautiful. I wish I could have seen it," I said, and he made a sympathetic noise.

"And here is another photo of the family, this one of Mary and Conrad Hoppe with their grandchildren." He pointed to a plastic-covered photo of the couple surrounded by three small children. The girls again wore sailor dresses and huge white bows in their hair, and the one boy—John—wore a boy sailor outfit with white socks and saddle shoes. His light hair flopped into his eyes, which were wide, and he seemed to look right through the camera.

"John, right?" I said, and Gerry nodded. "What can you tell me about him?"

He shook his head. "Very sad story. He was deaf." He paused for emphasis and seemed disappointed when he realized I already knew. "And he and his mother disappeared tragically." He again paused, irritation flashing across his face when I didn't react.

He stood up straighter and cleared his throat. "They disap-peared from their steam yacht during a storm on the night of Jane Hoppe's wedding, on May 28, 1923." He flashed me a small smile when my eyebrows lifted. "Jane Hoppe was Amelia's sis-ter, so it was her nephew and sister who vanished on the night of her wedding.

"Like I said, very tragic, especially since the boy was so young. Mr. and Mrs. Hoppe, Amelia's parents, never quite got over it, or so the story goes. Additionally, Mr. Hoppe lost every-thing during Prohibition, since the family had invested in breweries. The family just collapsed." He sighed and glanced at the photo of Monarch Manor. "Like the house, I suppose. Even the yacht, which was dismantled sometime in the 1930s."

"I read something that labeled the accident as 'bizarre.' Why is that?"

His eyes sparked with excitement as he leaned forward conspiratorially. "Well, there were rumors that something nefarious happened with the accident. Some on board swore they saw Amelia jump off the boat, and pull the boy overboard with her. A murder-suicide. There were whispers that she couldn't handle life anymore after her husband died."

My eyes wide, I turned this piece of information over in my head, letting it trickle across my previous assumptions. I couldn't imagine that was true. The mother I saw in the photograph couldn't have done that. I felt it deep inside. He cleared his throat and continued, "Of course, there were also rumors that she was spotted leaving town that night, after the accident. Unsubstantiated, of course."

I took a quick step back, stumbling over my purse and knocking the contents onto the floor. I crouched down and cleaned up an embarrassing number of tampons and quarters.

"It's quite a good bedtime story, isn't it?" Gerry said with a smile. He glanced at a clock on the wall. "I'm due to give a lecture at George Williams College shortly, but please let me know if you would like to chat further. Very few people are as interested in these kinds of forgotten events as I am," he said with a wink.

I thanked him for his help as he nearly pushed me outside and locked the door behind me. I drove to Powers Lake, thoughts of Amelia and the terrible rumors never far from my mind.

Luke was already waiting in the foyer when I walked in the door later. Both kids had their shoes on.

"We're going out to dinner at Take Five," he said firmly, and took a step toward the front door behind me.

"What? No—I can't. I'm exhausted." I rubbed my forehead and bent down in front of the twins. "Do you guys want to order a pizza?" I stopped myself before I could add *again*.

Will ignored me and studied the diamond patterns in the red

foyer rug, but Charlotte pulled her white headband down over her forehead with a frown.

"No. I want to get French fries and play on all the games like Daddy promised." She crossed her arms over her chest.

I sighed and looked up at Luke. I shook my head as I slowly stood. "You promised?" My head began to pound as I thought of trying to keep Will quiet and sitting down long enough to eat a meal. "I don't know if I have the energy."

No one said anything, a standoff. After a moment, I sighed, my white flag waving. "Fine. Let's go."

"Drinks?" the waiter said as he appeared. The twins were transfixed with the huge televisions on the walls, silent for one of the rare moments in their lives.

"Yes!" Luke and I practically shouted at the same time. My shoulders were already rigid with stress. It was our second table. Will had screeched when the hostess tried to seat us near the windows, so we allowed him to pick a different table for the sake of peace. Charlotte had immediately grabbed my phone and zoned out on a Disney game. I had pretended not to notice all the other diners staring at us, wondering why we gave in to our children so easily.

We ordered and the food came out quickly. Will ate two French fries before he started fidgeting in the booth. He reached for my phone, but Charlotte had pushed his hand away and they both screamed. Luke and I exchanged a glance and wolfed down what we could of our food.

As we were preparing to leave, a family next to us caught my eye. There were five of them. The boy and the girl looked to be around four and six and next to the mom was a small baby carrier with an infant inside.

As I slowly helped Will put on the shoes that he kicked off under the table, I stole glances at the baby carrier. Luke and I had always talked about having three, maybe four, kids. But, of course, that was before we entered the world of special needs and our present became much different than we had expected. I knew it was almost impossible to add an infant to our already-muddled mix, but I still couldn't help but smile at the infant's tiny knit cap and curled fingers.

On the way out of the restaurant, we bumped into Alicia Leeland, whose son, Mark, was two years older than Will. They had attended preschool the year before in the same autism program in our school district.

"Hi, guys," she said. "I haven't seen you all in ages." Her eyes slowly slid to Will. "How is school going?"

Luke and I exchanged a glance and I looked to her and cocked my head to the side. "Okay . . . for now. You know how it is. One day at a time." I lifted my palms in the air. "How's Mark?"

"I sure do." She rested her large arms on the ledge above a booth. "I have to tell you, he's doing amazing things. I think we might try and mainstream him next year."

I raised my eyebrows. "Really?" The thought of mainstream, of a typical classroom, was still something that seemed so far off for us, and yet it was within Alicia's grasp.

"To tell you the truth, I don't even know if he will qualify for services next year." She shook her head slightly. "All that therapy, all that intervention." Her face twisted into a smile. "It worked. One day it just all clicked for him."

"That's great to hear," Luke said, leaning forward. I could practically hear his thoughts. *See? Don't worry so much, Erin.*

"To think that we considered a therapeutic school at one point because we didn't think public school was a good fit," she added. She glanced over at Will, who turned and made eye contact and smiled at her briefly before looking away. My heart leapt in that moment, less than a second long, when I saw another flash of him enter our world, our situation. I squeezed him to me.

"That's wonderful. We should get the boys together for a playdate," I said. The playdate usually involved Will and Mark playing separately, ignoring each other, while Alicia and I made a few futile attempts to engage them before we gave up and chatted over coffee. Yet we both watched the other's child, with the silent, shameful, constant question: *Is my child better or worse?*

"Well, I should go grab our dinner: takeout again." She turned around but then stopped and called to us, "Good luck!"

"Well, that was encouraging," Luke said as she left.

I waited until we were in the car before I said, "Yes. It was." I couldn't bring myself to tell Luke that Alicia's son's autism was always much less severe than Will's. In preschool Mark was completely verbal, doing math problems, and reading books, whereas we still had yet to hear our son's voice. It didn't seem like an apples-to-apples situation.

"Why do you sound like that?" Luke said with a frown as he started the car.

"I don't sound like . . . anything. I'm just thinking about what she said." My throat constricted, as my eyes burned with tears. There it was, a real-life example of a mother who had fought hard enough for her child and made progress. Real, measurable progress. And yet instead of it making me feel inspired, the weight of defeat crushed my chest. *Why isn't Will progressing, too? What am I doing wrong?*

I was so lost in my painful thoughts that I didn't hear Charlotte calling my name until she was practically shouting, and Luke had to nudge my arm.

"Mom? Mom? Mom?" Charlotte said.

"What?" I said, and whirled around, my eyes flashing with annoyance.

Her bottom lip stuck out and tears formed in her eyes. I reached my hand back to pat her leg, but she twisted away.

"I'm so sorry. I'm just . . . thinking about something," I said, but she refused to look at me.

I turned back around, swallowing everything I wanted to

say: that I felt like we were failing Will. That we were failing Charlotte. That we had failed. That I had failed, before I had even begun to try.

I was supposed to be Will's advocate, the gatekeeper to a life that was easier for him. I was supposed to discover the secrets that would allow him to talk, play, make friends. I had to be that resource for him. If I couldn't protect and help him—if I couldn't be the one to reach him—who could?

As I lay in bed that night, one question above all repeated itself no matter how many times I tried to silence it: What kind of a mother doesn't know how to help her child?

CHAPTER 7

AMELIA

Amelia saw her sister Eleanor when she was still halfway across the lake, on an arriving steam yacht. She sat at the back of the boat, the ribbons on her hat flowing behind her in the breeze. One of her gloved hands secured the hat on her head, and she held the other in the air, waving to her sister.

"Look, it's Aunt Eleanor," Amelia signed to John as they stood on the white pier. She smiled and pointed toward the boat, a feeling of light moving across her forehead. Eleanor had always come to her rescue, with Jane or otherwise. She wished she could ask for help now, with everything before her. But it felt like no one could truly help her, not since Henry died.

John turned his face and looked out across the lake, shielding his eyes with his hands. His face broke out into a brilliant smile before he turned back to his mother, signing his aunt's name.

As the yacht grew closer, the steam from the engine filled the air, and Amelia waved it off, pressing a finger to her nose and breathing through her mouth. When the captain slowed the engine and the deckhands began to jump out and secure the boat to the pier, Amelia and John ran down the dock.

"Has she started screaming yet?" Eleanor asked with a smile when Amelia released her from a tight hug.

Amelia raised her eyebrows in response and they broke out in laughter. It felt so good to laugh, she realized. A momentary relief, like slipping her head under the lake's surface on a brutally hot summer day before the heat returned and suffocated her.

"I figured as much," Eleanor said. "Poor Father. This wedding will nearly break him." She shook her head and her mouth turned down into a frown.

The sisters were silent for a moment as they reflected upon how much stress the financial burden of the wedding had to have caused their father. Since Prohibition began a few years earlier, the brewery had tried to shift to selling Near Beer, with the same taste but none of the alcohol, but it didn't amount to anything close to what annual sales used to be. For Jane's sake, and the sake of every other party that happened for however long the law remained, thankfully it wasn't illegal to consume alcohol, only to manufacture or purchase it. The people with means—the sisters' parents and everyone in their social circle— had stockpiled liquor before the law went into effect. Heaven forbid any of their parties be affected. And certainly, Jane's wedding would put a large dent into their parents' stash.

Eleanor lifted the white skirt of her summer dress and knelt down on the dock until her face was level with John's. "And hello, my handsome nephew. I've missed you so much." She held her arms out, and John slowly leaned forward, allowing her hug. His arms fell at his sides for a moment before he felt safe, and then, slowly, he hugged her back. "There it is," Eleanor said, and she hugged him tighter. "Such a strong little boy."

Eleanor turned and pointed to the yacht, where her husband, George, and her daughters, Emily and Louisa, were being helped onto the pier by a dockhand. The girls wore matching starched white dresses, short white socks with black mary janes, and enormous white bows on top of their dark curls. As soon as their feet hit the wooden boards, they ran toward their mother, bookending her skirts.

"Girls, you remember your cousin, John?" Eleanor said.

Three-year-old Louisa buried her face in her mother's skirt in response, but five-year-old Emily nodded slowly and took a step toward John. "Hello," she said.

John looked at Amelia and she signed, "Your cousin Emily." She reminded him that he had last seen her two summers before, at the Midsummer's Eve party at Monarch Manor. They had both been three years old, and young enough for them not to notice there was much difference between them. They ran around the front lawn, holding sparklers, making the nannies worry. Their pressed white clothing had been stained from the grass and the dirt of the garden, but what Amelia cared about the most was how often she saw John smile. It felt as though that was the last time he was able to be just one of the children. The last time before the chasm between him and other children grew too wide to broach.

"Mother, can John and I play in the garden and look for monarch butterflies?" Emily asked as she tugged at Eleanor's white skirt.

Louisa gave a squeak in protest and Eleanor sighed. "As long as you take your sister with you."

"Come on." Emily grabbed John's hand. He startled for a moment, before he relaxed in her grasp. "I want to see if I can find my favorite one, with the three black spots on the right wing." She began to run off, pulling John behind her, with Louisa trailing them and whining in protest.

"That's very sweet. I'm not sure if John remembers her, but it's wonderful for him to have a playmate. As you know, this place is best explored with other children." Amelia winked at Eleanor and they clasped hands and began to walk across the lawn, toward the house. Amelia felt a pang of sadness when she saw Emily chatter along, a familiar feeling whenever she was faced with a child the same age.

"Truly, our summers here were the best summers a child could possibly have," Eleanor murmured. "What wonderful times we had, before . . ." She trailed off as she watched her husband, George, trudge across the lawn, ignoring his own family and Amelia.

Amelia squeezed her sister's arm in sympathy. Eleanor had written that George hadn't been the same since the financial troubles in New York two years before, his existence barely that above a ghost. Being alone was one thing Amelia understood. Tears, impossible choices, and loss were the steel framework that encased her soul.

"I presume the Cartwrights have not arrived yet?" Eleanor asked with a frown, scanning the lawn.

At the mere mention of her in-laws, Amelia's stomach turned and fear ran through her body like an electric shock.

Eleanor saw her sister's face and squeezed her hand. "I'm here now," she said, her voice low.

They silently walked toward the estate, Amelia steadying her breath. The Cartwrights would certainly not let the event pass without the suggestion that John not be allowed at social functions . . . or, really, anywhere at all.

"How I've missed this place," Eleanor said as they walked up the wooden steps to the large veranda that overlooked the lake. She breathed deeply and closed her eyes before staring out at the water.

"And I think it has missed you, too," Amelia whispered as she leaned on the porch railing.

They settled into the white wicker chairs at the far end of the porch, closest to the water. The floor was painted a light blue, a color that mirrored the lake water. The veranda was scattered with white chairs and tables, and a few rocking chairs that faced the water. Amelia had spent more than a few hours in them when John was young, rocking him to sleep as the cool breeze off the lake lifted her hair from her neck, waving away the irritated nannies.

Eleanor took off her hat and leaned back in a chair. Amelia saw new lines on her face, around her eyes and forehead. "I remember thinking that it was the most beautiful house in the entire world the first time we came up here," Eleanor said. "It was like something out of a fairy-tale book."

Amelia was just ten and Eleanor thirteen when the construction was finished on the estate. Their father, Conrad, had found the exact spot to build while visiting a business partner who was building his own estate on a different part of the lake. It took three years to build, and once it was complete their family spent every summer there, from Memorial Day to Labor Day. As was customary for all the families, their mother and the girls stayed there all summer while their father took the train back into Chicago to work each week.

The women held tea parties and meetings for the Lake Geneva Garden Club on the lawns of their estates, competing with one another for the best event. The children were cared for by a rotation of nannies, who hopelessly tried to get them to pay attention to lessons instead of running through the grass barefoot, picking berries off the bushes, and trying to capture the butterflies with nets stolen from their fathers' fishing equipment.

As she looked back from her place in adulthood, it felt to Amelia like it was all a dream, a time and a place separate from the world they lived in. It was close enough, though, for her to step back into if she closed her eyes and reached her hand out, through the thin veil that separated the worlds. And then she could only touch it for a moment, before it went away again.

"Let's stay here forever," Eleanor said.

Amelia smiled, yet her nose pricked with tears that she could not allow Eleanor to see. "I like this plan," she managed to say. She could feel her sister's gaze on her, but she didn't meet it, keeping her eyes trained on the water ahead.

They silently sat on the veranda, ignoring the commotion around them, their eyes focused on the lake while their minds were in the past, in a time when their dreams were possible.

In the light of Before. Everything was Before.

CHAPTER 8

ERIN

This can't be it, I thought as I turned down the long gravel driveway just outside of Williams Bay on Geneva Lake. I quickly glanced down at my phone, which still impatiently pointed ahead, the dropped pin quivering as though tapping its tiny red foot. A canopy of trees, leaves beginning to turn brilliant autumn colors, shaded the rocks below as my car bumped and hopped along the uneven path. I winced every time I heard the car's undercarriage squeak and grind, hoping a wheel didn't come off and strand me in the middle of nowhere. The late-afternoon sun was blacked out from all the foliage as I passed a long field of grass overgrown with wildflowers, cattails, and wispy prairie grass.

Finally, the tree line began to thin out and the path wound to the right, toward what I assumed was the lake. It bowed out like the mouth of a river, into a larger gravel circle, and I pulled my car into Park and got out.

I took a step forward, squinting in a way that I could feel accentuated my crow's-feet and other wrinkles. I shielded my face with my cupped hand and exhaled. The house that I had thought about so much over the last few days was now in my gaze, rising above the lake like a beacon, as it had for more than 100 years.

Monarch Manor.

I took a step toward the estate and felt a rush through my bones that ran from my head to my toes. I once read a study that said memories can be passed down through DNA and I had the strange sense that Monarch Manor was both like nothing I had ever seen and yet an old familiar friend.

I heard the roar of my mom's motorcycle make its way down the gravel driveway, and I turned in surprise. Earlier, at the end of the day at my grandmother's house, I had invited my mother to go on a treasure hunt with me to find the estate, armed with the geographical location from Gerry at the museum. She had quickly declined, stating she and my father had a poker tournament with friends that night.

"What happened to poker?" I said as she killed the engine.

She frowned and stepped off the bike. "I'm not that good anyway. I figure your father can figure out how to lose our money all on his own." She took her sunglasses off and whistled, stepping back slightly. "Shit," she said.

"Agreed," I said.

Our necks strained as our collective gaze moved along the turret on the left side of the house. It reached toward the cloudless fall sky, like an upright pointer finger. An expansive front porch faced the lake, with one deteriorating white wicker rocking chair left. I could picture the Hoppes gathering on a hot summer day to feel the breeze off the water or enjoying afternoon tea when the air held the crispness of a McIntosh apple from the orchard that I spied on the edge of the property.

Various dormers and levels graced the front of the house, additions over the years as the whims of the owners changed with the times. I tugged on my mom's sleeve and pointed to tiny, delicate cherubs carved into the roof and, I imagined, having long begun their return to the heavens. The entire outside was made of wood, but the foundation looked to be stone. The house was edged in rows of milkweed, the blooms long having been spent for the summer. I didn't see any of the namesake monarch butterflies around the plants, though.

"What do you think is inside?" my mom said as she eyed the rickety wooden front porch.

"My nightmares." I shuddered as I pictured decades' worth of animals and bugs residing happily inside. My own old house was overrun every spring, even with the aid of tea tree and peppermint oil to keep out the mice, and a seasonal spray from the only natural exterminator I could find in a thirty-mile radius. I couldn't imagine years of pestilence having free rein.

"What a beauty it must have been, huh?" She walked toward the wooden porch steps and carefully toed the first one. Her boot went straight through the wood like it was wet cardboard. "Well, I guess that settles that," she said as she backed away.

"Yes. And don't forget, it's condemned. Which, seeing it now, seems like it was the right move. Such a shame, though." I paused and lowered my voice to a whisper. "So many things are so sad about this place."

My eyes moved down to the worn white piers that were still in the water, the cold autumn lake lapping against them in the wind. I followed a line out to the center of the water, as I tried to picture the steam yacht that Amelia and John rode during the night of their disappearance. I could feel a heaviness in the air that surrounded the house, like it remembered. Like it was in mourning. And sadly, the house would be put out of its misery soon.

"You're thinking about the little boy and his mom, aren't you?" my mom said as she kicked aside a pile of leaves on the driveway.

"Of course I am," I replied.

She gave me a look before she patted my shoulder. "But what is it that you're really looking for?"

I want to know that Amelia didn't give up. That she didn't do something to John. That she kept fighting, even when it felt hopeless.

"To solve a family mystery," I said to her with a small smile, my lips closing around all that I wasn't ready to say.

She shook her head. "All right, kiddo. If you want to go with that, I can deal." She glanced over at her bike and took her sunglasses out of the pocket of her cracked leather jacket. "Now I really do have to go. The estate sale company is coming to the house at nine tomorrow morning. Don't be late." She stared at me from behind her black glasses.

"Seeing as how I have beat you there every morning, even though I live three times as far away, I will be on time," I said.

"Have a safe drive home, kiddo," she said with a laugh before she sped away.

I didn't get back into my car right away, although I knew I should leave to avoid traffic. I stood on the patchy grass, bumpy with spots of chickweed and clover, and stared at the lake. I pictured John running through the gardens and Amelia watching from a distance, and I couldn't imagine how anyone wouldn't be happy there, in such a magical place.

After the twins were in bed that night, I collapsed on the couch next to Luke. His laptop was perched on his lap and his eyes were glazed over as he stared at the screen. I thought about asking him about work, but lately that had just been a source of stress. His division had recently changed what they could sell, and it meant that he had to work twice as hard to sell the same amount as last year. He had warned me when the change happened at the beginning of the year that his commission checks might decrease, a prospect which terrified me. We were already teetering on the edge of just getting by, and anything less would push us into crisis mode.

"How was Wisconsin?" he said without looking up.

"Well, I saw Monarch Manor. Or what's left of it." I told him about the rotting front porch and how all of it seemed mid-crumble, like it had been falling to the earth when someone pressed Pause. "I want to spend more time investigating the accident. I feel drawn to it, in a way I can't quite describe. But it's like I was supposed to find that picture, supposed to learn more about these people."

He slowly looked at me, his mouth twisting to the side as he adjusted his tortoise-rim glasses. "It's a pretty neat mystery," he said evenly.

I played with the strings on my gray zip-up hoodie, winding them around my index finger. "I know. And I have to at least try and see what I can dig up. Especially because the little boy looks like Will. Because . . . because I'm the only one who cares anymore."

He considered this, shifting on the couch to face me a bit more. The glow from the television across the room flickered across his glasses, obscuring his eyes. "Don't take this the wrong way—I'm not trying to sound like an asshole when I say this—but don't you have enough to worry about? With everything going on with Will, and the estate sale, and stuff around the house?"

I gave him credit for not glancing around the room, although I'm sure he wanted to. Charlotte had attempted to do a puzzle earlier, which Will had thwarted, sending pieces scattering everywhere. Their clothes littered the floor from when they had changed into their pajamas (hastily pulled out of the laundry pile still waiting to be folded on the dining room table), and stacks of papers from school—fund-raisers, flyers, PTA announcements—all rested on the end table next to me.

I did look around for both of our benefit, slowly taking in the work that would never be done, the chores that would never end, before turning back to him. "Yes, I do. I have more than enough to worry about. But I want to worry about this, too."

He opened his mouth to say something but then closed it, turning back to his laptop. "Then you should do it. If it will make you happy," he finally said.

I nodded and waited for him to say more, but he never looked away from his computer. Although he studied some kind of spreadsheet, his face flashed with doubt and concern.

I quickly gathered the papers on the end table and stacked them together as I walked toward the kitchen. I made a half-hearted attempt to go through them before I opened the trash and shoved them inside.

I tried to sleep that night but couldn't. I lay in a half-awake, half-dreaming state where my real thoughts were mixed with dreamy encounters, like what I should pack for the twins for a snack the next day as a unicorn walked through my kitchen. I opened my eyes and glanced at the clock: 3:15 am. Luke's side of the bed was empty, still rumpled from where he had gotten up the day before. He must have fallen asleep on the couch while working. Again.

Some days, it felt like we were two people living in the same house but in different orbits. Occasionally, our paths would circle close enough to barely touch, but only for a moment, before we were pulled away by the choices we had made and the circumstances we could not control.

The room was flooded with light from the full moon in the sky. I peeked through the side of the plantation shades and saw it was a huge orange ball of fire in the sky, directly above the house next to us. One benefit to living in such an old house was that it was built before any of the current codes, so it was taller than any new house, and it always seemed like we were reaching up to the sky.

I lay back down and tried to sleep, but I kept thinking back to my conversation with Luke. The guilt of focusing on something other than the twins seeped into me like groundwater. Yet shouldn't I allow myself to do something interesting? I had given up so much over the years: my body, my career, my sense of self, friendships. My sanity.

I sighed and kicked the covers off my legs. I tiptoed out of our bathroom and into the hallway. (Another quirk of our house. There wasn't a bathroom upstairs when the house was built, so someone, at some time, had built one in the master bedroom . . . except they built it where you walked through the door. So the only way to access our bedroom was through the bathroom.) I winced as the uneven floors creaked under my feet, even though I tried to step in spots that I remembered were silent.

I slowly pushed open Charlotte's door, smiling when I saw she was twisted perpendicular to her bed. She was always a fidgety sleeper, kicking her legs and spinning around in her sheets as she slept. I gently moved her back onto her pillow and brushed the sweaty strands of hair from her cheek. I leaned down and kissed her forehead, taking in a deep breath. She smelled like laundry detergent and toothpaste, with the faintest, sweetest odor of little-kid perspiration.

She rolled over again and threw an arm over her face. "Pancakes," she muttered. She had always talked in her sleep, so much so that whenever she had a nightmare and asked to sleep in our room, I let her lie next to Luke while I went into her bed. I never could sleep with her chatting all night long, but he snoozed right through it.

"Sweet dreams, my amazing, silly girl," I said as I gave her another kiss on her head and tiptoed out of the room.

Next, I went into Will's room. I was startled at how peaceful he looked. He was curled on his side, his hair flopping over his face. No anxiety, no worry, no meltdowns imminent. Just a child sleeping, resting.

"Are you at least happy in your dreams, baby?" I wanted him to answer so badly, to tell me what to do to make his life easier, to bring him peace. To say anything, really. For me to hear his voice.

The full moon outside lit up his room as I gently lowered myself onto his bed, curling my hand around his palm, so that he was holding my finger. I put my head next to his on the pillow, closed my eyes, and breathed in the smell of his little-boy hair, a mixture of shampoo and playground dirt.

And I made a promise to him that I wouldn't stop fighting for him, that I would find out what I was supposed to do to help him. Then, I whispered a promise just between me and the moon, to John and Amelia. I promised that I would find out what happened to them, even if their story didn't have the happy ending that I so wished for.

I watched the full moon move across the starless sky for far too long that night, the promises I made to myself and to others lingering in the air and whispering against the tall eaves of my old house.

CHAPTER 9

AMELIA

Long after Eleanor had left the veranda, Amelia remained, rocking in one of the same white wicker chairs that she sat in as a child. Being there, in that safe place, reminded her of a time when the world was beautiful and full of possibility. Before she knew how cruel people could be and the terrible choices she would be forced to make. In the city, she was reminded of it on every block, on every corner. But behind at Monarch Manor, all of that pain seemed far away, hazy, like she was looking at it through the dense fog that rolled across the water in the morning.

She thought of her sisters and their sun-kissed youth. Of her teenage years, tangled with Matthew Cottingsley, who lived on the estate next door, and who had once been her closest friend. Of her adulthood and Henry, and John, and . . . darkness.

She took a deep breath and looked around at the familiar porch, unchanged through the years. And she thought back to when it all began, to when she first saw the estate and tried to reach through time and pull out a whisper of that joy.

The first time Amelia saw Monarch Manor, it was raining. Long, dark sheets of water fell from the sky, roughing up the surface of the lake around her in the steam yacht as she traveled from the train station in Williams Bay to the house. She could barely make out the uneven horizon of the Queen Anne jutting above the trees through the water that dripped down into her eyes from the roof of the yacht. She sighed and draped a shawl over her head, her curls limply falling around her shoulders, as her nanny, Mrs. Brown, shot her a disapproving look.

As the boat drew closer to the lakeshore, a deckhand appeared on the white dock, shielding his face from the water. He held out his hands as a crew member tossed him a knotted rope, and he wound it around one of the pristine white posts, newly painted after the house was completed. Only then did Amelia lift her chin and gasp at the full sight of the house.

"Mama, is that really it?" She reached forward and grabbed the sleeve of her mother's yellow printed dress, tugging on it.

But Mary was motionless, a statue nailed to the bottom of the rocking boat.

Conrad saw her expression and walked over, putting a hand at her elbow. "Welcome home, darling," he said. He swept a hand toward the house, like a vaudeville performer showing off his newest skill.

Mary slowly turned toward him. "It's . . . breathtaking."

Conrad gave her a wide smile and looked up at the house with pride. It was no secret to anyone that he had wanted his own estate on Geneva Lake. When he was just a child, after the Great Chicago Fire in 1871, he and his parents had traveled to the area when their house burned. His parents' friends the Sturges family had generously offered space at their lake cottage. After the destruction and heat of the city as it burned, the lake became the most beautiful sight he had ever seen, and he had carried that feeling with him throughout adulthood. The Sturges family eventually built a large estate called Snug Harbor, and Conrad often dreamed of being their neighbor or sharing a piece of their paradise. Until finally, he did.

Conrad looked down at Amelia, who still clung to her mother's sleeve. "Imagine all of the adventures you and your sisters will have here, Lia."

Amelia wrinkled her nose at the nickname, even though she secretly didn't mind when he called her it. At ten years old, she was practically a grown-up and should be called by her full name, not something fit for a child. At the back of the boat, seven-year-old Jane began to cry, wailing that she was hungry and cold.

"Stop it," Amelia hissed before Mrs. Brown gave her another disapproving look. She couldn't help but roll her eyes. Jane had cried the entire train ride from Chicago to Williams Bay, sniffling that the maids hadn't packed her favorite dresses and that her hair bows were certain to get crushed in the perfectly packed steamer trunks. With Jane, there was always something to cry about. When Mrs. Brown didn't think anyone was listening, Amelia heard her whisper to one of the maids that Jane should have been named Mary Mary Quite Contrary.

Mrs. Brown leaned down and hissed something indistinguishable to Jane, who quieted her sobs. Amelia hid a smile. She knew what the nanny had likely threatened: helping the kitchen staff scour the pots and pans after that evening's dinner. Their father had announced they would be served a delicious pork roast. It was their mother's favorite, but the staff's least favorite due to all the grease and fat.

Eleanor, seated at the front of the boat, walked back and gave her father a kiss on the cheek. "It's even more beautiful than what you had described." Then she turned and stepped out onto the slick dock, waving off an umbrella from the deckhand, letting the rain bounce off her shoulders. At thirteen, she had the long limbs and grace of a show horse and none of the awkwardness or sharp edges of most of her friends.

Mary and Amelia huddled together under one of the umbrellas, followed by Jane, Mrs. Brown, and Conrad. Amelia heard her mother's breath quicken as they walked across the stone path toward the looming estate. With each step, the rain slowed, first from a steady tap-tap to a light mist, to nothing. By the time they reached the large stones that stood on either side of the steps leading to the porch veranda, small rays of sunshine began to poke out of the clouds.

Amelia looked up, and a beam of light hit the top of the tower at the very tip of the estate, making it look like God himself was blessing the house. She stopped suddenly, transfixed at the way the light moved across the wooden carvings at the top, tiny cherubs with huge wings dancing in a row of molding across the top of the roof, anointing the estate.

"Ow!" Jane ran into Amelia's back and screeched, sobbing once again.

Conrad stood at the bottom of the porch veranda, his suit coat drenched with rain, a smile beaming from his lips. "My love, look."

Mary took a step toward the east garden and brought her hands to her mouth. It took Amelia a moment to realize what her mother saw. The plants looked like they were moving, brilliant orange, yellow, and black spots waving through the flowers. Monarch butterflies, seemingly hundreds of them, lightly tended to the landscape.

"I've already purchased a stack of train tickets for our friends and family, so that we can share this home with everyone, all season long," Conrad said. He frowned at a sobbing Jane. "Jane, if you don't stop, we may send you back on one of those train cars. You wouldn't want to miss the famous Fourth of July celebration this year, would you? I've heard the fireworks display goes on for hours and the boat regatta is strung with thousands of red, white, and blue lights," he said.

Jane immediately stopped, swallowing her next sob, and gave Conrad a brilliant smile. "No, Father."

"Welcome to Monarch Manor, girls." Conrad swept a hand back behind him, across the expansive lawn, through the colorful gardens, up to the porch kissed with lake breezes, and the snowfall of butterflies on the yard.

Amelia's heart felt as though it would burst. She had never loved anything more.

After lunch, the rain finally stopped, and the sisters ran outside.

"Come on, come on! Before she sees!" Eleanor tugged at Amelia's hand as they ran across the lawn, black patent-leather shoes caked with mud from the soft ground. As the girls formed a daisy chain of sisters, Amelia held Jane's hand as they ran toward the brilliant gardens, to get a look at the monarch butterflies up close.

Amelia stole a glance back at the house, where Mrs. Brown was certainly scouring each room looking for them, cursing Conrad and everyone else for bringing her there for the summer. She had made it well known that she disapproved of Conrad building a summer home, as she thought it to be unnecessary and wasteful. Yet everyone knew that it was because she didn't want to leave her husband, a railroad worker, back in Chicago for the summer. Amelia had heard Eleanor and her friends whispering that he had a reputation for going to the taverns at night and finding comfort in various warm beds around the city. With Mrs. Brown up in Lake Geneva all summer, the whole city would be his playground.

"Watch," Eleanor commanded as she stood close to a butterfly and held out an index finger, waiting. One came close, flitting very close to her finger, but kept on going. "Picky, picky," she said with a shrug.

"Look at this one!" Jane began to follow a particularly large and colorful monarch through the milkweed, trampling through the grass and coneflowers with her usual carelessness. She didn't look back as she went deeper into the garden, until she had almost disappeared from her sisters' sight.

"Wait!" Amelia called as she hiked up her skirt and began to follow her through the orange and purple blooms, butterflies and grasshoppers scattering around her like confetti. The long flower stems scratched at her ankles and the grasshoppers brushed against and tickled her arms. More than once, she was certain a spider or some other scary insect had bitten her legs, yet it was only the feathery leaves and dry branches of the underbrush.

"There she is," Eleanor said from behind her. Amelia followed her older sister west, toward the lake, where Jane stood. In front of her was a row of hedges that seemed to be in one solid line, a wall of greenery, but as they got closer Amelia realized there was a slight gap in them, a secret passageway.

The sisters looked at one another, faces beaming with glee. Eleanor grabbed Jane's hand and held out her other for Amelia. Together, they walked toward the hedges. It was a small circle, surrounded by tall arborvitae. A private hideout, where no one would ever find them.

Jane broke away from her sisters and squealed in delight as she ran a hand lightly along one of the green walls. "Is this where the fairies live?" Jane asked in a breathy voice as she slowly twirled in a circle, her blue-and-white gingham dress floating around her legs like the sail of a sailboat blowing in the breeze.

Her shoes sinking slightly in the soft grass of the clearing, Eleanor walked over to her youngest sister, knelt down, and held her hands. "Yes." She leaned forward and kissed Jane on her round cheek.

Amelia saw a flash of something gray out of the corner of her eye, near the opening of the arbors. She took a step toward the movement and pointed. "Bunnies! Baby bunnies!" At the noise, the tiny rabbit scampered back into a concealed nest.

The sisters ran toward the nest, which was covered in a thatch of grass and leaves. Eleanor reached for the leaves, even as Amelia protested, and carefully peeled back the cover. Inside were six bunnies, huddled together into one mass of gray fur

and soft ears, eyes closed. At the light, they squeezed tighter together, relying on one another for protection and comfort.

"Are they boys or girls?" Jane said as she crouched in the
grass, her hands sinking into the dirt.

Amelia looked down at the tiny babies and from side to side
to her sisters, kept safe in their secret garden, and said, "Sisters.
They're all sisters."

Eleanor nodded. "Yes. And they only have each other . . . and
us." She smiled at Amelia and took her hand and squeezed it.

"This is my favorite place in the whole world," Jane said as
she stood up and ran her pointer finger along some striped
grass near the hedges.

Amelia wasn't sure if she meant the secret garden or Monarch
Manor as a whole, yet she said, "Mine, too. I never want to leave."

Many years later, as Amelia rocked on the veranda on the
day of the wedding, she whispered those same words to herself:
"I never want to leave." And yet she knew she would have to
say good-bye long before she was ready.

CHAPTER 10

ERIN

When I was eighteen, my grandmother once told me that her house was her favorite place in the world. "Everything I want is here, just the way I want it." At the time, I remember thinking that it was sad, that she should want to explore the world, try new places. Yet as I got older, and after Luke and I bought our house, I understood. I realized how lucky I was to live in a house and love it so much that I would choose it over anywhere else. And so, on the day of the estate sale at my grandmother's house, I couldn't help but feel a sense of invasion as people walked through, browsing the items. After all, this was her sanctuary; this was her safe harbor. And these people walked through it with muddy shoes and a critical eye, licking their lips as they searched for a bargain.

"How much for this piece? I know it says three dollars, but I only have two dollars." A brunette with hair draped over her shoulder and a knowing smile held out eight quarters. In her other hand she held a license plate frame that read VIVA LAS VEGAS. A name tag on her shirt read SHANNON and it shifted as she thrust the money closer to my face.

"Done," I said as I grabbed the quarters from her hand before she could reconsider. A look of disappointment crossed her face, as though she was locked and loaded for a fight to the license plate death.

I walked outside and saw a couple staring at a rake in the front yard. "I just don't know," the wife said as she watched her husband take it for a test drive against the leaves. "We only have that one maple tree, and we already have two rakes. . . . I'm not sure there's room in the garage for a third."

"Then don't buy it," my mother muttered under her breath as she stood off to the side, on the sidewalk in front of my grandmother's house. She grunted when she saw me. "Jesus, this is a lot of conversation for five bucks." She threw up her hands when the couple walked away, the rake unsold and lying on the grass. "Thanks for coming!" she called. "I hope neither of your two existing rakes break."

"Stop." I elbowed her in the arm, and her skin moved back and forth easily. "Remember what . . ." I trailed off as I tried to remember the name of the perky blond woman with short feathered hair who had arrived that morning from the estate sale company. "Camille," I finally said, "told us? 'It might not seem like we're making any money, but we're going to get everything taken care of, easy peasy lemon squeezy.' "

I cocked my head to the side. "Except lemons aren't that easy to squeeze."

"Yeah, but don't tell Camille that." My mother turned and looked back at the house, shaking her head. People had started lining up at 6:30 am even though the sale didn't start until eight. We knew this because when we arrived at 7:00 twenty people stared at us, whispering about their thirty minutes already spent in line.

"Garbage pickers," my mother had whispered as she saw the crowd assemble that morning. Several were already trying to crane their necks to peer into the windows. "Can they really be that excited for a few old Barry Manilow albums? Weirdos."

When I had tried to protest and say that maybe they were just normal people, looking for a deal, she pointedly turned around and looked at me. "Just like Grandma, huh?"

Two hours later and most of the Precious Moments figurines had been sold, to people with eager hands who carefully watched us wrap them in newspaper before placing them in a plastic grocery bag, and all of the bedroom furniture was gone as well. The curio cabinet was next, and it was only when someone bought the freestanding dishwasher that I saw my mother's face flash with any sign that these had once been the things that surrounded her as a child.

"Fond memories of washing dishes?" I asked her as we stood guard over the table of Christmas records, including one with the carols sung entirely by cats. (Camille said that theft was a huge problem at any estate sale and we had to be vigilant in watching the crowd, although I couldn't imagine the cats' Christmas hits would be a hot shoplifted item.)

"The day my father brought that thing home, you would have thought it was the Hope Diamond, the way my mother reacted. 'Can we afford this? It's too much! I can't accept it!'" She smiled, her brown eyes catching the sunlight that streamed through the picture window in the parlor, as my grandmother called it. "I had never seen her so tickled by any gift he gave her before, or would give her again."

She crossed her arms and glanced at the space where it once was in the kitchen. Next to the end of the cream Formica countertop, on the linoleum floor, was a small square less faded than the rest of the room. "Never mind that we had to walk sideways around it to get through the kitchen."

I nodded. "I get it. To go from hand-washing to a dishwasher would feel like a miracle." Just last year, Luke had bought a Roomba and it made me feel like I was Queen Elizabeth. Charlotte tried to ride it like a horse the following week, and it started smoking and never worked the same after.

An hour earlier, Luke and the kids had met us so the twins could see their great-grandmother's house one final time before we had dinner, but within the span of fifteen minutes Will tried to co-opt the drink coasters to build a tower and Charlotte cried when she saw my grandfather's creepy ventriloquist dummy. Luke had quickly carted them off, muttering about finding a lakefront park and an ice-cream shop.

An hour later and the sale was over. All that remained of my grandmother's things was an odds-and-ends collection of ashtrays and lanyards from Branson, Missouri, and a few plastic necklaces, in addition to a stack of old books. Camille scooped all of it up into a cardboard box, to be donated to the local Salvation Army. At the last moment, I grabbed the books out of the box and put them in my car.

My mother and I took one last look around the house, emptier than we had ever seen it—and so much bigger than it ever appeared before—before we shut the door and locked it behind us.

I didn't ask her if it was hard to see it empty, how she felt about seeing it all gone. Even if she felt some sense of loss, she likely wouldn't have told me anyway. She was never one to dwell on negative feelings, as she preferred the "if you pretend it's not happening, maybe it will go away" approach for all things, big and small. When I told her we were worried that something larger was going on with Will, she thought we were crazy and told us to give him more time to reach his milestones. Even when I told her what the doctor said, she showed no signs that she fully grasped what it meant. I often wondered if it was her way of coping or if she really didn't understand what we dealt with every day.

Sometimes I wished I could be like her, that I could keep my eyes focused on the present, and not what had happened in the past. If I could, then I wouldn't feel the burden of finding out what happened to Amelia and John, of thinking about all that we had gone through with Will. I imagined I would feel much lighter, sleep sounder, if I didn't feel as though I constantly had to try to find the meaning of our struggles.

"Before we all head home, do you guys want to see something neat? Like, really, really neat?" I said as we picked over a plate of fries at Champs, a sports bar in downtown Lake Geneva. Will didn't turn to look and Charlotte's head bobbed slightly, her eyes glazed over. They were both flushed from spending two hours outside, in a park and on the lakeshore in nearby Fontana, across the lake.

Luke eyed me with suspicion, but I just told him to follow my directions once we got to the car.

It looked even more magnificent, and even more decrepit, the second time I saw Monarch Manor. I noticed the roof wasn't just in disrepair, it was caving in, pieces falling inside, disappearing into the dark void at the center of the structure. Yet I saw that the shingles that remained glinted with a mother-of-pearl stillness as they overlapped in the fish-scale pattern. It looked like small hands folded over one another, keeping the secrets of the former inhabitants safe, until they disintegrated into dust, no longer tasked with the charge.

"It looks like a haunted house," Charlotte said as she climbed out of our minivan and hopped off the running board.

"Should we go inside to be sure?" Luke said with a grin, and made a motion to grab her arm. "I'm sure the ghosts won't mind."

"No way!" She stepped back, pressing herself against the car. "They'll eat my face and steal my body."

I looked at Luke. "Maybe no more scary cartoons? Just a thought." I turned back to the house. "Well?"

He took a step forward, his mouth bending into a small, bemused smile. "Well, it's . . . a craphole just like you said. And yes, probably haunted."

I folded my arms over my chest as I walked toward it, my

eyes scanning the rotting wood and the peeling paint. "It's amazing." I stopped and looked out over the lake, at the crumbling pier that still jutted into the water. "Amelia and John were here, right where I'm standing." I bent down and put my fingertips on the yellowing grass and chickweed on what I imagined was once a magnificent green lawn, dotted with ladies carrying parasols and butterflies flitting in the breeze. I could picture children playing on the once-grand veranda, their knees skinned and palms sporting a dusting of dirt. Out on the water, pristine white sailboats formed a regatta, the children pointing at them and rooting for their favorite one.

I pictured Amelia on the steps, with John in her lap, as they watched the boats. The summer air caused the backs of his legs to stick against her skirt, and she brushed his hair from his sweaty head, so the lake breeze could touch his skin and cool him. I wondered if she ever knew how lucky she was to have this place, to have this sanctuary.

Still crouching down, I turned to Luke, my voice swelling. "They were here."

He studied my expression for a moment before he relaxed his arms and walked over. He nodded. "What a view," he said after taking in the scene again. "I can see why they built it right here. You can see almost the entire lakeshore."

Will gave a screech from inside the running car, where he was strapped into a five-point harness, watching a Pixar movie from the flip-down TV screen. He started thrashing his arms in frustration. Luke turned and walked to the car, leaning inside. I saw him hit the Chapter Forward button twice before Will stopped flailing, his body calm once again. Almost all of our DVDs had been "well loved" to the point of freezing and skipping, something that drove Will nuts. Which I totally understood. It would have driven me nuts, too.

"Mom, is that Geneva Lake down there?" Charlotte called, brave enough again to step toward the house.

I held out my hand. "C'mon."

"O-kay," she said slowly as Luke stayed with Will in the car while we walked toward the water. Her eyes shifted to the crumbling house every few seconds, as though she wanted to make sure all the ghosts stayed put. (And her face stayed on her head.)

When we reached the water's edge, the lake sparkled in front of us, a deep navy blue. Choppy waves splashed against the edge, where a beautiful rock wall once stood but was now a mess of tumbled boulders and moss-covered edges. I stopped just before the pier, as I didn't dare set foot on the rickety wood. But that, too, I could picture as it once was. The wood was a gleaming white, polished every day by deckhands. The children would run down from the kitchen with stale bread to entice the sunfish to come to the surface. When the sunlight would hit the water just right, their silvery bodies could be seen in between the strands of seaweed sprouting from the rocky bottom. Maybe John had a favorite fish, one he fed each day, his secret summer pet.

"The water looks really dark here, Mommy," Charlotte said as she leaned forward and tried to peer down. "I can't see the bottom, even."

"It does look really deep. I wonder how far it goes down." As I said the words, my heart beat quicker as I thought of Amelia and John, surrounded by all that dark water. Were they at the bottom somewhere, their bodies resting together forever, a permanent part of the lake?

Charlotte shivered as a breeze came across the water and whipped against our bare arms. As we turned to walk back to the car, I looked up again at Monarch Manor, wondering which broken window had been Amelia's bedroom, wishing I could reach through time and hold her hand.

After the twins were in bed that night, I sat awake in my bedroom. On my phone I had tapped *Monarch Manor* into the search bar, again scanning all of the available photos online and rereading every blurb about the house. I knew it all by heart at that point, but it was comforting to read the words again and see the same pictures. Like the house was frozen in time and wasn't the pile of debris on the lakeshore that I had seen that afternoon.

I wondered if it was the same for Will. When he insisted on reading the same books over and over or eating his food off of the same plate, did he feel that same sense of comfort? In that a lot of things didn't make sense to him, but he could control this one small thing, this one tiny corner of his universe? In the same way, the yacht accident and Amelia and John's fate was a glaring question to me, yet I could reread the blurbs online about the mansion's construction and the tea parties and feel some sense of accomplishment.

I set my phone down next to a sleeping Luke and looked over at the stack of unsold books I had grabbed from the estate sale. They were haphazardly set on my dresser, a collection of rough-hewn covers in light blue and red. I walked over and picked up the first one: *A Tale of Two Cities*, a likely leftover from when my mother was in high school. I opened the inside cover and saw the stamp for the library of Wilmot Union High School, where my mother had gone to school.

"Hopefully the overdue fines aren't still collecting," I said with a laugh. I grabbed another book, an old Bible, and flipped through the pages like an accordion, the paper crinkling and the spine giving a satisfying crack after years of hibernation. I was about to set it back when I saw a small card resting at the bottom, underneath a physics textbook.

I bent down and fished it out with two fingers. It was a funeral prayer card, for Emily, my great-grandmother. It read: BORN ON OCTOBER 25, 1918, DIED ON APRIL 1, 1988, with a caption under a picture of Saint Theresa the Little Flower on the front. On the back was a short blurb:

EMILY KOEHLER,
BELOVED DAUGHTER, AUNT, SISTER, MOTHER, AND WIFE,
WAS PRECEDED IN DEATH BY: BELOVED SON, EMIL;
HER GRANDPARENTS CASSANDRA, THEODORE,
CONRAD, AND MARY;
MOTHER AND FATHER, ELEANOR AND GEORGE;
SISTER, LOUISA;
AUNT AND UNCLE JANE AND EDWARD; AND OTHERS.

Two things immediately occurred to me: It confirmed that John and my great-grandmother Emily were first cousins. And, more important, John and Amelia weren't listed in the deceased relatives. "What the . . ." I whispered as I turned the card over, certain I had missed something. I couldn't imagine why they weren't mentioned. Even if they had survived the accident, surely Amelia would have died by 1988. They must have been intentionally left off.

I texted my mom a picture of the prayer card, noting the confirmed family connection and the glaring omission. She immediately texted back: *Looks like you have a family mystery to solve, Watson.*

No way, I'm Sherlock, I sent back.

You're cute, was the reply.

I set my phone down and relaxed back against my pillow. I put the prayer card on my nightstand and closed my eyes. Yet sleep didn't come for hours later, as the questions from the card haunted me every time I started to drift off.

CHAPTER 11

AMELIA

Amelia was brought out of her wistful contemplation on the veranda by Jane screeching. Again. This time, all it took was one lone, slightly off-center teacup to set her off. Long tables, covered in freshly pressed cotton tablecloths, lined the front of Monarch Manor's yard, with gold spindle chairs placed at each setting. Mary's best china, bought in London several years ago, was on each table, a white teacup with etched pink flowers neatly placed to the side of each plate. At the front of each place setting was a folded pink place card, with names such as *Mrs. Charles Wacker* scrawled on the front by a calligrapher. Down the center of each table were pink roses in silver vases lined up in military precision.

Everything was perfect. Except for one place setting.

"We may as well just cancel the luncheon," Jane hissed to Amelia after she came down from the veranda and onto the lawn. Jane grabbed her arm. "Why do these things always happen to me?"

"Stop," Amelia said as she shrugged her sister's arm away, rubbing where there would certainly be a bruise later. She followed her sister's trembling finger to the place setting for Mrs. David Whittingham, the mother of the groom.

"She's already noticed that the handle of the bread knife isn't pointed at exactly eleven o'clock. She said"—Jane straightened her spine and held her head at an angle, her wide-brimmed white hat tilting on her head—" 'I hope this oversight isn't any indication of how the rest of the festivities will occur.' " Jane slumped her shoulders forward and sighed. "It's already a disaster."

Amelia leaned over the table and straightened the teacup, so that it was in line with the others. "Fixed. Now, please, worry about something important." She gave her sister a wry smile before Jane pursed her lips and walked over to a gathering crowd of admirers in long white dresses and white gloves.

Amelia tapped at the sweat already forming on her hairline, under her own straw hat. She took a deep breath, trying to gather the strength to have meaningless conversations while politely nodding. The traditional pre-wedding bridal luncheon was something she would have happily skipped, had she not feared that her mother would string her up should she miss it. It all seemed so pointless—why have an event for everyone to socialize when the entire evening would be spent socializing and catching up? It felt like one more opportunity for the guests to enjoy free food and drinks while the parents of the bride spent more money.

There were so many other things to think about, worry over. Plan for.

She walked over to the table with refreshments, her heels sinking in the grass, and a maid poured her a glass of lemonade. "Again, pink," she said when she saw the sticky sweet liquid in her glass. "If I never see pink again before I die, then . . ." She stopped, and exhaled slowly.

"You'll what?" Margaret Cartwright, Amelia's mother-in-law, appeared at her side and Amelia startled, nearly spilling the pink lemonade down her printed dress.

Amelia hadn't been alerted of her arrival, despite Alfred promising to send word when she arrived. "Excuse me," she said as she put down her glass and patted her dress. "I was just remarking how beautiful the pinks are in the wedding. How it complements the roses in bloom on the property." Her hands shook and her throat closed, holding back all her words and cracking her composure.

Margaret narrowed her eyes. "Yes. Of course you were." She sighed as she scanned the crowd of women gathering on the lawn. "One more day to endure, I suppose. It's nothing like the Dickerman wedding from last season. Now that was something to talk about."

Amelia nodded, her body loosening as she clasped her stomach so as to avoid a snicker. She had heard that a guest had far too many brandy cocktails and tripped on the front lawn, staining the front of her white silk skirt. She heard that the bride's mother had fired the gardener the next day, citing uneven terrain for her guests.

She should have fired the waiter who kept making the guest those drinks, Amelia had thought.

Yet Jane thought the gesture was glamorous, a glittering display of power. Firing a servant over something that was clearly not his fault. Real power, power over other people, could only come with that kind of wealth. The kind of money that scared other people into believing whatever it was you wanted them to think, whatever it was that they should believe.

Amelia tried to swallow, wondering if Margaret had asked about John, about where he was, about where he should be. She turned toward her, ready to ask one of her practiced questions about a new Monet they had purchased, but instead she saw Margaret staring at someone. She followed her gaze across the lawn, to where a handsome man with a swoop of brown hair stood, frosted drink in hand, smiling in her direction. She couldn't help but twist her mouth into a smile before she thought better of it. She lifted a gloved hand toward him, and he started across the lawn.

"Oh my," Margaret said, one hand at her throat in mock surrender. "Just who is that?"

"Matthew Cottingsley. An old friend." It was the truth, but so much more was left unsaid. The way they ran through the lawn of Monarch Manor when they were kids, daring each other to find another toad. She and Matthew collected them in metal pails that they took to his family's estate, Cottingsley Glen, and then released them close to the pond on the property. His summer tutor, Miss Olverio, hated the sound of the toads as they closed out the day and the dusk fell into the night. Matthew had hated the way she made him sit on the stuffy porch each morning, the one built erroneously on the south side of the house, without so much as a breeze from the lake. It became the punishment porch, a place to idle away the mornings under the watchful and often in-motion ruler of his tutor. Amelia and Matthew would watch from outside as she paced around in her room, throwing her hands up as the toads croaked away in a disorganized symphony for hours.

As the chorus would die down, she would lean out her window and yell, *"Finalmente!"* They never knew if she saw them down there, giggling, running back through the maple tree woods to Monarch Manor, but they both secretly hoped she did.

"Amelia, finally." Matthew moved toward an embrace, but after he saw the way her eyes widened he stopped and took her hand. "So good to see you."

His touch was like a favorite dress, one she wasn't sure would still fit but always did. A relic of the past, which would always fit against her. Amelia's eyes darted from Margaret to him, her heart beating against her sundress so hard she was sure they could see her chest quiver. "And you as well. How was your trip into town?"

"Long," he said, and for the first time she saw the crinkles around his eyes and the lines on his forehead.

How long has it been? So very long. Too long. Too late.

He ran a hand through his hair, the thick brown locks brushing against his forehead. "Yours?"

She nodded, slightly tilting her head to the side. "And each day leading up to the event is longer than the last." She heard how breathy her voice had become, how she sounded like a child again. But Matthew always made her feel that way, like the past was something she could touch, feel, hold. Like her soul was bright and untouched by all that she had felt. With him there, at Monarch Manor, it felt as though she had dipped a hand into the well of her childhood and pulled out a few shimmery drops of magic.

He smiled. "I can only imagine how crazed Jane has become. I remember the year she had her sixteenth birthday, and how she ordered all of us to dress in stark white suits."

"Ah, yes. And then you and several of your friends drank too much champagne and slid down the hill into the lake." She laughed. She could still see her sister's red face, veins popping out of her neck, a crooked finger pointing toward them, before she screamed so loud it woke up the children at Havighurst, three estates down the road.

"I don't regret a thing," he said. He looked at her intensely, their eyes meeting briefly, and her stomach dropped at the memory. The night of the party, she had escorted the boys into the dairy barn and handed out towels and fresh clothes. Matthew had been the last to arrive, and the barn was empty, save for the two of them. As she had handed him his towel, her hand had brushed his chest. He brought his hand up, his fingers lightly resting over hers. In that moment, everything changed.

It was like the first time she noticed how beautiful the hydrangeas along the south lawn looked in the morning. They had always been there, yet she had accepted them as a normal part of the garden. It wasn't until she was older that she truly saw them for the first time, the way their blooms exploded against one another and their heart-shaped leaves framed them like a fan. Her mother told her the gardeners had added food to the soil to make them bloom, to reach their full potential.

After that moment, Matthew would never simply be her childhood friend again. She knew their childhood together, their closeness, their friendship, was their own food in the soil in which they were planted.

The memory of their intimacy made Amelia's cheeks turn pink and she looked away, fanning her face with her hand.

"It's such a warm afternoon," she said quickly, keenly aware of Margaret's presence. She took a quick breath, steadying her voice, before she held a hand out toward her mother-in-law. "Please, meet Margaret Cartwright."

Matthew took Margaret's hand and bowed his head slightly. "Pleasure to meet you."

There was a long silence, in which Margaret's mouth curled upward like a marionette, a signal that her internal recording was turned on and anything that was said would be stored for later use.

"Where's your handsome boy?" Matthew's voice broke the silence, a tiny pebble rippling against a smooth lake surface.

"He is playing on the south lawn with his cousin Emily, Eleanor's daughter." She shifted uncomfortably, watching Margaret out of the corner of her eye before she squinted toward the lawn, but she saw that it was empty. She whipped her head around, searching the lawn for any sign of the children, but it was only adults milling around. She took a faltering step toward the water, her pulse quickening as she searched the rocks, looking for John's tiny frame.

He knows not to go in the water.

He knows.

"Do you want me to search for him?" Matthew said, his hand at her elbow, as he took a half step toward the lake.

"No, no. Thank you. I'm sure he's inside, tormenting Alfred." She gave him a shaky smile before she turned and quickly walked toward the house, her ankles wobbling against the tree roots and uneven spots in the grass.

"And do you see this here? This is the beautiful fairy who grants wishes to the toys. She's the one who makes them Real. She knows when a toy is loved so much, when it's so special, that nothing can ever be done to it. She—" Amelia heard her mother's voice break, and she swallowed hard. She stood outside the nursery, after having scoured nearly the entire estate looking for John. She startled one maid who was arranging roses in vases in the parlor, who wordlessly pointed upstairs.

She had heard her mother's voice reading *The Velveteen Rabbit* as she walked on the polished oak floors. She began to tiptoe, listening, careful not to step on any creaking spots. She still knew the floors well, from when she and Eleanor would sneak out under the cover of darkness, strip off their nightgowns, and go for a midnight swim beneath the stars so numerous and bright, it looked like a carafe of milk had been spilled across the sky.

When she heard her mother's voice tighten with emotion, and she could no longer speak, Amelia stepped into the doorway. She saw that while her mother knew John couldn't hear the words she said, she had pointed to the pictures and gestured with her hands. Amelia had read the book to John so many times, despite it being published the year before, that John remembered everything in the story. When her mother didn't look up, Amelia cleared her throat.

"Oh!" Mary put a hand to her chest and smiled, eyes closing briefly. She closed the book and patted John on the head before carefully standing, fanning out the skirt of her dress before she rose.

"I was looking all over for him. I suppose I should have thought to look in the most obvious of places," Amelia said as she smiled at John. She watched as he took the book, opened it back up, and began to trace the pictures with his pointer finger.

"I'm sorry if I frightened you. He was sitting alone at the luncheon, looking wide-eyed as you always did when your father and I had one of our big parties. He saw me, and walked over and grabbed my hand." Mary looked over at John and raised her eyebrows. "It was wonderful timing, since I was able to avoid a conversation with Mrs. Bartlett about her prestigious home award . . . twenty years ago."

Amelia laughed. Mr. Bartlett had built their summer home as a gift to his wife and insisted it be done in time for her birthday. Apparently, the construction took longer than expected, so he borrowed a circus tent from his friend the circus man P. T. Barnum to tent the house so the work could continue throughout the snowy winter. It was all worth it, as Mrs. Bartlett never failed to mention at a social event, since *Ladies' Home Journal* awarded it one of the most beautiful country homes in America. Nearly twenty years ago.

"Thank you for rescuing him, even if he rescued you right back," Amelia said.

Mary didn't say a word but simply walked over to John and kissed his head. He looked up at her and smiled, reaching his hand upward. She clasped it and whispered, "Sweet angel. I will always be with you."

CHAPTER 12

ERIN

I felt like time stopped as the side doors of the school gym opened and the kindergarteners began to process out, toward the empty risers. The teachers went first, the morning group and the full-day group, smiling as they led the kids toward the stage. Each kid fell into step behind the one in front, sneaking glances out toward the crowd, where parents stood and waved frantically. I could tell that none of the kids remembered where they were supposed to go, as the teachers frantically arranged them, asking them to stand still and stop poking one another.

The group of mothers in front of me nudged one another, their stylish patterned tops and leather earrings swaying back and forth. I realized with embarrassment that they must have been fellow kindergarten moms . . . and I had no idea. I had seen them walk in together, their hair curled around their shoulders, their nails painted shades of gray. They waved to the redhead in front of me, who gestured toward the empty seats next to her. They sat in every other seat, waiting for husbands to fill in the A-B pattern. And I watched as the husbands, too, appeared, dressed in expensive suits with large watches on their wrists.

It had been so long—college, likely—since I had been part of a group. That I had people I could ask to carpool or to save me a seat at the recital. My friends faded away after Will was diagnosed, although I can't say I was responsive before that, being overwhelmed with having twins, let alone twins with special needs. Will had no real friends, and I realized as I sat there I no longer did, either.

Over the perfect blond waves in front of me, I saw Will come out of the door, his special ed teacher, Miss Ball, holding his hand, as she led him to the end. She put her hands on his shoulders, on the blue polo shirt that I had picked out for him, marveling that morning at how handsome he looked in it, and gently scooted him closer to the little girl on the end. Her yellow braids bobbing, she smiled at Will. I saw him study her face for a moment, and then he frowned. That familiar frown that signaled his anxiety pot was about to boil over.

"Oh no. Oh no." My ears started to ring and I looked at Luke, a white-hot chill running down my spine. He shook his head slightly, in what I'm sure he thought was a calming gesture, but I could see the fear on his face, too.

I know that look.

"Why does your face look like that, Mommy?" Charlotte asked from her seat next to me. Her fall recital had been two days before, at our home elementary school, and they sang a song about spiders. Well, most of them did. Charlotte mostly twirled her hair and played with her dress.

I didn't answer her as I half-stood, ready to dart up to the stage and pick him up should he start to cry. Then would come the collapse to the floor, like all of his bones were removed, followed by the wailing. It was the sequence of behavior that usually meant we had to leave a public place.

I was ready for a repeat, this time on a much more personal stage, but his teacher bent down and whispered something in his ear and his expression changed. The tension left his face, and while he slowly looked around the room with a wary eye I could tell that his nerves weren't as elevated as they usually were.

I sat back down, my spine straight, perched on the edge of my chair, ready to spring into action. Luke tried to put a hand on my leg, but I brushed it away. I didn't need anything impeding my movements when I needed to rescue him (and the rest of the recital from being ruined). The piano started, and the first few lines of a kindergarten song, something about going for a walk to a pool, began.

"Mommy, Mommy, this is the same one that I sang!" Charlotte whispered excitedly as she grabbed at my arm.

"Yes, honey. I know," I whispered. Charlotte had sung the song nearly every day, seemingly on the hour, every hour, for a month. I could perform it in my sleep, and I'm sure some of the neighbors could as well. But I hadn't realized that it was the same song Will was learning at his school, maybe as part of a district-wide decision by the music department.

"Come on, buddy," I said under my breath as I watched Will stand silent, hands over his ears, through the first verse of the song.

Charlotte grabbed my hand and squeezed tight. "Mommy, he looks like he's going to cry."

"I know, honey. Please, please, just let him be okay," I whispered.

By the time the second verse began, he shut his eyes. I dropped Charlotte's hand and stood up quickly, tunnel vision forming. I couldn't see anything but Will up on stage. I stepped over all the parents in my row, not hearing their grunts of annoyance as I tripped in front of their recording phones. Finally, I made it to the side of the gym and half-crouched as I got to the front row. Will had opened his eyes and seen me approach, and we made eye contact for a brief moment. In that split second, his shoulders seemed to relax a bit.

He is going to be fine. He will calm down now, I thought as I watched his face.

And he might have been, if the song hadn't ended right then and the crowd burst into loud applause. Applause to show how proud they were of the children, applause to boost their confidence.

And yet, as with most things that other children loved, Will hated it. He let out a high-pitched scream of terror and clamped his hands over his ears before collapsing on the floor. I tore up to the front of the stage, my heartbeat in my ears, my face turning red, as I scooped him up into my arms. I don't remember how I got outside of the gym with him, as everything went blank, but I did see Luke and Charlotte come out seconds later.

Will was still screaming in my arms, his body shaking in terror. "It's okay. You're safe," I whispered to him, pressing my arms tightly around him. I slid down onto the floor, curling him into my lap, rocking him gently.

Charlotte came over and put a hand on her brother's face. He stopped screaming once he felt her touch, although his body was still racked with sobs. I looked up and then saw that Charlotte, too, had started to cry.

"I'm sad," she said with ragged breaths. "He's scared."

I reached a hand out and pulled her toward me, too, and hugged both of them.

Will's teacher, Miss Ball, came out of the gym and found us in the hallway. "Poor guy," she said with a sympathetic frown. "It's so loud in there. Who can blame him?" Her long blond hair twisted around her shoulders like a waterfall.

"So loud," Luke repeated woodenly. His cheeks creased as he rubbed a hand across his face.

"He did great in the rehearsals yesterday, so we were hoping for the best," she added. She looked at me. "I'm so sorry he's upset."

"Me too," I said. I pressed him more tightly to me as I stood up, holding him to my chest. I reached down and put a hand on Charlotte's shoulder. I looked to Luke. "Did you get our coats? I think we should go home."

I saw him hesitate before he went back into the gym, as though he had assumed Will could rejoin the group or that we should try to stay. It was forever our dilemma: How hard do we push? But this time, I knew that pushing was a terrible idea.

"Good-bye, Will. See you tomorrow," Miss Ball said as she leaned over, Will's head still on my shoulder.

We walked out of the school in silence. As I buckled Will into his car seat, smoothing back his sweaty hair, I wondered where we had gone wrong. Was it too much to expect him to be in a recital? Was that fair to him? Was it fair to assume he *couldn't* do something?

I knew that we shouldn't set him up to fail, but I had no idea how to do that when I didn't know where the goalposts were most days. If I had any sense of what was possible and what wasn't, I could make that choice. But even after five years, I still didn't know what to expect from my son.

On the way home, I heard my phone beeping with a text message, and I ignored it. I ignored it on the chance it was my mom or my sister, asking how the recital went. Finally, after the twins were in bed, I looked at it.

It was my mom, but the message wasn't at all about the recital. It read: *Going through one of the boxes from Grandma's house that we set aside. Found something interesting. Call me.*

"Well?" I said as she picked up.

"What took you so long?" my mom replied. I took a deep breath, prepared to tell her what happened, but she didn't wait for me to answer. "Remember all those boxes that we set aside, filled with what we laughed were 'memories'?"

I grunted in response. Most of the boxes contained things like old newspaper articles from the local *Powers Lake Gazette,* with articles circled about how such-and-such distant relative had completed their first marathon or how their pig had come in fourth in the Walworth County Fair's 4-H competition.

"Well, at the bottom of one I found an old prayer book that belonged to my grandmother Emily. It's covered in ratty white satin material, and I thought it was blank, but just as I was about to toss it back in the box, a newspaper article came fluttering out of it."

"Okay?" I closed my eyes and sank back down on the pillow, trying to push away my annoyance that she didn't remember the recital, even though I didn't want to talk about it.

"Well, dear daughter, the article is dated May 30, 1923, two days after the accident with Amelia and John. And while most of it is just a recap of what happened, there is one quote from the article by someone who claims to have seen her on the train platform the next day, on a train bound for the Big Apple." Her voice ticked up in triumph as she finished.

"New York? Really?" I sat up and rubbed my forehead. "No, that can't be true."

"You said there were rumors that she jumped and took the kid with her, right? Maybe she had to get rid of him and run away to New York. Probably had a boyfriend out there, secret lover, the whole shebang," my mom said. "It makes sense."

I thought about it for a moment, the idea that she staged the whole accident to run away with a secret boyfriend, and again my gut said, *No. She didn't do that.* "Well, people say lots of things. Who knows? Who was this that said they saw her?"

"Hang on." I heard rustling in the background as she muttered to herself. "A . . . Georgina Lindemann. Listed as a close friend of the Cartwright family. And a Matthew Cottingsley was quoted as saying, 'I simply can't believe that Amelia and John are gone. I still hold out hope that they are alive, somewhere.' And then—get this—it says: 'When reached for a comment, Mr. and Mrs. Hoppe declined to comment.' Sure sounds like they think she did it, too."

I pressed my lips together for a moment before I exhaled loudly. "So what? It doesn't mean anything."

My mom chuckled. "Whatever you say, kiddo. Just thought you would want to know. The bigger question is: Why would someone keep it? Seems like a pretty weird thing to hang on to, especially if the family had no official comment, right? Listen, kiddo, I have to go. But just wanted to tell you the news."

After I hung up, I searched for *Matthew Cottingsley, Lake Geneva* on my phone. I quickly learned that his family was one of the first investors in the Cottingsley Tool Company, which later became a major hardware chain. His family had an estate on the north shore of the lake called Cottingsley Glen, which was ravaged by fire in the 1950s.

At the end of one article, one particular fact made me swallow hard: Matthew Cottingsley never married, as it was rumored his true love was his childhood sweetheart, Amelia Hoppe, a widow who died in a boating accident with her young son.

I slowly put my phone down and looked out the window at the ancient maple tree in the front yard, watching the leaves sway in the cool fall breeze as I wondered if Matthew ever released his hope that Amelia and John were alive or if he had reason to believe they had survived the accident.

I then looked up Georgina Lindemann, the close family friend who claimed to have seen Amelia on the train. I learned that her husband came from New York society, old money, and owned half of the city. When I clicked on the image search, the first photo that came up was of her and Margaret Cartwright at a ladies' tea. The way they stood together, hips touching, made me believe that they were, in fact, best friends. I imagined that Georgina must have known Amelia well, or at least well enough to recognize her easily.

How could it be a case of mistaken identity if Georgina was Amelia's mother-in-law's best friend?

I stood up and pulled open the front door, the old wood creaking as it always did, and stepped out onto the crooked front porch. The air had the unmistakably crisp autumn smell of crinkled leaves and browning leaves. The streetlights illuminated the sidewalks, and I watched as the fallen leaves danced down the street with each kiss of wind. I sat down in my porch swing, making a note again to ask Luke to bring it inside before winter came. I wrapped my gray cardigan tighter around my waist, and I closed my eyes and breathed in deeply, trying to make sense of what my mother told me.

CHAPTER 13

AMELIA

It was sounds that kept Amelia alive and connected to the world during the summer of 1918. She spent two months in her bedroom at Monarch Manor, the window open and the lake breeze flowing through her room that held the smell of sickness no matter how windy the day.

The sounds began each morning as the sun would barely begin to peek over the horizon, of the engineers as they gathered on the white piers. She would already be awake, staring at the grooves on her bedroom ceiling, waiting for them. Patrick would always be first, grunting orders with his thick Irish brogue, his voice still heavy with sleep. She would hear the shoveling of coal, of the metal tip being thrust into the pile and depositing it into the yacht's engine with a rat-a-tat-tat of spilling rocks. Soon she would smell the fire as the engine was lit and then hear the testing of the whistle, a low, sweet tone that woke everyone else in the house.

She could picture it all in her mind, the white pier gradually illuminating with the brilliant yellows and oranges of the sunrise, first lighting the lake and then softly moving across the white boards of the pier and then, finally, across the *Monarch*

Princesses slowly bobbing in the water. She could hear all of it, picture it as though she were there, but she couldn't see any of it. Nor did she see anything else but the ceiling tiles—there were exactly forty-four of them—and anything else she could spot if she turned her head to the right or left.

She didn't see anything for two months, almost the entire summer, when she lay in her room, sick from influenza when she was six months pregnant.

She had first felt ill when she and Henry rode the train up to the estate for the weekend, after he was done with work for the day at the bank. As the train listed from side to side, she suddenly felt hot, like her insides were burning, and the mass of people in front of her began to swirl. She had grabbed Henry's arm to steady herself.

"Is everything all right? Do you need some water?" Henry had asked. Since she had told him about the pregnancy, he had been at her side constantly, asking how she felt and what she needed. She had heard from her friends that their husbands were never as interested in their pregnancies as they were, but with Henry it was different. She sometimes felt as though he wished he could be the one carrying the child.

By the time their train reached the Williams Bay station, she could barely stand, and Henry had to carry her up the porch steps with the aid of one of the deckhands. He laid her in her childhood bedroom, calling for the doctor. He came and examined her, and she heard him grimly say, "Influenza," outside of her door. "It's widespread," he had said. "She needs to rest, especially given her condition."

So there she stayed for the entire summer, as Henry went back and forth to the city on the train. He came the first few weekends, until the doctors convinced him to stay in the city. "Work obligations," her mother had said as she smoothed Amelia's hair back. The sheet was pulled up to her shoulders, and her skin was slick with sweat, despite feeling cold all over.

She shivered so hard that her stomach bump jumped around, like it was dancing.

She turned her head away from her mother, a task that felt monumental. She knew why Henry stayed in Chicago. It was for him to stay healthy in case she didn't make it. In case either of them didn't make it. She closed her eyes slowly and said a prayer that if one life had to be taken, let it be hers.

On Sundays, she would wait for the afternoon sun to move high above the lake and strain her neck to hear the sounds of the Crane steam yacht approaching. The boat would drop anchor off of Monarch Manor, and their large Victrola on deck would come to life, playing a selected opera recording. She would hear the family and staff gather down on the veranda overlooking the lake to listen to the music and then, when it was done, cue up their own Victrola and volley music right back, usually one of her mother's favorites by Vivaldi.

"Do you want me to ask the Cranes to stop the tradition? Does it bother you or disrupt your rest?" her mother had asked her one Sunday evening when she stopped in to bring her fresh water.

Amelia weakly lifted a hand in the air. "No. Please—no." It was all she could say, but there was so much more. It was one of the few times when she was reminded that there was a world outside of her bedroom, that there were people laughing, eating, drinking, and listening to beautiful music. They walked around without struggle and breathed without coughing. Maybe, someday, she could do those things again, too.

The evening of the Fourth of July, she listened to the fireworks outside of her window. They flashed red and blue and white throughout her bedroom, illuminating the bedsheets that covered her stomach.

"Just think, next Fourth of July you will be able to bring the baby to watch all of the festivities," Mary had said brightly, yet Amelia heard the catch in her voice.

And so, as she lay in bed for another day, another memory missed, she made a promise that her mother's words would come true and that her son or daughter would watch the fireworks the next year, from her lap. That the child would be startled by the sound of each one and cry, while the adults would lovingly laugh and try to soothe him or her.

The next morning, she was able to sit up in bed and slowly sip a cup of broth. The baby inside her shifted as she did so, and she took it as a good sign. A sign of encouragement.

Later that afternoon, she listened again, this time to the sounds of her mother hosting afternoon tea, promptly at four o'clock. She heard the kitchen staff trudging their way to the vegetable garden to pick the cucumbers for the sandwiches, and eventually, the sound of the steam yachts approaching the dock as the women came for tea.

When she heard them leave, her door opened.

"You are looking so much better. I told the ladies that I think you will be better in no time," Mary said. She sat on the edge of the bed, her white sundress splayed underneath her and her feathered hat perched on the side of her head. In her hands she held a clear glass bottle. "Frances brought some witch hazel for you."

Frances Hutchinson's estate, Wychwood, was famous for the witch hazel plants grown on the property, and she was always extolling the benefits of the plants.

Mary leaned over and took a cotton handkerchief from the bedside table and dotted some witch hazel on it. She slowly rubbed the cloth against Amelia's forehead. The liquid immediately cooled her skin and made her feel like she had slipped under the surface of the lake, water soothing every pore.

The following week, she was able to stand, albeit for a brief moment before she collapsed down into a maid's arms. A few days later, she took a step forward, toward the window, toward the water that stretched before her. From her vantage point in the bed, she couldn't see the other side, and it looked like the water went on forever, that there was no other shore. That everything in the world had been swallowed up by the water. Yet when she stood, she could see that there was another side and that the water did end.

She pressed a palm against the window and opened her eyes wide, taking in everything that she had missed seeing that summer: the white sailboats lazily floating on the surface during a regatta, the ducks waddling around the perimeter of the property, the dome of Yerkes Observatory jutting above the tree line in Williams Bay. It all looked the same, yet the world was different. She was different.

She placed a hand on her stomach and felt the baby shift under the weight of her palm. She pressed down on what seemed to be his or her bottom, and she cupped it in her hand, patting it slowly, rhythmically.

"It's you and me, together, forever," she whispered. "We have been each other's constant this summer. And next summer, you will get to see and hear everything that I do."

The noises of the house kept her alive that summer, reminded her that there was an outside to her room, that there were things to experience beyond fevers and night sweats. She never could have imagined that her son, due to her illness, would be robbed of the ability to hear those same things.

CHAPTER 14

ERIN

I turned my car down the worn gravel path that led from the road to Monarch Manor, holding my breath the entire way. Even though I had driven by the house from time to time after the first time I saw it a couple of weeks ago, it never ceased to amaze me. There was something so magical about the juxtaposition of great beauty and terrible decay. There wasn't a time when I approached it that I didn't nearly gasp with admiration and sadness. Yet this time, the gasp that left my body was all sadness.

The wrecking crew was already there, big yellow machines lining the property, while men in hard hats pointed toward the structure and nodded, their feet shuffling in the rocky driveway. I pulled my car off to the side and their heads snapped in unison toward me, like an unwelcome visitor entering a locals-only bar. A man with a dress shirt and a plastic name tag clipped to his pocket walked toward my car.

"You from the township?" He had a weary look in his eyes, like dealing with the township had slowly been killing him with each house he tore down. Or, maybe, it was the houses' revenge for destroying them, I thought. In exchange, they stole a little piece of his soul.

"Um, yes?" I said before I could stop myself.

He nodded and walked away, jerking a thumb back toward my car and saying something to his crew. Whatever it was, it wasn't glowing praise, as they all glared at me in one singular yellow-hatted ball of hate. Yet they didn't require any more of me, so I stayed in my car and watched without making eye contact with any of them.

I watched as the man in the dress shirt whipped his arm in a circle over his head—*Let's get to it.* Four of the men climbed into enormous yellow machines and whirred them to life. I watched as they approached Monarch Manor in a combat line, pausing for a moment before driving forward, knocking easily into the rotting wood and crumbling plaster.

My heart began to pound as I saw the back of the house collapse forward, the roof caving in and down toward the ground, surrendering to a fate that had been decided decades before, when everyone abandoned it. The bulldozer pressed forward toward the lake, the rubble pile growing bigger, until it reached the veranda, the place where I pictured the Hoppe sisters—and Emily and John—sitting and staring out at the lake. I had imagined that they sat on the porch, eyes trained over the sparkling water, and assumed the house would stand witness throughout the decades.

The bulldozers pushed forward again, and the porch collapsed, also gone forever. All that was left was rubble, and the sadness of neglect that permeated the air.

"You look like you need a drink. Beer?" my mom said as she disappeared into her kitchen. She didn't wait for me to answer and appeared with two bottles, thrusting one in my direction.

I took a long pull of the beer, wincing at the bitter, hoppy IPA taste, before I set it down on the scratched oak end table that had existed in their house since before I could remember. "Since when did you start liking craft beer?"

"Someone brought over a twelve-pack for our neighborhood Fourth of July party, and I've been slowly pawning it off on unsuspecting guests." My mom settled down on the couch next to me, tucking her legs up underneath her, a proper light beer in her hand.

Across from us, my dad snored lightly on the love seat, his glasses still perched on his nose and his iPad on his chest. We always joked that he fell asleep whenever he was at any angle greater than ninety degrees. He had welcomed me with a hug, asked me to sit down, and fallen asleep thirty seconds later.

"I just keep thinking it's all such a shame: Amelia, John, the house. The last piece of all of it was torn down, oh, three hours ago. I'm sure some new mansion will go up on the lot, for the low bargain price of ten million." I had seen the houses around the lake, the ones that were meant to look like they had been there forever, bearing a perfectly worn Craftsman cottage style, but they were less than a decade old. They were priced with so many zeros on the end that it was hard for me to imagine who owned them. And almost all of them were summer houses, and none of them looked well loved. It baffled me to think someone had spent multiple millions on a summer house (after all, what did their regular house look like?) and then never used it. At the rate Luke and I were going, our summer house would be a tent in the state park—and even that might be stretching it.

"So what's next, kiddo?" my mother asked as she drained the rest of her beer, glanced down at the empty bottle, and shrugged.

"I'm not sure. I guess I should start researching Amelia, but I'm not sure what to do first. I don't know much about her, other than what the illustrious Internet has told me." I held my hands in the air, full IPA in my right hand. "I did read a whole bunch about that time period, and about how they all had these huge estates, with servants, and nannies, and cooks, and how the women spent all summer up there with the children, while the men came up on the weekends. There was even a special train for them on Friday afternoons, nicknamed 'The Millionaires' Special,' that went straight from downtown Chicago to Lake Geneva so the men could get to their lake homes right away after work."

"Rough life, right?" my mom said as she rolled her eyes.

"Totally. And all these famous people visited at one point, like Monet and Einstein—"

"Probably just there for the booze and parties," my mom said with a laugh.

I nodded. "Why wouldn't they? I read the estates all had crazy names, like Harrose Hall—Harry Selfridge's house—named after him and his wife, Rose."

"No egos at all," she said. "And let me guess: It was *Days of Our Lives*, with everyone sleeping with each other."

I pointed my beer at her. "You got it. Like, if your wife died, you married her sister, or whichever rich, single daughter lived next door."

"These people sound peachy. Sure you want to even research any of this?" she said.

I looked down at my beer bottle and ran a finger along the label. "The little boy, Mom. John and his mother." *Will and me,* I added silently.

"As you wish, kiddo." My mother leaned over and snatched the iPad off my dad's chest.

"What did I miss?" he said, sitting upright and reaching for the tablet.

My mom held it out, away from his grasp. "Nope. We need to do some important research. And you're sleeping."

He shook his head. "No. I was just resting my eyes for a minute." He looked at me. "Sorry, honey."

I smiled. "Don't worry about it, Dad. Besides, I'm not sure what Mom is planning to research, anyway."

She started pecking away at the screen. "Well, since we don't know much about Amelia, let's start with someone we do know something about: Emily, my grandmother."

"Okay," I said slowly. "What do we know about her?"

"That she had two kids: my mom and my uncle Emil, who died sometime in the sixties, I think. And that she lived in Milwaukee, or at least somewhere outside Milwaukee, from the few times I visited her before she died." She peered down at the screen. "Let's see what else we can find."

"Oh! Look at that!" I pointed to a blue link, and my mother clicked on it, taking us to a page on wedding announcements from a 1937 article in the *Milwaukee Sun*. Halfway down the page was Emily's name.

> Mr. and Mrs. David Koehler happily announce the engagement of their son, Scott, to Emily Rochester. The bride, raised in New York City, is the daughter of Mr. and Mrs. George Rochester. A fall wedding in Chicago is planned, after which the couple will honeymoon in Italy and in France. Upon their return, they will reside in Milwaukee, with the groom working at a law firm.

"New York City," my mom said quietly. She turned to me, eyes wide. "Wasn't there some report that Amelia was seen on a train bound for there the day after the accident?"

I nodded slowly, reading the engagement announcement once again. "That might be a coincidence, right? New York City is a big place. That still doesn't mean anything, even if the report was true."

My mother exhaled slowly and handed me the iPad, sitting back and drumming her fingers against her beer bottle. "Or it could mean everything. It would mean that her sister Eleanor might have been involved in helping her escape . . . or that she was possibly involved in John's demise."

I chewed on the inside corner of my mouth, pulse quickening. "That can't be true. So the whole family was involved in some kind of conspiracy to murder a little boy? That's pretty dark."

"I didn't say murder. It could have gone down a number of ways. But still, kiddo, I think this one is worth considering," she said. "After all, her husband was dead, and she was alone. Who knows what frame of mind she was in at the time?"

Later that night, as I lay in the guest bedroom, after Luke convinced me to spend the night at my parents' house and drive home in the morning, I considered the possibility of what my mother said. As I stared up at a picture of my parents on their wedding day, I thought about Amelia jumping off the edge of the yacht, pulling John down with her. And I couldn't help but think of Will.

Life with him at times felt like the brightest of sunrises and the darkest of thunderstorms. The day and the night, and we were never sure what we were going to experience. And during those blackest of moments, when we had no road map to tell us which way to steer, all we had was hope and blind faith. I failed more than I wanted to acknowledge in those times, and that always brought me to my own midnight. My own dark thoughts, of how I was making things worse, not better, for him. Thoughts that I didn't know what I was fighting for anymore, of what I hoped would happen. Of what was fair for me to hope for anymore.

Despite what my mother believed and despite what my worst self whispered to me in difficult times, I still couldn't allow myself to consider the possibility that Amelia did something to John. Even considering whatever she felt at the time, whatever terrible options were in front of her, she couldn't have chosen such a horrible fate for him. No, something else happened, and maybe if I found out I could somehow figure out how to navigate my own difficult choices.

CHAPTER 15

AMELIA

Amelia watched as Cecilia Grant, Jane's soon-to-be sister-in-law, struggled to pull up her pale pink bridesmaid gown over her large chest and hid a smile.

"Mother, this is not the size we ordered. That wretched seamstress must have measured me wrong. I knew we should never have allowed their family to choose who made the gowns!" Cecilia yanked on the silk sleeve so hard that it slipped out of her hand and she smacked herself in the face.

Amelia let out a laugh, and Cecilia turned, her eyes burning with fury, but she said nothing, her face growing redder where she had slapped herself silly. Thankfully, Jane was dressing in the bride's room, with only Mary and a maid attending her. She had wanted to make a grand entrance, even for her wedding attendants.

There were five of them in the room upstairs: Eleanor, Amelia, Cecilia, and two of Jane's friends from school, who lived in Chicago. Jane had requested (*demanded* was more of a proper word, yet the letter stated: *I request...*) that they wear pink silk tea-length dresses with impossibly full skirts and puffy sleeves. They were to be made in Paris by Mary's seamstress, no variations. The bridesmaids' hair was to also be worn swept up, with a spray of pink roses on the side, and the pink satin shoes would have rhinestone buckles on them.

Amelia thought the wedding party looked like a troupe of rouge-covered marionettes.

Somewhere on the other side of the house, in the children's quarters, John was in his room, resting. She had promised him that he could have one of Alfred's treats, a rose-gold-dusted petit four, if he went to his room and lay in his bed. It was bribery, but the only way she could be sure that he wouldn't wander off with so many people milling about the estate, prepping the house.

"Let me help you," Amelia said when she saw Cecilia was still struggling with her gown. The woman glared at her but nodded slightly. Amelia grabbed each side of the gown. "On the count of three. One, two . . . three." On the final count, she jerked upward, hard. At first the dress resisted, but then it slid up to Cecilia's shoulders with a silken sigh of relief.

Amelia waited for a thank-you, but Cecilia turned her back and walked over to a vanity table, barking orders at the maid to style her hair so she wouldn't be late. Amelia walked over to the large window that overlooked the east side of the house, toward the apple orchard and dairy barn. It didn't have a view of the lawn, so all she saw was the glittering lake water below the tree line. The apple trees' white-and-pink blossoms released a light, fruity scent throughout the orchard, signaling that the trees would soon bear fruit in the fall. Amelia could see the farmhands in the dairy barn carrying pails of milk out, lugging them toward the house for Alfred to store in the icebox.

She ran a finger along the glass, just below the leaded octagonal design at the top, and looked toward the familiar outline of Cottingsley Glen, Matthew's childhood home. Only the top tower was visible from Monarch Manor, and she wondered how many times she had stared at it as a child, trying to will Matthew to escape his lessons and come swimming with her.

Henry hadn't believed her when she told him that she used to jump in the water with all of her clothes on as a child. The first time she brought him to Monarch Manor, he looked at her skeptically as they stood on the pier after disembarking the steam yacht. He glanced down at the dark waters below and shook his head.

"Amelia, you've never been one to bend the rules. I just can't picture you running from the nanny and leaping into the deep water, feetfirst." He had outstretched an arm, wanting to pull her close, toward the house, and toward the safety of her familiar role.

She had taken a quick step back, just out of his reach. She knew he was, in his own strange way, trying to compliment her, by implying that he couldn't imagine she was anything but the proper lady he saw in front of him. Yet, in her mind's eye, she could see that dirt-streaked little girl running down the pier barefoot, splinters be damned, Matthew chasing behind.

And so she had turned, kicked off her black heels, and jumped into the water before he could say anything else. It was September, and the water had already begun to turn cold, the springs at the bottom of the lake overtaking the dwindling summer sun. The water felt like a glove on her skin, moving up her spine to the crown of her head. When she surfaced, she saw Henry's slack face, mouth opened, and laughed louder and longer than she could remember.

Of course, the official story became that she had fallen in ("clumsy, adorable Amelia!" as Henry would giddily relay at parties) and he had rescued her, holding his hand out to pull her from the terrifying waters. It was only Patrick, the one deckhand who was still tying up the yacht, who saw. Whenever they crossed paths in the future, only the tiniest of head nods proved neither of them forgot the real story. When he had left to go back to Ireland a year after John was born, Amelia had slipped him an extra purse of money, which he initially refused but accepted after she threatened to throw it in the bottom of the lake.

When Henry would tell the story in front of Margaret, she would purse her lips in satisfaction, Amelia's apparent clumsiness a kind of equalizer between them. Margaret had resented their relationship from the beginning, a wedge between her and her son.

Everything else about Henry was easy, nearly too easy. He loved her. He wanted to marry her, have children together. He was safe. Stable. Perfect. Except for the one blemish that only Amelia had to navigate: Margaret. More than once, she had heard Margaret refer to her first as "his friend," followed by, "his wife." Like the first party they attended at the Cartwrights' home after they were first married, introduced as "Mr. Henry Cartwright and guest."

Amelia was brought out of the memory by a knock at the door of the bedroom. The girls gasped, and covered themselves, even though they were already dressed. She sighed slightly and cracked open the heavy wood door with transoms above that let in the lake breeze.

"Oh. Yes?" Captain Scott stood at the door, his white hat in his hands. He had a short gray beard and a long, lined face that was etched with lake wind and cold spray from the water.

"I'm sorry to bother you, Mrs. Cartwright, but I'm afraid I have some bad news." He pointed toward the other side of the room, at the window that faced the west side of the house.

Amelia turned and her eyes widened at the sight of thick gray clouds beginning to gather over the tree line in the distance, toward Buttons Bay. The rest of the sky was a beautiful blue, with the occasional white puffy cloud daring to float lazily across. Yet to the west, the weather looked different.

"My goodness. That doesn't look promising." Amelia kept her voice low and hoped it sounded calm, a rouged, powdered veneer over her insides, which began to churn at the thought of flashing lightning and booming thunder. Rain would certainly rough up the lake's surface and make it impossible to navigate.

"It might not be. I just want you to be prepared that if that storm hits we will need to postpone all boat trips out of safety," he said.

"No," she said automatically, her stomach churning in alarm at the thought.

The captain gave her a quizzical look. "Safety should be our first priority."

She swallowed hard, thinking of the hundreds of guests who were due to arrive via train and then be transported on the *Monarch Princesses* for the festivities. And the boat cruises that Jane had specifically asked for after dinner, so that the guests could see the estate illuminated from the water.

Not to mention the white tablecloths and beautiful roses that would be soaked with rain and covered in mud, and the handmade gowns and delicate shoes sinking into the wet grass.

The wedding could very easily be a disaster, and then Jane would make sure they all felt her wrath, Mother Nature's fault or not.

All of the plans for the night would be ruined should a storm appear.

"Thank you for the information," Amelia managed to whisper before she walked over to the west-facing window and saw that the cloud in the distance was growing larger and seemingly darker. She pressed a palm against the glass and closed her eyes until she could stop the tears that threatened to form. She took a long, slow breath before she turned back toward the bridesmaids, smile on her face.

There may have been a storm approaching, but she needed to will the sun to shine.

CHAPTER 16

ERIN

"*Who knows what frame of mind she was in at the time?*"

My mother's harsh words about Amelia were still very much on my mind as I drove home from her house the next morning, and throughout the following day while the twins were at school. I tried to focus on the mounting chores and tasks I had at home: endless laundry, bills to be paid with a sad bank account, empty shelves badly in need of groceries, but in the middle of each task I would stop and stare off into space, trying to imagine how Amelia felt on that final day, in those final moments. Did she, too, have an unending sense that the chips were being loaded against her? That her equilibrium was on the most tenuous of scales? That it would be so easy for her comfortable existence to crumble away under her feet, turning to dust?

If so, would it be that hard to imagine that she tried to find a way to escape and failed?

Each time I would think the thought I wanted so desperately to not be true, I would stop and shake my head, a physical reminder that I was not to go to that place. I would even say it out loud: "No."

Earlier that morning, after school drop-off, I had sent an e-mail to the historical society in Port Washington, New York, Emily's place of residence as a child. The response came less than an hour later: *No, I'm sorry. We don't have any documents for someone of that name.*

I then thought of the Geneva Lake Museum and how excited Gerry was when I mentioned Monarch Manor. He seemed to be one of the few people alive who understood the importance of the house and the Hoppe family, and all that they represented. I shot him an e-mail, telling him about my research and what I hoped to uncover, and his response, too, came an hour later. This time, very different:

Wonderful! I'd love to help in any way. Let me do some digging. I adore a good scavenger hunt!

The message, despite its brevity, lifted my spirits. He cared. We were on a team. We would do this together. I was in the middle of rereading the e-mail for the seventh time when the alarm on my phone went off—time to pick up Will at school and time to shift into mom mode.

As I pulled up to the designated pickup area, on the side of the school away from the "regular" pickup area that was full of chaos, one of the aides from his class, Mrs. Cesare, opened the school door and gave me a perfunctory nod as she led Will by the hand to my car. I jumped out and opened the car door for him, a too-bright smile on my face.

"Hi! How was school?" I called to him, yet he stared off into the distance. I crouched down, hands on my jeans as they approached. "Hi!" I said again, my voice rising. "Ready to go home?"

Finally, he looked up at me, his expression seemingly looking right through me, to the open car door to my right.

"He had a bit of a rough day," she said as they walked down the sidewalk. Her hair either was permed or had naturally perfect spirals that ran down her back, and large, fluffy bangs like no one had bothered to tell her that the '80s had ended. "He had a meltdown over his lunch." A sympathetic look passed over her eyes as she dropped his hand while they kept walking.

"Oh. I'm so sorry. I will make sure to get his usual applesauce pouches this evening," I said. Two years ago, he developed a fixation on a certain brand of applesauce pouches, staring at the box on end, tracing his finger along the cartoon apple on the front. When I made the mistake of buying the generic brand, which was half the price, he first refused to eat it and then threw it against the wall, applesauce exploding all over Charlotte's new dress on school picture day.

Yet that was a year and a half ago. He had come so far in other things and hadn't stared at the applesauce box in months, so I thought it might be a calculated risk. Clearly, a miscalculation.

I was about to bend down and reach for his hand to help him into the car when he broke away from Mrs. Cesare and began to run full speed away from the car, toward the chaotic pickup area on the street.

"Will, no!" I screamed as I lunged toward him, but his backpack was just out of my grasp while Mrs. Cesare stood frozen in place as she watched him race toward the area where the buses were filling. The one in front began to pull away from the curb.

With everything I had, I ran toward him, waving my arms and yelling for him. Finally, I had reached him, pulling his backpack back roughly, out of the way of the bus. He jerked back in surprise and began to cry, not because he was scared, but because I had stopped him.

Several aides and crossing guards, having seen what happened from afar, raced over to make sure Will and I were okay. I fought back tears as I hugged him and walked him back to the building.

"It wasn't your fault," Mrs. Cesare said, patting my arm in a way that made me believe she most definitely thought the opposite.

I should have predicted that, my thoughts whispered. *But how can I always expect the unexpected—it's called unexpected for a reason.*

She saw my hands were shaking. "Do you want to come into the office and wait until things die down from pickup?"

I nodded, as I saw out of the corner of my eye the same group of moms from the recital staring in my direction, Starbucks cups in hands, black lululemon leggings on. I followed Mrs. Cesare inside, where Will's teacher, Miss Ball, was waiting. She put her hands on her head.

"Oh my goodness! I saw what happened from my classroom window. Is he okay?" She bent down, the long gold vector charm around her neck swinging.

"He's fine, but I think it took about five years off my own life." I managed a soft laugh, but it died as quickly as it escaped my lips.

She frowned and nodded. "Poor guy. He had a tough day, and now this." She crossed her arms in front of her pink knit sweater that she wore over gray leggings and black boots. I followed her into the principal's office. The school secretary, with a nameplate that read TRACI SCHUESTER, stared at me before she slowly looked to Will and then back at me, her eyes softer and her lips pressed into a knowing smile.

"Feel free to stay here as long as you need," Miss Ball said. "Have a great night, buddy!"

As she left, I saw the secretary roll her eyes before she turned to me. "I saw what happened. Are you guys okay?" She clasped her hands in front of her, and I saw that she wore sparkly hot pink nail polish.

I nodded and sank down into a chair, Will next to me, as I finally exhaled.

Traci gave me a sympathetic look. "I've been there. Believe me, I've been there." With her index finger, she slowly turned around a picture frame on her desk. "My son, Chris. He's on the spectrum. He's nineteen now, but man, those early years were brutal. Bru-tal. Or whatever word comes after 'brutal.'"

I leaned forward, taking in the picture of her son, dressed in a Cubs jersey and jeans, standing in front of Wrigley Field with the marquee in the background. He was smiling but wore headphones, to mute the sounds of the ballpark. But he smiled. With his entire face, up to his eyes. My heart leapt as I looked at it. I could feel his happiness through the glass frame, across the office.

Traci saw my face and nodded slowly, turning the picture back to her and glancing at it. "Believe me, it took years of therapy and blood, sweat, and tears to get to this point. And, honestly, this point wasn't something I even thought we would have to hope for. I'm guessing you know what I mean."

I looked at Will and thought about how we were still pushing for mainstream, still pushing for him to overcome everything. Still pushing for everything we thought we wanted for him.

When we didn't even have a picture of him smiling and I hadn't seen him look that happy in a long time. Maybe ever.

"Look, it's a tough road, and I remember thinking I wish someone got it. I wish someone understood," she said. She grabbed a pad of pink Post-it notes, the same color as her nails, and wrote a phone number. She peeled it off and stuck it to the desk in front of me. "If you ever want to meet for a beer, or coffee, or anything, I'm game."

I looked at it and slowly pulled it off the desk. It had been so long since someone extended any offer of friendship, I didn't know what to say. Finally, I said, "Thank you. I'd love that."

She nodded and I followed her gaze as it moved down to the picture of her son again. "I have to tell you something. If your son is having trouble with school, you should look at other options."

"Like what?" I said, thinking of homeschooling and how that might just kill all of us.

"Private school. Therapeutic schools. My son went to Lake-wood Academy for years, and it really made a big difference. Best, and hardest, decision we ever made. The tuition is . . ."—she raised her hand in the air and rolled her eyes—"but he did so great there that I would take out that second mortgage all over again." She smiled. "And might need to—who knows?"

I nodded slowly, remembering that Lakewood Academy was the school that Alicia Leeland had considered for Mark. The school that she considered to be "giving up" before her son progressed enough to join a regular class.

Will started to hum in annoyance, so I quickly grabbed his hand and thanked Traci, carefully folding her phone number and placing it into the back pocket of my jeans. Later that night, I pulled it out before I took off my jeans, staring at the numbers. I thought of the picture, of her son smiling at the camera. Attending a baseball game. Stopping to pose. So many times, so many things seemed out of our grasp, even simple things like participating in a school recital. Maybe at this point of our lives, a picture was enough of a goal.

Maybe that was what I should have been hoping for, despite the thoughts that whispered I was doing Will a disservice by setting the bar so low. But it was something that felt possible, a feeling I hadn't experienced in a very long time. And that night, before I went to bed, I didn't research therapies or read the blogs of moms whose kids had made progress overnight. Instead, I thought of Will, wearing a Cubs shirt, watching a base-ball game in between Luke and me, smiling.

CHAPTER 17

AMELIA

On the day of Amelia and Henry's wedding, it rained all afternoon. Amelia had woken up that morning and peered out of the window of her parents' home on Lake Shore Drive in Chicago, brushing aside the heavy velvet drapes and lifting a finger to the linen sheers. She looked out over the few automobiles on the road, to the warm glow of Lake Michigan. She had breathed a sigh of relief when she saw that the sun peeked out through a few white clouds over the horizon. It wasn't that she was worried about herself as much as what all of the guests—and her parents—might say if it rained.

Rain is never good luck for the bride.

Rain means the couple will never have children.

Rain nearly guarantees an unhappy marriage.

She didn't care so much what they all thought, but she knew her mother did, and she didn't want to sentence her to months—years, maybe—of having to insist that her daughter and Henry were very happy together, thank you for asking, and had a house full of children. Her mother already had trouble keeping up with the social customs and norms. Really,

Amelia couldn't blame her, since they seemed to change every day. But it was important to Mary to portray the family in a certain way, likely because she had grown up outside of all of it. The daughter of an Irish immigrant, during a time when being Irish meant she would never belong. And that stigma still existed, an extra layer of judgment against the family that, it seemed, could never be overcome.

"The Irish are well suited for cooking and cleaning. The good ones, anyway."

It was the first thing Amelia had heard Margaret say about her, after they met. She thought Amelia was out of earshot, after she left the Cartwrights' parlor and excused herself to the water closet. At least at first, she had assumed Margaret thought she was out of earshot. After a few more meetings, she suspected Margaret knew exactly what she had done. It was a test. The first of many. And the query seemed to be a calculation on how many times Amelia could pretend not to hear.

The skill served Amelia well, on the morning of her wedding. She had pretended not to notice when the coachman held his palm in the air and glanced at the sky. The rain had begun to lightly fall, but not nearly enough to form in puddles on the street. She held her head high as she stepped into the coach, her dress gathered by Eleanor and Jane, and rode to the church. The white horses and carriage arrived just as the rain picked up, a steady drizzle soaking the bottoms of the gowns and splashing mud on the men's black oxford shoes. She could feel the annoyance of the guests as they filed into the pews, dabbing at themselves with handkerchiefs and stoles, as though she had personally spoken to Mother Nature and given her blessing for the weather.

For Jane, there would be no such whispers. Despite the storm clouds looking ominous in the west, they stayed far away as the ceremony began. The bridesmaids went first, their pink dresses swishing down the aisle in a rhythmic pattern. Amelia held her breath the entire time she walked, until she reached the front, turned, and made eye contact with John, seated off to the side in between her mother and a nanny.

When it was Jane's turn to walk down the aisle, everyone stood. Jane waited a few moments, relishing everyone's attention, until the anticipation grew. Then, she began to walk, her heavily beaded drop-waist gown kicking in front of her. Their father, Conrad, proudly walked beside her, a large smile on his face.

"Do you think that's pride or relief that he's getting rid of the drain on his bank accounts?" Eleanor whispered to Amelia, who stifled a laugh with her gloved hand.

Her smile faded as she thought of the lines on her father's face and how they had increased tenfold in the years since he had to stop selling beer. She couldn't imagine how much strain the wedding had put on his accounts, not that Jane would have adjusted her plans otherwise.

In Jane's hands she held an enormous bouquet of pink roses and lady's breath accented with rhinestones sewn to ivory ribbons that trailed on the pale pink runner. Rows of gold chairs were set on either side of the runner, filled with guests blinding one another with diamonds and jewels. Finally, she reached the end, and the ceremony began.

Thirty minutes later and it was done. Once Amelia saw that the nanny was leading John over to the punch table, she grabbed her skirt with one hand and headed straight for the champagne bar filled with cases of the alcohol that her parents had stockpiled right before the laws were enacted. Next to the champagne bar was a bar for the Hoppe Near Beer, although the waiter stood bored, his tablecloth pristine, without one drink on it, and would likely stay that way all evening. She grabbed a glass of champagne off a sterling silver tray and took a large gulp, before anyone could stop her. She started to put it down but then finished off the rest in one burning swallow.

The bubbles made her eyes water, and she coughed, her throat on fire.

"It's champagne, not whiskey, Em," said a voice to her right.

Through tears, she saw Matthew holding out a sweating glass of water. She took it and let the cool liquid soothe her throat. "Thanks," she said. "It's been a while since I had any."

"Champagne? Or whiskey? Because if it's the latter, I can probably sneak us some from that gentleman over there." Matthew pointed to one of the groomsmen, Edward's brother, who already looked very unsteady as he leaned against a waiter, his cheeks flushed, animatedly telling a story. "I don't want to be within earshot if he falls over into the cake."

Amelia laughed. "That would never happen. Everything perfect on Jane's perfect—" The word caught in her throat, her stomach dropping and her nose tingling. "Day," she finished, not meeting Matthew's eyes.

He lightly touched her forearm, his eyes soft. "Is everything all right with you?"

Pull yourself together, she thought. *He knows you better than almost anyone.* She forced a bright smile. "Of course. I'm just glad the rain seems to be holding off."

His expression of concern didn't change. "It's me, Em. I know when something is happening with you. What is it?"

"Truly, it's nothing. It's been a very long day already, with all the preparations." She couldn't look at him again, for fear that he would see everything that she was thinking, and had thought, and she would tell him secrets he couldn't understand, so instead she lifted a fresh champagne glass from his hand and took another sip, this time relishing the way the bubbles popped in her mouth. "How are your adventures? I heard you landed in Charleston earlier in the year."

He nodded, his eyes bright. "It's a beautiful city, full of so much history, and right on the water. Before that, I was in Philadelphia for six months, and Washington, D.C., before that."

She gave him a small smile. "Always the explorer." Even as a child, Matthew talked constantly about how he was going to travel the world, and see everything he could, and meet people who were interesting, and different. He would always ask her, "Are you going to come with me?" and she would shrug and say, "Maybe." The idea of leaving her home and her family behind sounded lonely and scary, and not at all the great adventure Matthew believed it would be.

He would always frown and tell her she would change her mind.

She never did.

"Yes, well, Mrs. Crane again told me about her travels to Russia, back before the war. Each time she pauses to remember a detail, I've had to stop myself from finishing her sentence." He laughed. The Cranes had traveled extensively throughout Russia, even purchasing a replica of a Russian peasant cottage from the St. Louis World's Fair years ago and having it transported to their lake estate, where Mrs. Crane held afternoon teas.

"Some things never change," Amelia said, the words cutting through her heart like glass.

Matthew gave her a questioning look, but when she didn't meet his eyes he looked out into the crowd, scattered into various small groups, each stealing glances at one another, sizing up the gowns and the jewels and the hairstyles. "Then you are well? Your mother told my mother so, but it's not like they ever tell each other the truth," he said.

"I am," she said quickly.

He paused, studying her face with his brows furrowed, his mouth soft. "You know," he said quietly, "if you ever needed anything, you could ask me. I would be happy to help you in . . . any regard. With yourself, or for John. I would be happy to help both of you. Take care—"

She swiped the champagne glass through the air, the liquid dancing inside. "Thank you. That's very kind. How are you doing? Any marriage prospects? There are many beautiful women here. Let's see." She scanned the crowd, feeling the warmth from the champagne move up her face and loosen her limbs. "Oh! What about Dolores Silas? I've heard she is eagerly looking for someone to share her father's fortune. I have heard she loves to travel, as well."

His mouth turned down and his cheeks sagged, and he studied her for an extra moment, imperceptible to anyone but her, before she turned in the direction of her slightly pointed index finger, toward Dolores, a petite blonde dressed in a gown covered in peacock feathers. A group of admirers were clustered around her, ready to offer a cigarette or another glass of champagne or just to simply breathe the air next to her.

"Yes, of course," Matthew said evenly. He stood up straighter and took a sip of his drink. "Except she has one small flaw." He turned to Amelia, and her heart began to beat so quickly she was sure he could see the movement from the outside of her dress.

Oh, Matthew. What are you going to say?

Don't say it. You shouldn't say it.

Nothing good can come from you saying it.

Except, more than anything, her heart wanted him to say it. To tell her that he loved her, that he had always loved her, and that things, for the first time in so very long, might be beautiful again. It was the part of her heart that she kept hidden away, behind the lock and key of her reality, the small piece of her that was unchanged from her childhood. From the Before.

But Before didn't exist anymore. Or, at least, she didn't have the luxury of revisiting it. She had to focus on John and what his future would be, not her own. He was all that mattered.

Yet before Matthew could say anything—the words her heart wanted to hear or otherwise—a familiar cry turned the guests' heads. At attention, Amelia scanned the party to where she heard the sound, on the south edge of the lawn, closer to the pier. She saw his figure in the crowd, crumpled into a ball.

She thrust her drink at Matthew so hard that the liquid spilled down his front, and raced toward John, bumping into drunken guests on the way, not caring when Charles Hutchinson fell over at the slightest touch.

"Madwoman!" he called out, slurring his words, as his wife unsuccessfully tried to help him stand.

By the time Amelia reached John, his cries had turned into screams, as he looked down and saw the blood pouring from his kneecap. The nanny was huddled at his side, trying to cover his mouth and muffle his noises.

"Stop that!" Amelia said, and swatted her hand away. She pulled John toward her, into her lap, not caring about the grass staining her pale silk dress. She began to rock him, pressing his body against hers, his head tucked under her chin. When he was just a toddler and he would become inconsolable because he was startled by something that he could not hear coming, she would do the same, letting him feel her breathing in and out and the beating of her heart. With him at that age, she wasn't able to offer any soothing words, since he wasn't proficient in sign language yet, but he could feel her body and feel that he was safe.

She knew every guest was staring at her, and could hear their whispers and a few loudly proclaiming that this was why children shouldn't be allowed at wedding receptions, but she kept rocking, holding on tight to his head, until she felt his body relax. When he did, she opened her eyes, her gaze focused on him. She motioned for the nanny to put her hand over the wound on his kneecap, so she could sign and tell him everything would be fine, but the nanny balked, shaking her head.

Amelia shot her a look of fury before touching the blood running down his leg, putting her palm over his scrape. With her other hand, she lifted his chin to her eyes.

It's just fine, she said silently. *Everything will be fine. It's just a cut.*

She scooped him under his arms and stood up, blood staining the front of her dress. He collapsed into her like a baby, his head on her shoulder. Her eyes quickly scanned the crowd, who watched her with looks of disdain mixed with mild concern. In the back, she saw Margaret's lips pursed and arms folded over her chest as she stood next to Mrs. Hutchinson, still mopping off her husband from his drunken fall. The look in her mother-in-law's eyes made her blood turn to ice. She had seen it before, and it reminded her of all that Margaret had planned for them after the wedding.

She took a step toward the house, chin held high, and looked over her shoulder at the nanny. "You are relieved of your duties," she said before she walked toward the house, slowly enough so that the guests knew she wasn't escaping, but quickly enough for them to not be able to stop her.

She caught a few of their words and what they said about her and her son, and for once, she was thankful that John could not hear.

CHAPTER 18

ERIN

The air in my grandmother's empty house swirled with dust, even though my mother and I had hired a professional crew to come in the day before, to clean it prior to its going on the real estate market. As I looked around in the thick air, the house suddenly felt abandoned, hurt.

I felt guilt wash over me, like we were doing something wrong by putting it up for sale. I turned to my mom, who had a wistful look on her lined face.

"Any chance you and Dad want to keep it as a summer place?" I said lightly.

She laughed. "Oh, honey, no. We can barely keep up with what we have now. I'm still trying to convince your father to buy that RV I've always wanted so we can spend our summers driving cross-country. I need another house in Wisconsin like I need a hole in the head."

A year earlier, she had mentioned to my father that she would love to sell their house and buy an RV to travel around the country. Katie and I had laughed, but my father just shook his head, like he was almost resigned to his fate. Much like the time when my mother decided to paint their bedroom fluorescent purple.

"More houses, more problems." My mother laughed.

I nodded and walked over to the built-in shelves in the living room that had once been dangerously overflowing with the Precious Moments figurines. Without the statues, the shelves were straight instead of bowed in the middle with the weight of all that porcelain.

"Too bad we can't keep it as a vacation rental. Powers Lake is very fancy now, you know," I said. When I had visited with Katie years ago, Powers Lake was the rustic cousin to the more glamorous Geneva Lake. The lakefront was mostly dotted with modest ranch houses and a few diners, dive bars, and convenience stores. In recent years, it became a secret getaway, a place to tear down and build enormous lakefront houses at a fraction of the cost of Lake Geneva. And in doing so, it became exclusive. Even though my grandmother's house wasn't on the lake, it surely would fetch a nice dollar for its proximity to the water.

"It goes on the market on Monday," my mom said, closing the door on the thought.

I nodded, and she put an arm around my shoulders as we walked toward the door. "How's school? When are you meeting with everyone?" she said.

"Wednesday." I walked slowly, out of sync with her, so it was a continuous jostle as I kept my eyes carefully trained out the window on the twins, outside in the expansive front yard. "Truth is, I'm not sure what I hope they will say. Obviously, that they have a perfect solution and have total faith that he will meet all his goals." My shoulders shook with a laugh that didn't reach my face. Will had been increasingly agitated with school with each passing day, to the point where he was coming home and melting down almost immediately after he crossed the threshold, as though he could finally exhale, in his own Will way. So I had e-mailed Miss Ball and asked for a team meeting.

Yet the conversation with Traci was never far from my mind, and the questions of what exactly I should be hoping for were always pulling at my thoughts.

My mom nodded and tightened her arm around me. "And if you don't get those perfect answers?"

I inhaled slowly and shook my head.

"You know. You will figure it out. You always do. Even as a kid, you were always able to find your way to doing the right thing. Remember your gut feeling about the zoo field trip in fifth grade?"

I nodded. I had been looking forward to that trip for weeks. Then, on the morning of the trip, I woke up with an unshakable dread and begged my mom to let me stay home. She finally agreed after an hour of tears, and then we got word that the bus had been involved in an accident. No one was seriously hurt, but we always took my feelings as a sort of premonition that something would go awry. I tried to parlay that into a few faux sick days in high school, but she always called my bluff.

"I hope so, Mom. But . . . this is on a much bigger level than a minor car accident." I wished I could believe that things would all work out. It was so much easier with decisions that just affected me, not when it felt as though each decision we made was part of a larger ripple effect, one that could potentially set Will back.

My mother stopped before she got to the front door, and stared at the empty corner where the knight had once stood. A nice couple from Burlington had seen the ad on craigslist, driven to Powers Lake in their blue pickup truck, shrieked in delight when they saw it, and carefully loaded it into the bed of the truck. "Good riddance," my mother had said when it disappeared down Bloomfield Road.

Yet a look of sad nostalgia swept across her face as her eyes lingered for a moment on the empty space, but before I could say anything, she walked out the front door. Outside in the yard, Will and Charlotte walked around, collecting crab apples in a plastic bucket I had found in the back of my car from the last time we went to the park. Will had no sense of personal belongings, so it was always better to bring our own toys to the sandbox than be continuously apologizing to other kids when he took their stuff. It was a closed-ended task: defined beginning, middle, and end. Spot an apple, pick it up, walk over to the bucket, and drop it in. Repeat. Easy for him to understand. Calming. It made sense.

I stood on the front stoop and watched them, the sun peeking through the trees that lined the property, the smell of the lake permeating through the yard, with just the faintest smells of ripe apples from the tree. Charlotte's braids bounced around her shoulders, falling in her face before she impatiently brushed them away as she bent down. Will was more structured in his movements: bent over from the waist, pick it up, turn precisely toward the bucket, walk in a straight, undeterred line.

"Any word from Gerry?" my mother said as she watched the twins with a smile.

"Not yet. Although he did send me a very excited e-mail filled with exclamation points last night, saying that he was conferring with a colleague in Milwaukee. I think this is the most exciting thing that's happened to him in . . . ever," I said.

My mother turned and looked at my grandmother's house, her childhood home. "I bet. Think about loving something that no one else does. Things that you find fascinating and beautiful, and people don't see it that way. And then when someone shows interest in your beautiful things? Well, shit, I imagine that would be a pretty exciting day." Her gaze stayed on the house, on the place that once held all those strange, varied collections that my grandmother loved.

Things that no one else in her life appreciated the way she did.

I smiled and nodded, thinking of Will and his applesauce packets. I had bought the correct ones the week before and excitedly shown him. He had given me the briefest of smiles, a quick moment of connection between us, to show his appreciation. It was something so small, so insignificant to other people, but I knew it was important. I had shown him that I loved something as much as he did. That I loved *him* enough to honor his preferences.

Charlotte dropped an apple in the bucket and wiped her palm on her jeans. "Mom, I'm bored."

"Kids, I want to show you something. C'mere," my mom said. She pointed in the direction of the lake. "Want to see some fish?"

Charlotte skipped ahead, holding my mom's hand, as we crossed the street to the shared pier. I followed behind, slowly walking with Will, pausing every few steps when he wanted to examine something in the grass. The afternoon air had warmed thanks to the cloudless sky, and I pushed up my long sleeves. It was the time of year when the temperature shift from morning to afternoon spanned thirty degrees and it seemed like no matter what we wore, we were either shivering or sweating.

That morning, when we had left our house early, the kids off from school thanks to a teacher institute day, I had bundled them with blankets in the backseat and cranked on the heat. Right before we left the house, I paused at our old manual thermostat. We hadn't turned it on yet for the season, something that always required a few prayers and some sacrifices to the furnace gods. The unit was from 1966, something our furnace repair guy loved to remind us about. The last time he came out to service it, he asked if he could take a picture with it to prove to his coworkers that it really did exist. After the mailbox full of bills the day before, I didn't need "furnace repair" to add to the list, so I didn't turn it on. And with the afternoon temperature near seventy, my furnace anxiety would be put off for another day.

Ahead of Will and me at the pier, Charlotte dropped my mother's hand and ran down to the end. I held my breath as her little legs pranced too close to the edge of the still-Astroturf-covered surface. She stopped and put her hands on her thighs, peering down into the water.

"Grandma! I think I see one!" she said.

My mom plopped down on the pier next to her, crossing her legs. She put an arm around Charlotte's shoulders and pointed at something down in the water, their voices low. Will stopped when he saw the water.

"Do you want to sit here?" I offered a rickety-looking wooden bench still in the grass from years ago, perched just before the pier began.

I led him to the bench, praying it wouldn't collapse under us, and pulled Will next to me. He shrugged my arm off his shoulders but didn't move away. I looked out over the water, at the lake I loved so many years before.

"Wa-ter," I said to Will over and over, as I stared at the deep blue lake. It was empty, with only a few red-and-white No Wake buoys bobbing up and down. Almost all of the other piers had been taken out of the water, in anticipation of the upcoming winter freeze. The lake was a deep blue and choppy with the fall breeze blowing across the water. Just to the east, about ten piers (or, what would have been ten if they were all still standing) away, was the boarded-up restaurant formerly known as Harbor Lights. I remembered it from the summer when Katie and I were here.

One afternoon, when it had rained all morning, my grandmother gave her permission for Katie and me to walk down to Harbor Lights and play the video games. We ran the whole way there, the rain soaking through our jean shorts and flip-flops. Inside the restaurant, there were only four people at the bar, and they looked like they had been there for a while; the drinks in front of them certainly weren't their first. The bartender slowly looked us up and down before he pointed us to the back room, where there was a dusty Pac-Man game and a broken Caterpillar game with a cracked white rollerball joystick.

We had shrugged and emptied our pockets, playing Pac-Man and ordering too-sweet Cokes all afternoon, eventually sitting at the bar and laughing with the other patrons.

I didn't realize it at the time, but that afternoon was one of the most perfect I would ever have. It was a time before real life kicked in. It was before the time of mortgages, and savings accounts, and therapy appointments. Before the time when I would feel as though I was failing at everything I tried to do—and, likely, at the things I had yet to even attempt.

Charlotte walked over and brought me out of my dark thoughts. She sat down next to Will and pointed across the lake.

"See, Will? It's a lake. It's water. Wa-ter." She must have heard me say it to him. She tapped his forearm and said it again, "Wa-ter." I held my breath, waiting for him to screech or knock her arm away, but he stared at his arm, where she lightly tapped again. He slowly looked up and looked out at the water. A crooked finger made its way to his arm, and he tapped twice. No sound came from his mouth, but he understood.

I drew a ragged breath in, my chest constricting, as I saw him tap again.

"That's right! Good job," she said with a smile. "Mommy, did you see that?"

"I did, honey. I—" My voice broke like the limb of an old locust tree during a windstorm, swept away by the lake breeze.

Charlotte smiled and hopped off the bench, skipping back to where my mom perched on the end of the pier. It was the smallest of steps, almost indiscernible to the naked eye, but it meant everything to me. She reached him. She could reach him. It would be people like her who would change his life, help him to see the beauty in the world.

We needed to find a way to capture that magic, find the scenarios where he would feel comfortable, and extend a hand. And I finally realized that it might look very different from what I had first thought.

CHAPTER 19

AMELIA

After John had fallen, Amelia took him to Alfred, who threw his hands up in mock exaggeration and clutched his chest when he saw the smear of blood on John's kneecap. He soaked a towel in some warm water and pressed it to John's cut, smiling at him before tousling his hair and making a funny face. John smiled, his tearstained cheeks lifting as he sputtered between a laugh and a cry.

"I should get more of these cloths ready for when our prestigious guests begin to fall all over the lawn as well," he said to Amelia with a wink.

She heard them all outside, from her spot in the service kitchen, their raucous cheers as they drained glasses of champagne and brandy, one right after the other. The party was so loud that she didn't hear Margaret walking down the hallway and into the kitchen.

"Mr. Hutchinson is recovering from his injuries. He was quite upset, as I hope you realize." Margaret stood with her arms clasped in front of her, as though she believed she was holding back her anger in the most proper way.

"I think Charles should be more concerned with navigating

the bumpy terrain of the lawn after six cocktails. I'm quite sure those don't help his balance," Amelia said. She placed a hand on John's shoulder as his head snapped back and forth between them.

Margaret's eyes flashed and she pursed her lips for a moment, before a small smile escaped her face. "John has embarrassed us once again. You will not bring him to things like this again. People like Charles are too important to our family."

Our family. That implied she was part of it. When, really, she had never been a part of it, and Margaret had seen to that. From the first moment that she came home with Henry, Margaret made it very clear that there were two sides: hers and everyone else's. It was the smallest possible circle of trust, inhabited only by her husband, son, and best friend, Georgina. Amelia was already an outsider, by the simple fact that she was not born a Cartwright.

Amelia and Henry had met in Chicago, at a gala in 1915 at the Art Institute. Charles Hutchinson was the founder, and the Hoppe family were guests at the opening celebration. Amelia had wandered around the party, her deep green gown with black beading swishing against her legs as she took in the paintings. She had plans to sneak out later with Eleanor and go to a club, long after their parents were asleep, and she counted the minutes. She stopped in front of a painting of water lilies and read the plaque.

" 'Claude Monet, donated by Mr. and Mrs. Martin Ryerson.' Of course," she muttered. The Ryersons never stopped talking about their fabulously talented artist friend. She was about to walk away when she overheard the conversation of a group behind her.

"Had they not been on the water before? I'm sure any one of us would have seen right away that the ship was at capacity and gone back to the dock. If only they had been paying more attention," a woman behind her said.

Amelia's skin pricked with annoyance. She knew exactly

what the woman was talking about: the *Eastland* disaster from earlier in the year, when a ship meant to take Western Electric employees on a company picnic had capsized in the river and more than eight hundred people died, just feet from the dock.

She turned around and approached the group, fueled by the champagne she had gulped down out of boredom. She didn't recognize any of the two women and two men, except for one of the men, who had light hair and dark eyes. "Excuse me," she said, her voice sharp. "But I believe we should be expressing our sympathies, and offering prayers for those poor people, rather than questioning their decisions." She slowly looked around the group. The two women pressed their lips together in annoyance but didn't dare say anything back. One of the men, already bored with the conversation, surveyed the crowd behind her. The other man, the one who looked familiar, smiled.

"I couldn't agree more. Thank you for saying it," he said. When she didn't return his smile, he leaned forward slightly. "You don't remember me, do you?" He straightened up and nodded his head slightly. "Henry Cartwright, and I'm friends with your brother-in-law, George. We met at his wedding to Eleanor."

Amelia knitted her brows together and frowned. "I believe all of you drank enough that evening that it was hard to tell anyone apart, not that I would have wanted to."

Henry threw his head back and laughed, startling the rest of his group. "You're right about that." His eyes sparkled as he smiled broadly at her. "Any chance you would care for some company while walking around the exhibits tonight?"

She was about to say no, that she was just fine on her own, but she was tired of being alone at events like those and tired of having people ask when she might get married. Over and over and over again.

Henry wasn't Matthew, but no one was. Matthew was off on his grand adventures, trying to satiate his unquenchable thirst for travel, each time asking her to join. Until the past year, when he had stopped asking, already knowing the answer. She never told anyone how much she still wanted to be asked.

By May of that year, she and Henry were engaged, and the wedding planning only allowed for a few summer visits to Monarch Manor. She saw Matthew once, when she introduced him to Henry.

"He's a fine man," Matthew had whispered in her ear before she boarded the steam yacht. His hand brushed her shoulder, sending a wave of longing and nostalgia down her arm. It was her last moment to change her life. She could have stopped, stayed on the dock with Matthew, and let Henry return to the city. Instead, she turned and boarded the yacht. She knew if she stayed with Matthew he would once again ask her to join him. And she would say no, that Chicago and Lake Geneva were her homes.

He would, in turn, stay with her and give up his dreams of traveling and exploring the world. She couldn't imagine having to face him every day of her life, knowing he gave up everything for her. Knowing that he turned away from the plans he whispered to her during those childhood summers as they hid from the nannies, sweaty and covered in bug bites by the pond. She could never repay that debt. She might not be enough for him, and that was worse than never having him at all.

And so she became destined to a life of battles with Margaret, but at least anger was something she could process. Disappointment, letting Matthew down, was something she knew she couldn't.

Margaret, however, proved to be a more formidable enemy than she could have ever imagined.

In the kitchen, Margaret's smile grew larger. She lifted her eyebrows. "Good thing I have taken proper measures to ensure he won't embarrass us anymore."

Amelia's nose pricked with tears as she faced her, and her hands shook as she swallowed hard, again thankful that John didn't hear what was said. She straightened her spine, and with fire burning in her eyes she said, "It is you who should be embarrassed. You and your friends. He's an innocent child, and you are—" She stopped, searching for the words she had so desperately wanted to say for so long.

Margaret crossed her arms over her chest, waiting.

"Beneath my daughter. Beneath all of us." Mary Hoppe appeared in the doorway. Margaret turned in surprise, her arms dropping to her sides when she saw her.

"Pardon?" Margaret said.

Amelia's heart thumped against her pink dress, and her ears rang with tension. She had never seen her mother so much as raise her voice to anyone other than her family or staff members. Certainly not in a social situation and certainly not to someone as powerful as Margaret Cartwright. Margaret may not have grown up with wealth, but she had certainly made the most of her social standing. And Mary had just said the worst thing possible to her.

Mary looked past a frozen Margaret, to Amelia. "How is John?" She walked forward, her arm brushing against the skirt of Margaret's sparkling gown. Margaret leaned away, pressing her hands on the oak door frame.

Mary bent down to John's level and tweaked his chin. He smiled in response, still pressing his body against Amelia. Mary stood, her back straight. "They are almost ready to release the lanterns over the lake. Come." She looked down and held her hand out to John and nodded. He slowly took her hand, and Mary led them through the doorway, side by side, so that Margaret had to jump out of the way again.

Amelia looked back and saw Margaret shaking in anger, unable to speak, like a scorned child. She felt a wave of sympathy for her, for how sad and miserable she must be on the inside. For what she likely said to herself in quiet times: *You are not good enough. You will never be good enough. No one loves you.* Amelia had never once believed no one loved her, from her parents, to her sisters, to Henry.

To Matthew.

She knew Margaret had never felt that kind of love and it had darkened her heart and destroyed her soul.

Down at the lakefront, the guests gathered under the rapidly darkening sky. In the time since she went inside, Amelia saw that the waiters had lit the torches on the edge of the party. The flames danced across the lake, reflecting back up to the house, illuminating the front yard. The air smelled of fire and lake water, with a hint of sweetness from the roasted marshmallow station beginning to assemble just outside the porch.

Mary clutched John's hand as she marched across the lawn, her head held high in defiance. Amelia followed behind them, weaving in between the guests. When she passed Judge N. C. Sears, swaying slightly while animatedly telling a story about the most recent trial he had presided over, she rolled her eyes and wondered what the city voters would think of him, as he was labeled the "only honest judge in Cook County." As she continued on, her back stiffened ever so slightly and she heard the ever-present swish of Margaret's skirts behind her.

The fabric sounded like a warning to Amelia, a reminder of all that wretched woman had planned. Of everything she had done. Of everything Henry had empowered her to do.

Of his betrayal and how he had changed their lives.

When she reached the lakefront, Amelia felt Margaret push past her, to her husband's side, next to Simeon and Elizabeth Chapin. She didn't dare glance back at Amelia or at her grandson. Amelia joined her mother and John at the edge of the lake, next to Eleanor and her family. Emily grabbed John by the hand and led him close to her, bringing him into their circle, while Eleanor gave her the most imperceptible head nod.

I see you. I see John.

"Let's begin by making our wishes, and then we can each release a lantern. With any luck, our wishes will find their way home," Conrad said, his voice booming across the lake, amplified by too many sidecars.

One by one they released the lanterns, handed to them by a worker who lit the inside of each paper bag filled with air, and the lanterns floated up in the sky, over the water, creating a cluster of floating orbs high above the tree line. Each lantern held the wishes and dreams of the person who released it, lazily floating upward. Surrounding them, Amelia could feel the presence of all those wants and requests, pressing down on her shoulders. They hung like fairy lights around them, flickering on people's faces and reflecting on the water.

When it was Margaret's turn, she held the lantern in her hand for a moment longer than the others, the flames reflecting against her stony face. Amelia's blood ran cold as she suspected what John's own grandmother wished for, for what she was likely thinking about him. It repeated through Amelia's head as though she had actually heard it, a nightmare that Margaret had found a way to wish true:

I wish to never see him again.

CHAPTER 20

ERIN

On the Thursday afternoon after my mother and I closed up the house in Powers Lake, I sank down onto a bar stool at the Lake View Tavern and ordered a glass of wine. The sports bar was mostly empty, save for a few other depressed-looking souls scattered around the bar, wearily glancing at a college football game.

As I took my first sip of the sticky sweet house white wine, I felt Traci brush my elbow and sink down next to me.

"Hey there. Sorry I'm late. Traffic was a nightmare." She took a quick glance around the bar. "And sorry again. This place usually isn't this dead."

I had called Traci two nights before, after a disastrous school meeting that left me feeling bruised and battered. I asked if we could meet for coffee, and she quickly agreed . . . but only if it was for "real" drinks.

Without her asking, a large draft beer slid in front of her, and she took a long sip before she turned to me on her stool, hands clasped on the bar.

"Nice and cool out, huh?" she said as she surveyed my damp forehead.

I wiped my face. "Heat index of eighty today, I think. This has to be the hottest fall on record." I fanned my cheeks with my hand. The meteorologists were already predicting that the upcoming winter would be cold and snowy, the typical mood swings of Mother Nature in the Midwest.

"So, how's everything going? I know you said the meeting with school didn't exactly give you a warm and fuzzy feeling," she said as she jiggled a charm bracelet around her wrist.

"Ha. Nope. Understatement of the year," I said. I had called the meeting to try to brainstorm ways to help Will be more successful, to help him be more regulated and calm throughout the day. Every suggestion that I had come prepared to offer had already been put in place and was failing to a spectacular degree. He was spending most of the day in the sensory room, trying unsuccessfully to calm himself down. Each time he achieved equilibrium, the teachers and aides would try to put academic work in front of him, and then he would melt down again. It became obvious that while everyone was trying everything possible and truly seemed to want him to be successful, Will was still incredibly stressed and wasn't learning anything.

"Well, I know you aren't going to want to hear this, as it provides absolutely nothing in the way of concrete advice, but here goes: The problem with school is school." She tucked a strand of long, dark hair behind her ear. "School will always be a square hole, and it will always be a challenge. Point-blank. Some districts might work more with you, on shaping that square to be more round for your kid, but it will always be a square, just in another name."

I nodded slowly and chewed on the side of my lip. I knew this. It was becoming more evident each day. "So, what then?"

She took a long swallow of her drink and wiped the corner of her mouth. "For Chris, it was Lakewood Academy that made all the difference. A school designed for kids just like him. A school that was made to be round in the first place, if you know what I mean." She slowly turned to look at me. "I can see what you're thinking: Is it giving up?"

I opened my eyes wide and twisted my mouth into a frown. After a long pause, I said, "Okay . . . is it?"

She laughed. "It sure as shit feels like it in the beginning, I can tell you that much. Look, I've been where you're at. We thought Chris would just need a few years of speech therapy. Oh, now just a few years of special ed. Oh, just a few years in this autism classroom. And so on. Am I right?"

I sighed and didn't answer as I hung my head, tracing a finger along my glass.

"I thought so. But at some point, we have to face who our kids are. Sure, there are kids who are the one-in-a-million kids. But I didn't have one of those. So you try and figure out what they need, not what you want them to have. And that brought us to Lakewood. The first week he was there"—she paused and looked to the ceiling, smiling—"oh Lord, I had never seen him so calm, so happy."

I nodded. "That's wonderful. Will is . . . not happy. At all." I tried to imagine him leaving for school each day, his backpack on, walking into the building without having to be dragged toward the door. Yet the idea of him leaving public school still seemed like such an extreme thought, like we were taking steps backward.

"What about your husband? What does he think?" she said.

I smiled. "Not exactly on board." I had brought up the idea of Lakewood again to Luke, after he got home from work the other night. I hadn't even gotten out the entire sentence before he shook his head. "Will can do this; I know he can," was his response. "It's the school's fault for failing him." When he said it, I realized that while I used to feel the same way, I now believed that it didn't matter whose fault it was. The school was trying, but our biggest concern should be making things easier on Will. And maybe Lakewood was it.

"Well, you better get him on board if you are considering going the therapeutic route. The tuition is an arm and a leg, and you need both signatures for that second mortgage." She laughed but stopped quickly when she saw my face.

"What about the district? I read that some districts will pay for the school," I said as I took another sip of wine and winced.

Traci gave me a sympathetic look and patted my arm. "Some will. I can tell you that yours won't. Or at least, they won't without a fight involving lawyers. He would probably have to be allowed to fail for another year before you could push them."

"Another year? That's ridiculous," I said as I rubbed my head. None of us could continue on the same path for a year. It would kill all of us.

"Welcome to the world of special education," Traci said as she lifted her beer glass and tipped it to her lips. "Where almost all the options are shitty ones."

In the parking lot, before we got into our cars, she turned to me and said, "I've been where you are, and I know how hard it is. But there is another shore; you just can't see it yet. But it's there. And it's not perfect, but it's good. There's a lot of good things there. Different things than you probably had planned. Once you get used to that idea, everything else will come easier."

I swallowed hard and nodded, her words ringing in my ears. I waited until I got into my car before I let the tears flow. Gratitude, loss, and guilt all mixed together as I sat in my piping-hot car and cried until I couldn't breathe.

Other parents with children Will's age were shopping for markers from the school supply list and picking out pristine polos and khaki shorts for their children to wear on their first day of real school. There would be pictures and hugs and special treats.

We would experience all of that with Charlotte. But Will, likely, would miss out in one form or another—even though I hoped against hope it would be different.

After the twins were born, I had thought about their first day of school. They would have matching backpacks and Will would wear a cute button-down shirt, cargo shorts, and loafers. Charlotte would have a dress in the same color as Will's shirt and black mary janes. They would be nervous to go to school but excited to make new friends, since they spent most of their time together. I would have tears in my eyes, knowing how much I'd miss them, but I'd make sure to make a special dinner for them that night. They'd have a bunch of new friends and learn how to read sight words.

I wiped the tears from my face and took a long, ragged breath and turned on the air-conditioning. I had to let that all go. Traci was right; it was time to make decisions based on what was, not what might be, no matter how painful.

I held the image of a smiling Will walking into school in my head as I drove home to hug him. Yet as I reached the driveway my phone rang with a 262 area code.

"You are never going to believe what I just found." Gerry's words ran together like melted ice cream and chocolate syrup.

He didn't wait for me to ask. "It's a letter from Louisa, your great-great-aunt, to her mother, Eleanor. My friend at the Milwaukee Historical Society has the original. It doesn't appear Louisa ever mailed it, as she died in childbirth about a week later, and her family must have donated it along with some of her other things at some point."

"Louisa? So that would be Emily, my great-grandmother's sister? And Amelia's niece?" I said as I sat back in the driver's chair, my brain mentally drawing a picture of the family tree, searching for Louisa.

Luke pulled up next to me in the driveway and got out of his car. (Another perk of living in an old house is that we didn't have a garage. The house behind us was a coach house years ago, but we were told by the previous owner that it was sold off to become another private residence. So all we had was a patch of concrete and asphalt on the side of the house.)

I waved Luke inside and stayed seated in the driver's seat.

"Yes, that's right. And your missing child—John—would be Louisa's cousin." He cleared his throat. "Rather than paraphrase, I'm going to read it:

> *My dear mother:*
> *I apologize for not writing sooner, and telling you about my trip to visit Geneva Lake, but I have been busy with preparations for the baby. As I said in my previous letter, Jackson finally agreed to visit your summer home as we traveled through the area from Madison back home to Milwaukee.*
>
> *When we reached Monarch Manor, I was certain we were mistaken, and that I had the wrong address. It looked nothing like what I remembered! Of course, it has been many years since I have been there, but I still expected that it would look the same as it did from my childhood. I'm afraid it does not, and the entire house seems to be rapidly decaying. The paint is peeling, the garden is being overcome with weeds, and the dock is crumbling away into the water. I did not get a chance to go inside, yet I'm sure it would be more of the same condition.*
>
> *One thing that will cheer you is that I did see a nest of rabbits on the edge of the flowers, near where you always told me about your secret garden. I like to think that they are, at the very least, one last holdover from your childhood— maybe some relation to your rabbit. I wish I could remember more of my few summers there. I know they would have been magical.*
>
> *I also did have a visit with Aunt Jane, as you requested, and said hello. She was just as acidic as ever, and asked why I did not bring her more*

*petit fours from the bakery in Milwaukee. She
prattled on and on about how her husband is
always playing cards with his friends, and how her
friends never come to visit anymore. I can
imagine why after speaking with her for only a
few moments!*

*I hope your visit to Adare Village in Ireland
with Emily went well, and that you gave the
family my regards. I miss you and Emily very
much, and look forward to both of you visiting
next month. It will be just like our childhood—
except I hope you two do not communicate in
your own language still! I still have never
understood why you both continued your studies
of sign language, and were so emphatically
dedicated to it.*

*The doctor says the baby may come any day
now, and I wanted to be sure I wrote you before
she is born. I am still quite sure it is a girl, and I
very much look forward to sharing the name with
you once she is here.*

My deepest love and regards,
Your daughter Louisa

There was a long pause as Gerry finished, the static crack-ling on the phone between us. I was frozen in my seat, trying to absorb the information. Yet my brain felt full, and it was like wet ground trying to absorb rainwater.

"Hello?" he said. "Did you hear anything I said?"

"Yes. I'm sorry. I just need a moment to figure out what it means," I said. Inside, through our large living room windows that framed the porch, I saw Luke bend down and tickle Will before hoisting him over his shoulder and walking out of the room, Charlotte trailing behind.

"Do you want me to read it again? It took me a few go-throughs to unpack everything," he said.

"No, no. Please, tell me what you think it means," I said. Through the window, I saw Charlotte walk back into the family room, climb on the back of the couch, and stare outside, her chin in her hands and her lips pursed together. She spotted my car in the driveway and began to frantically wave. I knew I only had a few moments before she ran outside and interrupted my conversation.

"Well, the mention of sign language for one gave me pause. Why would Emily and Eleanor have continued their study of the language, well after John's death?" he said.

I cocked my head to the side and I saw Charlotte run toward the front door and pull on it. "Maybe they continued studying it as some kind of tribute to John? To keep his memory alive?"

"That seems far-reaching," he said.

Charlotte bounded down the cracked concrete front steps without holding the railing and with such speed I nearly gasped. She ran toward my car, waving frantically. "That does seem strange. What are you thinking?"

"I'm not sure. But maybe there was some reason why they kept the language alive. Maybe . . ." he trailed off.

"Maybe they were still using it. With John. Who was out there somewhere," I finished. The words vibrated as I said them, emotion threatening to close off my throat. A tingle ran down my arms, to my fingertips, as I imagined them practicing in secret, their hands moving around in conversation.

He was silent, and I jumped as Charlotte began to knock on my car's window and make funny faces, sticking her tongue out and pulling at the corners of her mouth.

"Well, that certainly could be an explanation, but we have no way to prove that"—he paused—"yet."

I smiled and stuck my tongue out at Charlotte. "I like your optimism. And I love that you seem to care about all of this as much as I do."

He laughed. "Yes, well, H-H-Haley says that I sometimes seem to care more about people and things that have been long dead, as opposed to what's right in front of me. She says—" He stopped suddenly and I could almost hear his blush through the phone.

Charlotte began to press her nose against the window, licking the glass. I shook my head and waved my hand, which only encouraged her to do it with more enthusiasm. "Well, I think my husband would agree with her in this instance."

He cleared his throat. "Yes, well, I will keep digging then," he said, his tone as crisp as a McIntosh apple.

I dropped my phone and opened the car door, Charlotte shrieking and running toward the house. I quickly caught up to her just before the steps leading to the front porch and wrapped an arm around her waist. She shrieked again and tried to wiggle away, but I bent down and attacked her face with kisses, until she begged me to stop.

"Never," I said as I pulled her toward me for a hug so tight, she shrieked again.

CHAPTER 21

AMELIA

"It must be eight layers tall," Jane had said when she ordered her wedding cake. "Eight layers tall, with a spray of pink roses in between each layer. "

The baker had looked at her in bewilderment, her eyes flashing from Jane to Eleanor to Amelia to Mary, who slowly shook her head. The tallest cake she had ever made—a chocolate and buttercream monstrosity with muddled raspberries as a filling, and white fondant placed over the top for Betsy Letts—was six layers tall, and she did not breathe one single, satisfying breath until it was cut into perfect wedge-shaped slices and placed in front of every guest.

"Did you hear me?" Jane took a step forward, her back straight in her drop-waist dress, her hair pinned up against her head in perfect curls.

Amelia's head snapped, bristling at the phrase. She had heard people say that many times to John, usually adults who had no idea he was deaf, assuming he was just another misbehaving child with selective hearing.

"Of course she heard you," Amelia said as she crossed her arms over her chest. Her black dress suddenly felt tight across her chest, and she took a slow, deep breath. "It's impossible not to hear you, Jane," she added.

Eleanor stepped forward, in between them, as she always did, and placed a hand on Jane's wrist. "Eight layers might be too large, Jane." She looked at the baker, who nodded in relief.

Jane's eyes narrowed before she turned to the baker. "Eight. I want eight. One for each of the months in our courtship."

And there it was. No one could argue with sentiment for a wedding cake, even if it was terribly inconvenient. Nor could the baker squeak in protest when Jane had described exactly what she wanted: a traditional Swedish princess cake—covered in fondant, dusted in powdered sugar, with each layer consisting of white cake, custard, chocolate chips, and fresh strawberries. Then, repeated seven more times.

It didn't matter that they weren't Swedish or that Jane had never even met someone from Sweden. She had seen the cake in the latest *McCall's* magazine, described as one of the most difficult, yet enchanting and delicious, cakes one could serve at a wedding. The cake shown in the article was only three stories. But, come hell or lake water, Jane would have the most difficult version possible.

So when Jane went to cut into the cake at the reception, after the guests had released their lanterns on the lakefront, the crowd seemed to collectively hold their breath as she carelessly plunged the sterling silver cake knife engraved with her and Edward's monogram directly into the center of the bottom piece, making the entire five-foot-tall structure sway back and forth gently.

Jane, oblivious, hastily removed the knife, rotated it forty-five degrees, and stabbed at the cake again, attempting to make a perfect triangle cut. Again, the cake wobbled, and Amelia saw the baker off to the side put a hand over her eyes, peeking out in between two fingers. Miraculously, the cake found its footing and stopped wobbling. Edward helped Jane pull the piece out, the custard filling moving back and forth before slumping to the side. A waiter appeared and handed them two forks, and they gently fed each other, not even a wisp of Jane's lipstick smudging. The guests clapped politely, and the waiters began to wheel the cake off to the side, to begin disassembling it for service.

From their vantage point off to the side, John tugged at Amelia's dress and signed, "Cake, please."

She smiled and nodded. "Of course. You can even have my piece. Sweets for my sweet," she signed back. She dropped her head toward her lap and closed her eyes, whispering the phrase again: "Sweets for my sweet." She had said it automatically, the phrase sewn tightly into her life, a part of her. But it was Henry who had stitched the words. She hadn't spoken them since he died, she realized, and she clasped her hands so tightly in her lap that her knuckles turned white.

Henry, why did you have to leave us? If you were still here, we would be safe. John would be protected.

So many questions, so many regrets, especially in the last few days of his life. So many broken promises.

She slowly opened her eyes, whispering the phrase again as she thought of the first time he said it to her. It was on one of their first dates, and he had brought her chocolate-covered cherries from a farm in Michigan. "Sweets for someone sweet," he had said as he stood in the foyer of her parents' estate on Lake Shore Drive in downtown Chicago.

She laughed and said, "While I appreciate the gesture, I'd much rather have saltwater taffy," with a wink. Her heart swelled as she realized how good it felt to laugh with someone and how long it had been since she had done so. Matthew had left for California two months before, but not before asking again if she would come. It took everything she had to press a sheet of paper into his hand and ask him to write. And for the past two months, she had kept her feelings—her regret, sadness, loss—in the locked jewelry box of her mind and tried to look ahead. Until finally, Henry appeared.

And so after that first date, "sweet or salty" became their whispered phrase; whenever they were at a party and a man was obviously trying to court a woman, they would say, "Do you think he wants to give her something sweet or salty?" and then they would have to pin back their laughter. It became their first shared experience, a private joke, that would carry them to the next date, and beyond. It was the seed in the dirt, ready to be watered.

They had said that at one such occasion, at her father-in-law's birthday party at the newly opened Drake Hotel in downtown Chicago. John was only two years old and everyone already knew about his inability to hear, but the Cartwrights were trying desperately to pretend it wasn't true.

"He will start speaking soon," Amelia had overheard Margaret say to Tracy Drake and his wife, in a voice loud enough that everyone knew she didn't care who heard. "Heavens, Henry didn't speak in full sentences until he was almost five."

Which, of course, wasn't true. Before John was born, Margaret told everyone that Henry was a precocious child who came out of the womb practically skipping and negotiating deals.

Thankfully, the Drakes didn't seem at all interested in John. Amelia overheard them switch the conversation to the sugar maples on their property in Lake Geneva. He had one hundred of them dug up from Williams Bay and planted at Aloha Village, his estate, so named after he and his wife took a trip to Hawaii, a place they mentioned so often in conversation it was hard for Amelia to keep her face pleasant.

Later that night, after the party, when Amelia and Henry were home in their bedroom and John was in bed, Henry had sat on the edge of the bed, his back to Amelia, as he untied his shoes.

"She mentioned it again," he said quietly, slowly removing one of his black oxford shoes and placing it off to the side.

Amelia froze, her blue-and-white tea-length dress half off one shoulder, limply hanging down her arm. "Oh." Her breath quickened and her body went rigid as she balled up her skirt in her fists. Her shoulders were already knotted with stress, as she had heard a group of women gossiping about the Hoppe Brewery and how word was out that the family was beginning to struggle after the Volstead Act was passed the previous year.

Henry turned, his eyes deep with worry, and lines on his forehead. "Yes." He rubbed his chin slowly.

"And what did you tell her?" Amelia raised her eyebrows, a fire starting in her spine and radiating through her body. It was the anger that fueled her, to do anything, to anyone. The first time she felt it was when she was on a walk on a cool spring morning, pushing John's pram along the lakefront. He was six months old, but they didn't know about his deafness. She had stopped the stroller, and bent down, and cooed his name. But his gaze remained fixed at something off in the distance. She said his name again, and again, louder each time. Yet he never turned his head at the sound. Sweat running down her back, she said it one more time, her voice coming out in a fractured tone. Another mother walking near with a pram startled and gave her a disapproving look and John a questioning one. Amelia had wanted to reach across the park and slap the frown off the woman's face.

And in her bedroom, she struggled with the same reaction as Henry sighed, his shoulders slumping toward the bed.

"You told her no, correct? You told her that we will never consider sending John away to that . . . that prison of a place, yes?" She took a step forward when he didn't look at her. "Tell me that you told her, Henry. I don't expect that you told her exactly what kind of a person she is, or how black her heart must be, but tell me that you told her that he will never be away from us."

He inhaled slowly and then turned to look at her. "Of course. Yes, I told her that we would not agree to that."

Amelia's arms relaxed, releasing her dress. "Of course you did," she said. "How on earth can she believe that we would send John away to a school for the deaf and the dumb? She is his grandmother, for heaven's sake. His family. She is supposed to protect him, and care for him, like the rest of us."

Henry turned away from her again, removing his other shoe. "That's not her way. That's never been her way. She cares more about her standing with Ada Wrigley than anything else. You know this; we all know this."

"Well, I certainly hope Ada and her prized hogs will care for her in her old age, and pay her visits and listen to her awful stories. Somehow when she's even more old and gray and decrepit, I don't foresee that anyone but us will be forced to entertain her." The fire igniting again, Amelia began ripping her dress off, letting it fall to the floor in a heap, before kicking it to the side of the room. She walked around to where Henry sat and put her hands on her hips in front of him.

He reached out and took her hands, but she stayed rooted in place, rocking forward and then back. "You're right. She's awful," he said. "I always thought her to be a tough character, unbending, but the way she has been toward you, and toward John." He hung his head and shook it ever so slightly.

She softened like butter in the sun and let him pull her toward the bed. He bent back and she lay on top of him, her face buried in his neck.

"No one will ever take him from us," he whispered into her hair. "I promise."

CHAPTER 22

ERIN

I heard my mother's guffaw before I even put my hand on the door of Dilars Restaurant in Richmond, Illinois. I was walking through the gravel parking lot, trying to step lightly in my thin moccasins, the sharp white rocks piercing through the soles with each step, when I heard her laugh. Sure enough, when I took a quick glance around the side of the restaurant I saw her motorcycle parked, Ferrari-style and perpendicular, taking up two different spots.

When I opened the diner's front door, I spotted her and Gerry at a red plastic corner booth, mugs of steaming coffee in front of them.

There were only ten booths in the entire place, but my mother lifted a hand and frantically waved. "Over here, honey!"

"What took you so long?" she said as I slid next to her in the booth, across from Gerry, who looked half-uncomfortable and half-amused as he tightly held both hands on his coffee mug, a wary smile on his face.

She didn't let me answer and tell her that I was only three minutes late, thanks to construction on Highway 12 in Fox Lake.

"I was just telling our friend Gerry here about the last time my group rode through his neck of the woods. There were about twenty of us, on a nice, long Sunday ride, going for a trip around the lake. Well, we were stopped at a light in town when this jerk in some sports car pulls up next to us and gives us one of those looks. You know, like this—" She rolled her eyes in an exaggerated manner and flipped her nonexistent long hair over her neck.

Out of the corner of my eye, I saw Gerry's eyes glaze over a bit, and I wondered if this was merely the second time my mother had told this story.

"Anyway, so we are on Highway Fifty, near the lake, just before you get into town. And as we are waiting for the light to turn green, this huge flock of seagulls flies overhead." She leaned forward, palms on the table. "And right before the light turned, one of the birds pooped all over the guy in the fancy car. He started sputtering and cursing, bird poop all over his head, as we went on our merry way."

She laughed again, her bellowing, boisterous laugh that sounded like giant effervescent bubbles popping in the air. I didn't have the heart to remind her that she had told me that particular story no fewer than four times before. I turned to Gerry.

"Thanks so much for meeting us here. I thought this would be a good halfway point for everyone." I clicked my phone, illuminating the time. I had just over two and a half hours before I had to be back at Will's school to pick him up and drive him to group speech therapy. In it, he was supposed to be learning how to socialize with others, but three sessions in and all he had done was throw a tantrum each time he didn't win one of the games the therapist set up. So I would have to haul him out of the room each week in front of the other parents, whose children I never saw have a problem in the group.

"Well, I was quite excited after I discovered that letter from Louisa to her sister, Emily. All this time, it was sitting up there in Milwaukee, and I had no idea it had a connection to Lake Geneva. I wonder how many other things are out there of that nature." A faraway look passed across his eyes from behind his glasses.

Before he could mentally travel to another state and time, I said, "Yes, of course. So I really wanted all of us to meet, then, and figure out our next course of action. Where do we go from here? We have evidence that Emily and her mother, Eleanor, kept up with sign language, but for what purpose? It's worth investigating, but what next?"

Gerry nodded carefully, studying his coffee cup, as my mother said, "What about in your neck of the woods, Gerry? Any chance that there is something at your place, or maybe the library, with something on Emily or Eleanor? We've been looking at Amelia, but I think we should look at those around her, to see if there are any bread crumbs."

Gerry took a sip of his coffee, which I noticed was a light caramel color, like he had dumped an entire carafe of cream into it, and then smiled as he leaned back in the red booth, the staccato sound of the plastic shifting under his weight. "Yes. Of course."

"Great." My mother pulled out her wallet and threw down a twenty-dollar bill. "Let's go." She made a waving motion for me to get out of the booth.

"What? Now? Go up to Lake Geneva now?" I stayed in place and checked the time on my phone. We had met in Richmond since it was the halfway mark for me, wanting to avoid having to drive all the way into Wisconsin again. "I can't. And besides, even if I did, I could only stay for about thirty minutes, with all the driving back and forth."

"Then we'll go for thirty minutes. What do we have to lose? Adventure time," she said. I saw the same glint in her eyes as when she pulled up to church on her motorcycle for the first time. When I still didn't move, she added, "Now it's twenty-nine minutes, kiddo."

* * *

We met Gerry outside of the Lake Geneva Public Library, after a protracted battle with a family trying to get across Highway 50 to the public park on the lake, with them dropping various things like their picnic basket, a blanket, and a child trying to make a run for it.

Twenty minutes, a voice in the back of my head whispered.

Gerry stopped before we walked into the building, admiring the structure. "It always takes my breath away, no matter how many times I go inside."

I looked up at the Frank Lloyd Wright style A-frame building. Through the front windows, I could see that the back of the building was almost entirely made of windows, showcasing the sparkling blue lake just outside.

I smiled. "I can see why."

"You should see the library at the University of Wisconsin in Mendota, where I went to school," my mother said as she held open the door for us. "Now, that is a place. You have Lake Madison just beyond, and you can't go more than ten paces without finding somewhere to serve you a cold beer. This place is nice, but it doesn't compare."

Gerry pressed his lips together as he walked inside, and I gave my mother an admonishing look. "Can it," I hissed to her as I followed Gerry into the library.

"Back so soon?" a pretty redhead with big brown Bambi eyes said from behind the circulation desk.

Gerry's head turned and his back stiffened. "Oh yes. Hello there, Haley."

My head snapped back and forth between them as the name sounded familiar. I remembered he had said it before, on the phone, with a stammer.

"What did you think of the book? Yay or nay?" Haley put her elbows on the table, letting her wavy red hair fall around her shoulders, framing her tiny face.

"Ah, yes. I'm really enjoying it. Thanks so much for the

recommendation." Gerry nodded again, quickly adjusting his glasses.

"Great," Haley said. "So what can I help you with today?" Her eyes slowly moved over to me and my mother. "And your friends?"

"Right. Well, we are doing a bit of historical research," he said with a smile. He glanced at us, almost surprised that we were there, as though he and Haley were on a secret date. "A possible historical mystery, in fact."

Haley stood up. "Mystery? Well, I'm in." She walked around the circulation desk and held out her hands. "Where do we begin, folks?"

"Ah, yes, and here we have the obituary for Mary Hoppe," Haley said. Her voice was strong, confident, as she adeptly maneuvered the microfiche machine.

The rest of us were gathered around her chair, with Gerry standing and my mother and me sitting in rolling chairs we had stolen from nearby empty desks. To our right, the lake sparkled from outside the window. As on Powers Lake, most of the docks had been pulled in for the season, signaling the upcoming freeze when the ice-fishing season would begin. I was sure the lake temperature was far below swimming temperatures, yet all I wanted to do was dip my feet in the water and feel the lake pebbles under my toes.

We leaned forward and silently read Mary's obituary. It was fairly straightforward, mentioning her three daughters and grandchildren. The last line asked that, in lieu of flowers, Mary requested donations be made to the Irish Woods School.

"That was a school that was established for the children of the Irish immigrants who came to the area to help build the railroad. Some of the society women realized these children were in need of an education, and helped to establish a year-round school. You can still see part of the original farm off of Highway Fifty, just west of town," Gerry said.

"That's wonderful," I said quietly.

"One would venture a guess that she had a soft spot in her heart for children," Gerry said, "considering what happened to her grandson."

"That's good to see. I'm sure she felt like it was at least one thing she could do," my mother said quietly.

I didn't look at her and kept my head forward. I had tried to talk to her about my ever-changing feelings on Will but had never gotten past the thin surface stage. The stage where I said: It's hard. And then I would quickly change the subject or make a joke about it. I had never told her about the endless nights I cried myself to sleep, the nights even Luke had pretended to be asleep out of fear of saying or doing the wrong thing. The thoughts that horrified me, that destroyed me, the thoughts that I couldn't tell anyone. The things that I thought in the midnight of our struggles. Of course, as things often do, the clouds would break and a ray of light would shine through the next day, inflicting more shame and guilt on my soul, while lifting me out of the darkness. Yet I wished I could share some small piece of that with my mother, to have her share the burden of all the ways I doubted myself and my ability to be the mother that Will needed.

Haley clicked through a few more pages with expert ease and stopped at an article after Mary's death. It was a small blurb on her funeral, mostly detailing the famous names who attended and where her estate would go. "Looks like she also gave money to relatives in Ireland. In Adare Village," Haley said.

I turned to my mother. "I never realized we were that close to our Irish ancestors. I wonder if there are some still living over there, in the same place."

My mother nodded. "My mother talked about it once, and said that her cousins still lived in the same village, and owned a hardware store. 'Humble, kind, warm people' is how she always described them."

"Very neat," I said. "And also neat that Mary included them

in her will. Although how much was really left at that point? I wonder. Didn't you say that Prohibition killed a lot of their fortune?"

She shrugged. "I would think—"

"Actually," Gerry interrupted with a polite hand in the air, "if I may, from what I understand, the Hoppes did lose money in Prohibition, but they had diversified their investments in things like real estate so that they still had something. Of course they didn't keep the estate up, but maybe that was because of what happened."

"It was too painful," I said quietly, and my mother nodded.

Gerry continued, "A lot of estates weren't kept up at some point, though. Like, take for example, Otto Young's house, called first The Younglands and then Stone Manor."

Haley stifled a laugh. "Ah, yes. The famous—or, I should say, infamous—Otto Young." She swiveled around in her chair, her eyes bright. "After the Great Chicago Fire, he bought up half of the city for a song, and made a fortune, and built a huge house up here. And when he tried to join the country club, he was denied access since the properties he had bought once belonged to the current members, so he basically made his fortune off of them, selling back their real estate at a huge increase."

Gerry waved his hand around excitedly. "So then, when the members denied his application, listen to what he did: He built a barn in the exact same architectural style as the country club, and then named all of the farm animals after the club members. Like Mrs. Hutchinson, and so forth."

My mother let out a bellowing laugh that echoed across the library's tall ceiling. "What a great guy. I wish I could have shook his hand. Genius," she said as she wiped her eyes.

I saw Haley and Gerry exchange a triumphant glance. "What a great story. You should put that in the museum," I said.

Gerry raised his eyebrows. "It's more of a local legend than historical fact," he said. He looked down at Haley.

"He's the gatekeeper, that's for sure." Her tone was light,

teasing, and I had the sense that this was part of an ongoing inside joke.

Way to go, Gerry. Make your move, I thought with a smile.

Haley swiveled back around and clicked the machine again. She stopped briefly on the article that quoted a Georgina Lindemann, who said she had seen Amelia on a train to New York the next day, which we already knew.

"Well, guys, I think this might be—" She started to turn around but stopped as a new headline came into view.

NANNY FOR CARTWRIGHT BOY CLAIMS FOUL PLAY

We collectively leaned forward and skimmed the article. The first part was the nanny crying about how John couldn't swim in the lake and how she was always so careful that he not go in past his ankles.

" 'He could never swim. I told Mrs. Cartwright so, and pleaded with her not to take him on the yacht," the nanny claims,' " I read aloud. I looked at my mother, and she raised her eyebrows.

My mother squinted at the screen and pointed to the third paragraph. " 'A guest, who asked to remain anonymous, but was a passenger on the steam yacht when Amelia and John went overboard, claims that she saw Amelia jump and pull the boy with her, as he cried out. She claims they went under and never appeared again. Sources say the lake's surface where the crash happened was illuminated from the party, from the Chinese lanterns that were released earlier, despite the rain. Two other passengers report the same: that everyone scanned the water for them, but saw nothing. Even the captain is certain that they perished in the lake.' "

I stood up slowly and let out a breath. I could feel my mother and Gerry looking at me as Haley clicked a button to print off the article. The printer whirred to life next to her and spat out a black-and-white copy of the newspaper page. I lifted it and read it once again before I looked up.

"So it sounds like they died?" Haley slowly twisted around in her chair, and her smile faded when she saw my face. "Oh. I didn't realize you guys were pulling for a certain outcome."

"That's the thing about research. Sometimes it leads you in directions you don't want to go in, or never thought were possible," Gerry said.

"Or maybe those rich people on the yacht were wrong. Or maybe they had some kind of grudge against the family. We should all know by now that just because someone says something doesn't make it true, yes?" my mother said. She took the paper from my hand. "It's just another piece; we still don't have the whole puzzle."

I tried to keep my mother's words at the forefront as I raced home to pick up Will for his after-school speech therapy. When I was about a half hour from home, my phone rang and my heart sank as I saw it was his elementary school.

"I'm so sorry to bother you, but I was hoping to grab you for a quick chat." Miss Ball's voice came out light.

"Of course," I said, swallowing hard. The only times she had ever called, rather than e-mailed, were never for a good reason.

"Great. I just wanted to give you a heads-up that Will had another tough day today. He seemed agitated from the beginning, likely because another student was making a lot of noise, and stimming near him, and spinning near Will's desk." She paused, and I couldn't help but think, *Can you really blame him?*

"Thank you for everything," I said finally, my voice cracking. "We really appreciate it. I know it's been a rough start to the year."

"Of course. I do want you to know that I think Will is an amazing kid, and will do everything I can to help him," she said.

I hung up the phone and thought of how awful Will must have felt all day, alone and scared. And how that morning I had to drag him to the car to go to school. He had collapsed down on the ground as I held his hand, turning into a jellyfish. After several unsuccessful attempts to lift him off the ground, I finally picked him up and carried him to the car, all while avoiding the fists flying at my face. By the time I reached school, both of us were red-faced and shaking.

All I had ever wanted to do was help him, to see him happy, to see him grow and learn. It was time to make a change. And so before I could stop myself, I left a message for the administrator of Lakewood Academy, asking to set up a tour. I held the image of Will smiling, walking into school, learning, engaging, being part of a community. Maybe even, someday, making a friend. I was still aware of how small and how sad the goals probably looked to someone who didn't live in our world, but they were ours. And they made sense.

By the time I reached Will's speech therapy clinic, the sun had gone down over the horizon, shrouding everything in darkness. While I waited in the waiting room, listening to him cry, I thought back to the library, and of Amelia and John, in the literal darkness of night on the lake. I knew that my own demons came out in full force when the sun fell below the horizon, and wondered just what she might have been thinking when she took her child, who couldn't swim, on a boat in the middle of a thunderstorm.

CHAPTER 23

AMELIA

By the time the last of the lanterns had been released over the lake, the cake was served, and the guests had settled in for the last part of the evening, the dark clouds had moved closer to the party, covering the sky and blanketing the stars. In the distance across the lake, near Fontana, occasional flashes of lightning peppered the sky, like the flashbulb of the wedding photographer's camera.

None of the guests seemed to notice that the storm approached, or if they did, they didn't care. The brandy still flowed from the crystal decanters by the bar, the waiters lifting them to pour more liquid into the guests' glasses. Champagne glasses were drained quickly and easily, with gloved waiters rushing around to refill the empty ones, held out with a flick of a wrist. The noise of the crowd grew, dotted with laughter a bit too loud and a bit less proper.

Amelia watched the party from an empty table on the edge of the lawn, John next to her, finishing the last of his cake. He ate around the raspberry filling, having tried it and crinkled up his nose, pushing it aside, before he eagerly dug his silver spoon into the custard dotted with chocolate chip pieces. She absentmindedly ran a hand through his soft blond hair, admiring the way it fell back into place after she ruffled it. He had the same hair as his father: fine and straight, always falling correctly into place, whereas she had to use sheer will and determination and more styling products than she cared to admit to tame her curls.

On the edge of the party, on the dock, she saw Captain Scott dock the *Monarch Princesses* and let a group of guests off the boat. The dockhands helped them off with outstretched hands, steadying their footing on the white wooden dock. The captain got off the boat, too, and stood on the dock, arms folded, shaking his head as he looked up at the sky. He gave a hand signal to the workers, and they began to pull the canvas cover over the bow, preparing the boat for the storm.

Amelia's heart beat faster, and she quickly stood, her chair nearly tipping over behind her, as she grabbed John's hand. He looked up in surprise, and she signed, "Come," and pulled him to standing. She walked over to the dock, ignoring the guests who tried to get her attention and congratulate her on the party. More than once, she heard a request to find another waiter for more drinks.

"Captain, I would like you to take the yacht out for one more ride around the lake," she said breathlessly when she arrived at his side. She ignored the way her chest constricted, as though her body was telling her with everything it had not to go.

He looked at her in surprise, his white brows lifting toward the starched cap on his head. He studied her face before cracking a smile. "Funny joke, Mrs. Cartwright."

She didn't return the smile. "Not a joke. I want to take a ride out onto the lake. One more ride."

Captain Scott dropped his arms to his sides, frowning. "There is a storm coming, the same storm that I mentioned earlier today. It's simply not safe."

"It's not here yet. It's still over Fontana, and seems to be taking a long time to get here." She looked down at John and swallowed hard. "I promised him. Please. We should have been on one of the earlier boats, but he fell and I was taking care of him. Please," she said again, her voice crackling. John's eyes were wide, his head snapping back and forth between her and the captain.

He looked down at John and then out again over the lake, toward the gathering clouds, and slowly exhaled. "Fine. But it will be a quick trip, and we can only stay on this side of the lake, not far from shore. Understood?"

She nodded and jiggled John's hand. "Ready to go for a ride?" she signed.

"Em, what are you doing?" Matthew called from the dock as Amelia and John began to step onto the gangplank to the boat.

Amelia faltered and made a motion for John to continue onto the boat, and she turned to Matthew as John settled into one of the wooden benches on the yacht.

"It's just a quick trip. I promised John." She slowly turned and looked at the dark clouds, still far enough away from the estate to interrupt anything. "We will be back before even a drop of rain falls, I promise."

Matthew took a step forward and placed a hand on her arm. "I know you're upset about Margaret, and I don't think your head's in the right place right now. Please, it's too dangerous."

Amelia took a step away from him, toward the yacht, and stood on the gangplank to the boat. "It will be perfectly safe. We will be back in just a few minutes. John really wanted to see the party from the boat. Please, have a glass of champagne waiting for me, and we can sit together on the porch and watch everyone be soaked by the rain, if they are even of sound mind enough to realize they're wet." She laughed, but it was hollow and fell to the ground and burst into a million pieces.

"Then I'm coming with you," he said, and took a step toward the boat.

"No." He stopped in surprise at her tone. "Please, no. I want to be alone with my son. Please," she said again before she turned toward the water.

"Amelia—" Matthew said, his hand outstretched, but she continued onto the ramp.

She sat next to John, her arm around him. She pulled him close and kissed the top of his head. "Ready?" she signed, and he nodded. She couldn't look up, into Matthew's eyes, for everything she had planned and arranged might fall into dust. She didn't trust herself to let him see her, and all that she was willing to do.

The captain wearily walked down the dock. As he did, Rose Savington saw him boarding and screeched in delight. She ran toward the yacht, her heels digging into the uneven grass as she tipped forward and to the side, her glass of champagne sloshing all over her pale blue skirt.

"Oh! I still haven't been on the yacht yet!" She lurched up the metal stairs, dockhands rushing to her side to prevent her from tipping over the railing and falling into the water below. She fell into a seat in front of Amelia, waving toward her friends on the lawn, until they, too, boarded the yacht.

"Rose, you know I get seasick on these things," Georgina Lindemann grumbled as she sat down next to her. She turned around and shot a look of disdain at John and Amelia before turning back to Rose. "And it's supposed to rain. If my gown gets wet, I'm sending you the bill."

Amelia peeked over the railing, down to the water around the boat. It was dark, but she knew the bottom wasn't far below. That part of the lake appeared much deeper than it was, with black water swirling around the edges. She swallowed hard and pulled John closer to her as she imagined how cold the center of the lake was and how deep it was to the bottom. The yacht rocked from side to side as the wind picked up, causing Georgina and Rose in front of her to fall into each other, dissolving into laughter as they tried to sit upright. Georgina lit a cigarette, barely making it to her lips.

As Amelia settled back into her seat, she saw a figure in a pale pink dress running toward the dock, one hand on her skirt and the other in the air. Eleanor kicked off her pink slippers as she ran toward the boat, leaving them next to the cocktail table at the end of the pier, where the guests had picked up glasses of champagne and brandy when they disembarked the yacht a few hours before.

Amelia rose and signed to John to stay, and he nodded and looked out again at what was left of the floating Chinese lanterns over the lake, just a few dotting the sky like lighthouse beacons, ready to steer sailors into safe passage. She stepped around Charles Wacker and hurried toward the staircase to the dock.

"Coming along for a cruise?" she said lightly, her hand resting on the wooden railing decorated with pink ribbons.

Eleanor reached forward and grabbed her by the wrist, tugging gently. "Matthew told me. He's worried. It's too dangerous, Amelia. Please don't do this." She pressed her lips into a thin line, tugging again at her sister, who didn't move.

Amelia gave her a shaky smile. "It's just a quick trip. Like I said, I promised John. He will be devastated if he doesn't get one ride out on the water." She held a hand up when she saw Eleanor's frown deepen. "I promise we will be safe." She leaned forward and whispered, "Captain said we will be fine." She pointed a finger behind her, in the direction of Rose Savington and Georgina Lindemann. "If anything happens, we will throw them off first." She laughed lightly.

"This is a terrible idea. There is lightning over there, Amelia. You can't put yourself or John in that kind of danger, no matter what you promised," Eleanor said. Her voice rose, and Amelia straightened her spine.

"We will be back before you know it," she said with a quick nod. She turned around and began to walk toward John on the boat. The vessel swayed back and forth again, and she stopped, steadying herself on one of the chairs. And a memory came to her quickly.

It was of the first summer at Monarch Manor, when she and Eleanor were ten and thirteen years old. When her father had presented the *Monarch Princesses* to Mary and asked the captain to take them on a cruise around the lake, Amelia was too afraid to step on board. The lake was choppy that morning, and the boat swayed back and forth next to the dock. Jane had happily jumped on, holding their mother's hand. But Amelia remained on the dock, frozen, unable to step onto the wooden walkway that led to the moving boat.

Eleanor was right behind her, waiting. After a moment, Eleanor grabbed her hand and whispered into her ear, "I will be right here. I promise I won't let go. Trust me."

Amelia had squeezed her sister's hand tighter than she thought possible, certain she was going to break a bone. But Eleanor didn't so much as flinch as she led her on board, sat next to her, and put her arm around her shoulders.

"*Trust me.*" Her sister's words echoed in Amelia's ears once again as she boarded the *Monarch Princesses*.

Amelia turned back to Eleanor, hand lifted in the air. "Eleanor, can you do me one favor?" Before her sister could reply, she continued, "I forgot to ask Alfred to feed the baby bunnies in our garden. With the events of the day, it slipped my mind. I don't think their mother is coming back, so please remind him to do so before any rain falls."

Eleanor's brows knitted together in confusion, and her mouth twisted to the side, open slightly. "Amelia, is that really—"

"Please do it, Eleanor. It will weigh on my mind heavily. Please," she repeated. She walked over to John and sat back down next to him, putting an arm around his shoulders and pulling him close.

Eleanor still stood on the dock as the captain approached, walking around her to the stairway, and boarding the yacht. She hitched up her dress, and for a heart-stopping moment Amelia thought that she was going to step onto the boat, but she remained on the dock.

"Don't forget!" Amelia called to her sister as the dockhands pulled up the staircase, folding it onto the yacht before they passed out life jackets to the passengers.

Captain Scott stood at the helm, his hands on the steering wheel. He turned around slowly and gave her a grim nod before he pulled the boat away from the dock, the steam billowing out from the top of the smokestack.

Amelia kissed the top of John's head and first looked out at her sister, and then up at the estate in the background, her eyes floating up to the corner room, her childhood bedroom. Where she and her sisters had spent so many nights whispering long after bedtime, telling one another stories about beautiful princesses, handsome knights, and evil witches. They all wore the same white nightgowns, with eyelet lace on the hems and sleeves, and their hair was long and fell around their shoulders.

It was the Before. Before engagements, and marriages, and decisions, and children. Before death, tragedy, and heartbreak.

It was like the lake water in the morning, crystal clear and perfect. Beautiful, before the rest of the world disturbed it.

Just as the lake was impossible to calm once the day had begun, they could never again touch their past.

She looked out onto the water and closed her eyes as the yacht headed away from shore.

CHAPTER 24

ERIN

On the day when we were due to tour Lakewood Academy, the private school for Will, I watched the sun come up for the third consecutive morning. It was a Thursday, and since the week had started I had fallen asleep quickly at night but woken up each morning around 4:00 am, unable to return to sleep as I let the demons of stress circle around my ankles and pull me over the anxiety cliff.

There were so many things to consider: What if we loved the school? How would we ever pay for it? What if we hated the school? What other options did we have? And most important: What was the best thing for Will? Would we even know anymore?

Every question, and thus every answer, felt like we were choosing a path for Will, with very little room to make a mistake.

It reminded me of something my grandmother once said when Katie and I visited her in Powers Lake all those years ago. Just around the curve of the lake, on a diagonal from the green-covered pier where we spent our days, was the only thing that could be considered a marina on Powers Lake. It was part of the restaurant Harbor Lights, with a couple of piers for boat rentals, and some houses. All of the docks were close together, and one afternoon my grandmother was sitting on the pier with Katie and me and she pointed to a rowboat approaching Harbor Lights.

The dad inside the rowboat was carefully navigating the water, heading into the pier to presumably return the boat or maybe to go inside the restaurant. The kids sat up front in bright orange life jackets, looking unhappy at their boat ride coming to an end. The dad seemed to be heading to the pier on the very end, closest to the mossy pond part of the shore where Katie and I always threatened to shove each other on our daily walks. Yet he miscalculated the exact angle to steer the boat and realized the boat would barely fit on that side of the dock. So he began trying to furiously row backward, to adjust and dock at a different pier, but it was too late. His adjustment, mid-docking, caused him to crash sideways into the pier and dump the kids out among the lily pads and seaweed.

The kids were fine, albeit covered in green slime and moss, since the depth was only a few feet, but their screams made everyone in Kenosha County believe otherwise. And Katie and I learned some new, creative uses for the curse words we already knew.

"See, girls? That's why you should always be sure where you want to end up when you start something," my grandmother had said.

Of course, at the time, at thirteen, I didn't think she meant anything other than parking a boat. Yet, as I sat and watched the sunrise nearly twenty years later, her words came back to me in a rush, and their meaning took my breath away as the sun began to peek out from the horizon, illuminating the enormous maple tree in my front yard.

We need to be certain of where we want Will to end up when we decide on his school.

Of course, it wasn't that easy. There was what I wanted, there was what he would want, and then there was what was possible. Before I had kids, it never occurred to me that I would have to make a decision about something so monumental when my child was five.

I always thought that I would do anything for my children and anything to help Will. Of course, I assumed that meant tracking down doctors, losing sleep, and spending all of our savings. I never once imagined it might mean changing my vision for his future.

The thoughts stayed with me that morning as I dropped the kids off at school. They stayed with me as I met Luke in the parking lot of Lakewood Academy, and as I got out of the car and looked up at the redbrick building and noticed that the sunlight was illuminating the sign.

"Hey," Luke said as I walked over to his car. He still sat inside, staring down at sales numbers in his black work notebook.

"I know you don't want to do this," I said quickly.

He looked up in surprise. "I just think it's such an extreme step. That we would be giving up on him in some way," he said quietly.

I nodded, brushing a piece of hair out of my eyes. "I know. Believe me, I know. But we have to see if this is even an option we should consider."

He got out of the car and I started toward the school, but he put a hand on my upper arm. "I'll try to keep an open mind, Erin. I really will."

I swallowed hard, glancing at the school again.

"And this is the sensory room, where each student is encouraged to self-regulate when they need." The school's director, a woman named Valerie Halas, walked us through a room filled with exercise balls to bounce on, mini trampolines, a corner filled with foam blocks, and an entire bookshelf filled with sensory toys such as rubber balls, chewable necklaces, and fidgets.

"And when do they come in here? During Occupational Therapy time?" I said as I observed a girl around Will's age, quietly and happily humming as she spun on a disk in the corner.

Valerie shook her head, her white hair floating around her shoulders like a permed cloud. "No. We believe a child cannot learn until they are regulated, so they are welcome to come here whenever they need. Who are we to say when they need OT or not? He will get as much as he needs, no limits." She took in our wide eyes and smiled. "We have a lot of flexibility here since we are a private school."

"Sounds like it." I thought of Will's last IEP meeting in preschool, when the weary OT told us she could only offer him forty minutes per week of therapy and then whispered to us as we left that he needed much more, but the district had tied her hands.

"And here is one of our classrooms," Valerie said as we stopped at an observation window outside of a classroom. In the front, a young, cute teacher stood in front of a smart board, teaching what looked to be a lesson on how to read a map to a group of children of various ages. Some looked to be learning the information at an age-appropriate time, and others, much older.

Valerie nodded, as though she could read my thoughts. "You'll see students of varying ages in each classroom. The learning is also student-led. If a child shows an aptitude for, say, math, that student can excel in grades beyond their age. If they struggle with another subject, they will be grouped with learners at that level also, regardless of age. Again, it's all student-led and about flexibility. It's somewhat of a Montessori approach to children with special needs."

Luke cleared his throat. "What is the staff to student ratio?"

"Very good. Two to one," Valerie said proudly.

"How can that—" I started to say when I looked around the classroom again and noticed the adults lingering around. One was sitting next to a girl who was fidgeting, and helping her pick up her pencil. Another appeared to be helping another student follow along on a modified sheet.

"Of course, our aides will certainly back off if a child shows independence, but the help is there for them should they need it. Shouldn't we give them every tool to learn as much as they can?" Valerie said with a smile.

We followed her down a hallway to her office, marked *Administration*. Luke and I settled into two brown leather chairs opposite her desk, and she pulled out a black folder and set it in front of her.

"This is the admission packet for new students here. I encourage you to look through it, and let me know if you have any questions," she said.

I gingerly reached forward, my chair creaking and cracking under me, and handed it to Luke. He opened it, and I saw his eyes bulge out at the first page. *Tuition,* I thought. I swallowed hard.

"It's a lot to process, and there are a lot of decisions to be made, I'm sure. I just want to reiterate, we truly do commit to each child. We believe that setting them on the right course during these early years does make all the difference," Valerie said.

"How many zeros to make a difference?" I said lightly as we walked to our cars. I laughed, but it never lifted, like a half-deflated balloon barely hovering above the ground.

"Close to what you thought," he said, the folder tucked under his arm. A look of sad relief passed over his face.

"Are you going to tell me or do I have to play *The Price Is Right*? Closest to the dollar without going over?" We stopped at Luke's car, and he wordlessly handed me the folder. There, inside, was the number: $60,000 per year.

Something between a laugh and a cry escaped my mouth. I quickly shut the folder. "Oh," was all I said.

"Well, we have our answer: not an option. We should have asked for the number before we wasted our time," Luke said tightly before he got into his car.

I watched him drive off and stared up at the school. There was no way we could ever come up with that kind of money, short of some kind of miracle. Yet I thought of Will, and him running away from school each morning, almost into traffic, and his unwillingness to even go inside, and couldn't help but feel even more like a failure. Here was an option that might help him, that might be an answer that we had been searching for, and we couldn't do it. The universe was dangling a carrot in front of my face and then snatching it away.

How can we accept his fate, and not keep trying, not keep pushing? I thought as I got into my car. I realized my phone was still in my pocket as I sat down with a bump. I leaned over and pulled it out of my pocket and saw that I had two missed calls from Gerry and a text.

The text read: *Where are you? I have tried to call twice. I found something interesting and wanted to tell you directly. I'm about to walk into a town council meeting, so here goes: Margaret Cartwright—Amelia's mother-in-law—registered John at a school for the "Deaf and Dumb" in nearby Bloomfield. The admission date was supposed to be June 1923, after the accident. Call me at your earliest convenience.*

Breathing quickly, I called Gerry back. His phone went straight to voice mail, and I threw my own down in frustration. I pulled out of the parking lot of Lakewood Academy, away from the unattainable best option, trying to wrap my mind around the possibility that John was alive after the accident.

I gripped the steering wheel as I thought of my own decisions and how maybe Will's and John's lives intersected in more ways than I possibly could have imagined.

CHAPTER 25

AMELIA

The *Monarch Princesses* moved away from the dock of the estate, rocking side to side in the lake waves. Amelia clutched John's hand tighter as she tried to steady her breath.

"Just a few waves, nothing to worry about," she whispered to herself. She knew she couldn't turn back and the dock was too far to stop everything that had already been put into motion.

She closed her eyes tightly and thought, *If only Henry were still here. If only he hadn't betrayed us, willingly or not.*

Before she could stop the memory, she thought back to the day when everything had started: the day not only when she had had to say good-bye to Henry but also when she first saw the battle that was ahead.

At Henry's funeral, Margaret Cartwright wore the same strand of pearls as she did to Amelia and Henry's wedding. At the luncheon after the funeral at the Fourth Presbyterian Church, Amelia noticed the necklace on Margaret's black silk shift, resting against her bony collarbone. Amelia had tightened her grip on John's hand as they made their way up the stairs to the Cartwright home.

She only noticed the necklace because Margaret had made it such a big moment when she showed it to her. "Someday, if you have a daughter, these will be passed down to her," she had said as she tapped the white pearls. Amelia could see tiny diamonds in between each round gemstone. "Of course, if I had my own daughter, she would receive these, but instead . . ." Margaret had trailed off, each of them filling in a different blank. Amelia later heard her tell someone at the wedding that she had worn the pearls every time someone close to her had died. She called them her mourning pearls.

Amelia didn't remember much from the funeral luncheon, nor did she remember much from the funeral itself. All she could think of was the last time Henry was lucid enough to hold her hand and to look into her eyes as himself, rather than the shell of the person who he was in his final days. His hand was so weak in hers, yet he ran his thumb over the top of her hand, like he always did when he held it. Then he turned it over and pressed his forefinger in the center of her palm.

"I will never leave you and John," he had said, gasping for air, before another wet cough racked his body. She had kissed his hand and closed her eyes, holding his hand as his body convulsed.

After that moment, he wasn't himself. He could barely speak, and when he did, his mind had already moved on.

The cough had started a few weeks before, just a slight rattle the morning after the Hutchinsons' annual Christmas party. There had been the usual revelry of trees decorated with glittering ornaments and sparkling ribbons in every corner of their home, with the ladies' gossiping about the attendance at Frances Hutchinson's latest horticulture lecture at her home. The men, of course, drank too much and played billiards until the wee hours of the morning, their cigar smoke wafting underneath the closed pocket doors. Margaret, to no avail, again tried to win

Frances's favor, but being that she was a close friend of Mary's through the Garden Club, she was firmly planted on the opposing side.

"Just a bit too much indulging last night, I imagine," he had said with a smile when she remarked the next morning that he looked pale. A week later, he could barely stand and the doctor said the word that they had been dreading: "tuberculosis." It was a word that changed everything. The doctor encouraged her and John to move out of their home, hire nurses, and dismiss the servants for fear of spreading the virus.

While Amelia heeded his advice on the staff, she stayed in the house, a white nurse's mask her ever-present accessory, and had John stay on the other wing of the house with a nanny.

One week later, Henry was gone, and all Amelia could think the first night she was alone was that he had broken his promise to never leave them. It would be the first of many betrayals, she would later discover.

Yet at the funeral luncheon, as she sat at a table with John and her parents, she understood what it meant: He would never leave their hearts. Not that he wouldn't die. No one could promise that. It was as inevitable as the freezing of the lake each winter, the waves crystallized in a half-moon shape before they finally surrendered to their icy fate.

Amelia could still feel Henry's hand in hers, and she looked down, flexing her fingers. She closed her eyes for a moment and wished more than anything that she would open them and he would be next to her, as he always had been. That he could right all of the wrongs he had left behind.

When she opened them again and the stillness of the air with him gone began to close in on her, she quickly stood from the table, nearly knocking over a crystal water glass. "Excuse me," she said in a strangled voice as she frantically tried to move her chair back and disentangle herself from the white tablecloth. Everyone at the table stared at her in fear, hoping she wouldn't make a scene. Finally, a gloved waiter came over and quickly moved her chair back so she could walk off, out of the room of people who watched her with a mix of pity and relief. Pity that her life had turned into such a tragedy, first with her son, and now with her husband gone, and relief that it wasn't them. That their life was just as charmed as it was when they woke up. They would get to fall asleep that night in the same bed, with the same dreams, same plans, same family and people around them, while Amelia didn't have the luxury of having the same life, or an ordinary day again. She didn't know if she would ever again have the peace of waking up in the morning and feeling hope.

She stopped at a large sterling silver mirror outside the room, staring at herself, trying to will herself to take a deep breath. *Calm down, and walk back inside, and show John your strength. Show all of them that you won't break. That even this will not break you.*

"People are beginning to whisper," Margaret said as she strode out of the room, her spine straight.

Amelia didn't respond, her hand on her stomach as it turned, at the sight of the pearls. "Funerals. You said you wear those only to funerals. Why did you wear them to my wedding?" Of course, she knew the answer.

Margaret looked down in surprise and patted the pearls.

"Why are you such a hateful woman? What is wrong with you? What did I ever do to you, other than to love your son, and to give you a grandson?" Amelia stepped forward, her eyes blazing, the emotions she had never allowed herself to express bubbling up through her. She pointed a finger in Margaret's face, inches from her nose. "Tell me. Why do you hate me so much?"

Margaret raised her eyebrows and slowly clasped her hands in front of her. "We still have not discussed the plans for the fall. For John's schooling."

Amelia's blood ran cold. Tiny pricks of panic ran down her back. She took a step back, her heel wobbling. "I have my own

plans for John. I have found him the best tutor in Chicago—
who knows sign language—who will be leading his studies."

Margaret didn't move. "That should come at a price, I believe."

Amelia swallowed hard. Her father and Henry's lawyer had
tried to talk to her about the finances right after Henry died,
but she wasn't ready to hear any of the discussion, so they had
agreed to table it until after the funeral.

She was frozen in her spot, heart beating wildly, as Margaret
continued.

"You might be now realizing that since Henry's money
came from his father, we were named the heirs of his estate, and
thus, we will be the ones to approve or deny any large requests
for money," she said. Her face had a look of resignation on it, as
though she was burdened by the responsibility of having to
deal with Amelia and John for the foreseeable future.

Amelia shook her head. "Fine, then. John and I will get along
without." She steeled herself. and lifted her chin in defiance.

Margaret's face remained neutral. "He also entrusted us with
John's guardianship."

Amelia laughed and clasped her hands across her chest.
"Now I *know* that you're a liar."

Margaret pressed her lips into a thin line and reached into
her small clutch, pulling out a folded piece of paper. "See for
yourself." As Amelia unfolded it, she added, "There are many
copies, so you may keep that one."

It was a statement, signed by Henry, awarding his parents
full guardianship of John when he died. Amelia brought a shaking hand to her lips and then stopped when she saw the date.

She shook her head and held the paper out. "This is dated
the day before he died. He couldn't speak, barely knew his own
name. This cannot possibly be legal, if it is his signature."

Margaret cocked her head to the side. "It is, I assure you. Our lawyer was there when he signed it. We are John's guardians now, not you."

Amelia took a step backward, her heel catching on the brightly colored red-and-yellow rug. "How could this have happened? How can this be possible?" she whispered.

Margaret didn't move to help her. "Perhaps Henry did not want you to have to worry about John's extensive care after he was gone."

Amelia blinked slowly and pressed her hands into her stomach. She could hear the chatter of the guests inside the ballroom and the soft tinkling of the flatware as it hit the china plates. Cold chicken salad with red grapes and pear soup was what the chef had suggested. Amelia barely remembered agreeing to it, her world unfocused, like the first few moments after waking up, before the world is real, and anything is possible. Anything happy, positive, or exciting, of course. A birth, an unexpected windfall, good fortune found.

Not death. Never death. Certainly not of someone so close.

And certainly not that someone so close would conspire to destroy what was left of their family.

"I've had my advisors look into some possibilities for your son," Margaret continued, "and everyone agrees that the likely best place for him is a school in Wisconsin." Her voice rose with each syllable, as though she had practiced exactly what to say.

"What kind of school?" Amelia's voice was hoarse, crackling through the air.

"For children who are like him. They will know how to handle him, and if he can be taught, they will teach him," she said quickly. "It's a good, fine school. Someday, he may return to you when he's older and more capable of being in society, and less of a . . . disruption to our events."

If. There it was, that word again.

If you survive the pregnancy with influenza, your child will surely not be born alive.

If your child is even born alive, it will surely die soon.

If he lives past the age of one, he will be a very sickly child, with many problems.

If you can afford it, place him in an institution, and have other children better suited to your status and lifestyle.

If . . .

"No," Amelia said. Margaret raised her eyebrows and Amelia took a step forward. "No. John will not be sent away to any school. Of course he can learn just like other children, with some things changed. He will stay with me. I will find him the best teachers. I will fight you, get back guardianship."

"I see," she said, her light eyes turning to stone. "And just how will you pay these teachers? I would assume they don't work for charity. And how will you contest a document that your husband signed, that was witnessed by three people?"

"I will find a way," Amelia said loudly. She saw some of the guests in the ballroom turn their heads, trying to peer into the hallway to eavesdrop on the conversation.

"And your home, and your allowances, and staff wages, all of those will need to be paid for as well," Margaret said. "Not to mention the legal fees if you choose to fight us. It would be terrible if you were declared unfit, and then not so much as able to visit him."

Amelia didn't reply and took another step forward, her face inches from Margaret's. "You will do no such thing. And I will never agree to your plans for John."

"Amelia"—Margaret's voice was measured, calm—"we do not need your permission. We can choose to do what we want with both of you. I can think of other, less comfortable schools he can be sent to should the need arise."

By now the entire room had turned to stare at them. Amelia could see her parents frozen, her mother's fork in the air with a piece of lettuce on the end, her face flushing. Her father had his head down, staring at his brown drink in front of him.

"What if I choose to sock you one, right here, in front of everyone?" Amelia hissed at Margaret. She lifted a fist toward her.

Margaret shrank back in horror and fear, her once-haughty face turning gray and old for a moment before it returned to its wretched state, a small smile on her lips. "A lot of witnesses to your hysterics here. Be careful."

Out of the corner of her eye, Amelia saw John walk toward her, weaving through the tables, a look of fear on his face. Amelia looked slowly at Margaret and then at her balled fist, and the redness she saw faded from view. She turned toward John and wrapped her arms around him, burying her face in his chest. She picked him up and carried him out of the ballroom and down the hallway, before she allowed the sobs to escape.

"Please, you must calm down." Amelia's mother, Mary, pressed a crystal glass of liquor she poured from a carafe on Conrad's bar table in his study. Amelia had followed her parents back to their house, unable to get herself home.

Amelia looked at it and set it down on the carved wooden table in front of her. After the scene at the funeral, she walked with John to her parents' home on Lake Shore Drive, where she found Alfred in the kitchen, preparing dinner. He fed John a lunch of buttered bread and apples and let him have a slice of cake from last night's dessert.

Alfred didn't ask any questions and merely handed Amelia a white linen napkin to dry her face as he offered her a glass of wine. She drank it in two large gulps and then took John upstairs, where they both fell asleep in the nursery. She woke when her parents returned from the luncheon, and they ushered her into the study.

"How can she do this?" Amelia said, lifting a shaking hand to her forehead. She rubbed it furiously. Her whole body felt like it was on fire, like it needed to be scratched by a thousand wire brushes. "How can she want to send him away?"

Mary and Conrad exchanged a look, and Mary sighed. "It is her way. She feels that John's presence is a blight on their social standing. You know this."

"And then what?" Amelia threw her hands in the air. "Everyone can pretend he doesn't exist? Throw him into some prison where no one will love him, or care for him, or—" Sobs cut off her words, lodging them in her throat.

Mary came over and sat down next to Amelia and smoothed her hair back. "That may not be true. It might be a lovely school."

"He will be with other children who are like him, with teachers who know how to help him. They will know what to do with him," Conrad said as he crossed his arms over his chest.

"Father, I know what to do with him. There's nothing *to* do—he's my son. I love him. They can't send him away from me," Amelia said, tears running down her face.

"It may just be temporary. See how he does in this school; see what it is like. Apologize to Margaret for causing a scene," Conrad said wearily. "We can all sit down and talk in a couple of months and determine the best course of action for everyone."

Mary nodded. "You know we love John just as you do, but you will catch more flies with honey than vinegar."

"You cannot be serious. You want me to—" Amelia stopped as her father stood.

"I need to lie down," he said. "It's been a long day and we all need some rest."

The women watched as he left the room, the discussion over. He was famous for doing so in business discussions. When he would negotiate no further with a client or colleague, he would simply walk out of the room. Deal over. Finished. Although there likely had been fewer and fewer negotiations going his way, as Amelia noticed the staff was leaner and a light coating of dust was on the furniture in the parlor.

"Listen to me, Amelia," Mary said in a whisper when Conrad had disappeared up the stairs.

"Please, Mother, don't take him from me. Please. I've already lost Henry. I can't lose him." Amelia put her face in her hands, her entire body constricting with pain.

Mary leaned forward and put her hands on either side of her

daughter's. "I know. I won't let that woman take him away. I don't know how yet, but I will help you protect him. He will be safe. She is ruthless, though, Amelia. You know that."

Amelia collapsed down into her mother's lap, face still in her hands, as Mary ran a hand over her head.

"It must be our secret," she whispered.

CHAPTER 26

ERIN

"To finally getting a night out together." Luke lifted his wineglass in the air, burgundy liquid sloshing inside, and clinked it against my glass. The Friday night crowd at Brissago, an upscale-but-still-comfortable steak restaurant known for thick cuts of filet mignon and enormous double-stuffed baked potatoes, roared around us, and I had to lean in to hear him.

"With the price of babysitting these days, we'll be lucky if we don't have to take out a second—make that third—mortgage after tonight." I shook my head. Our neighbor's fifteen-year-old daughter was babysitting, but we made sure to make the reservations late enough so the twins were in bed before we left. All she really had to do was sit on the couch and text us if the house burned down. Or if Will woke up.

"Well, it's worth it. I feel like your mind is . . . elsewhere these days," Luke said. He set his wineglass down and put his palms on the white tablecloth.

I nodded slightly as I looked down at the bread basket overflowing with warm pretzel rolls. "Maybe I have been a little distracted. I'm sorry."

He gave me a quick look before tearing off a piece of the

pretzel bread and spreading a pat of butter on it. "Don't apologize. I'm just saying it's been hard to pin you down, mentally. You've been knee-deep in the mystery of your relatives. And obviously there's a lot going on with Will." He raised his eyebrows.

I clasped my hands in front of me. "Look, researching Amelia and John has given me something that I can't quite name. Something other than just worrying about Will's latest therapies or the new trigger for his meltdowns. It's something I care about, something for me." I took a long breath in and tried to push down the frustration bubbling up at the inadequacy of my explanation.

He folded his arms across his chest and nodded. "I know. I'm happy you've found a hobby." I raised my eyebrows and he held his hands up in defense. "Poor word choice. An interest? Whatever is the proper term."

"Right. And I understand what you're saying. There's only so much I can give, and I have been focused on this a lot." I sighed. I didn't need to add what we were both thinking: that I was leaving again tomorrow and taking a day trip up to Wisconsin, to see if there were any archived documents for the Bloomfield School for the Deaf and Dumb that John may have attended. I had never left the twins as much as I had while searching for Amelia and John, but I kept telling myself that it was worth it, that this was bigger than all of us

Luke took a long sip of wine and then set his glass down carefully, considering it as he spoke. "I hope you find what you're looking for soon so we can get back to our normal lives," he said.

I chewed on the inside of my cheek, desperately holding back the words I wanted to say: *There is no normal life.*

Earlier in the week, I had taken the twins to the park. Charlotte ran all around, jumping up to the monkey bars and sailing down the slide. Will wanted only to sit in the swing—the bucket swing made for toddlers. His long legs dangled out of the leg slots and almost touched the ground. Soon there were a few toddlers and their moms waiting around the swingset, hoping for a turn. I could feel those other moms staring at me, thinking, *He's much too old to be sitting in that swing. Why doesn't he get out and let another kid have a turn?*

I remained calm, even as he started to tantrum when we had to leave. He lay on the ground and thrashed his body, screaming like a hungry infant. I picked him up, struggling under the weight of his limp body as I hissed at Charlotte to stay close. I had tried to duck each of his swinging fists, but one connected with my face and my sunglasses flew off, shattering on the ground. I left them there and continued toward the car.

During the entire incident, my face was neutral, pleasant. Like a mannequin. I wanted to tell the other mothers who stared at us to look away and not to help. Offering assistance would only upset him more.

Nothing to see here. Move along. Go about your day.

Don't look at him.

Forget you ever saw us.

Just five years before, when I was in the hospital after the twins were born, I couldn't stop showing them off. Nurses stopped in the room just to catch a glimpse of the full-term twins they heard were born on the floor. I proudly held them in my arms, relishing the attention.

"Look at my beautiful babies. Have you ever seen such gorgeous infants?"

"Look at them."

"Have you thought any more about Lakewood?" I said carefully. We had tried to have a discussion several times on the topic but always seemed to get interrupted by one of the twins or a late-night work call, so we had never talked about it in a serious way. Not to mention, my stomach dropped every time I thought of the zeros on the tuition bill. I reached a hand up and touched the silver earring dangling from my ear, twirling it with a shaking hand.

Luke looked down at the table, slowly running his hand

over the white fabric. "Does it really matter what I think? We can't afford it. It's not an option."

I leaned forward. "How can you dismiss it that quickly? I know it's a lot of money, but maybe we can work something out. Like selling the house and living in our car." I laughed and it shattered into a million pieces, broken by the silence between us. I took a sip of wine and stared at him, wanting him to laugh, join me in this, tell me things would be okay.

He sighed and looked up, his lips pressed together. "He's a great kid. And he's going to get there someday. He's only five. Who knows what he can do?"

I dug my nails into my palm. "I totally agree. But we can't keep living like this—he, I—can't keep on this way. The stress, and the meltdowns, and waiting every second for another call from school to tell me that he spent another day crying . . . that takes a toll."

"Just the other day, I read an article about a kid who didn't speak until he was six years old and now he's a vice president at a major corporation." He leaned forward. "That could be Will. And it feels like if we pull him out of school at this age, he won't even achieve his potential."

My cheeks burned with rage. "Really? You think I don't think he has potential? What do you think I've spent the last three years of my life doing? All I have done during that time is try to find a way to help him. Autism is my life, Luke. Believe me when I say I want more than *anyone* for Will to be the best that he can be." I noticed other diners around us staring at us, nudging one another and raising their eyebrows.

Luke didn't say anything and stared at his wineglass. After several long minutes, he said, "Maybe we should talk about this another time. A better time."

"When would that be?" I crossed my arms over my chest and waited for a response, but he never answered me. We ate our dinner in near silence, murmuring answers to the waiter and staring at our phones. My insides burned with rage at his words. *How could he not see everything that I had done? How was he so unwilling to consider an option that might truly help?*

I allowed the rage to build, even though I knew that a few short weeks ago I had felt the same. I knew the journey wasn't a straight line, but I was the unofficial general of an army I had no business leading, and I felt as if I had the responsibilities of leading the battle, I should also have the respect of being allowed to make decisions. Or at least my opinions should weigh more heavily than they apparently did.

After a silent ride home, I paid the babysitter while Luke went upstairs. After I closed the front door, I sat back down on the couch, a reality show on television, while I steeled myself for another fight before bed. When I was ready, I went upstairs, but I saw that our bed was untouched, still hastily made from when I threw the covers over it ten seconds before the sitter came. I tiptoed across the hallway and pushed open Will's door. There, on his bed, was Luke, still dressed in his clothes from dinner.

Will was scrunched into the fetal position, with Luke next to him, an arm over his body. I could hear deep breathing from both, the sleep heavy and deep. My anger bubbled away at the sight of them together. I knew that Luke wanted the best for Will and was just as lost as I was. We had the same goal and no idea how to reach it. I gently closed the door, my throat constricting.

My bed seemed too big, too empty in that moment, so I went into Charlotte's room and curled up against her just as Luke did to Will. Although unlike them, I stayed awake, watching the moon outside of Charlotte's window move through the sky, waiting for the first dusting of morning sunlight, awaiting my next drive to Wisconsin.

The sunlight illuminated the wooden WELCOME TO WISCONSIN sign on I-94 outside of my car window. I had left earlier in the morning, when it was still dark, and the twins and

Luke were still fast asleep. I had stepped outside, a momentary shock running through my bones at the early-morning chill, and I ran back inside and grabbed a wool hat from the bin next to the front door that served as our mudroom. Our slanted wooden front porch had creaked and groaned with each step of my UGG boots, no matter how much I tried to tiptoe, and a layer of overnight frost dusted my car in the driveway. I tried to use the ice scraper on the coating of frost on my windshield, but it didn't budge and the dry scraping sound made me cringe. I turned on the car and fired up the defroster and waited for the windshield to clear. I thought of the first winter we spent in the house, when we got a record number of inches of snow, and no garage to park our cars, when Luke repeatedly said, "Please tell me this is part of the old-house charm you love so much."

By the time I reached the Wisconsin-Illinois state line, the sun was finally rising above the trees, giving an orange glow to the cornfields and signs along the highway. An hour after I crossed the state line, I exited the highway toward the Milwaukee Public Museum. The parking lot was empty, and I stopped in front of the closed guardhouse. Moments later, the glint of a blue Prius appeared in my rearview mirror and Gerry waved. He got out of his car, wrapping his arms around his waist as his breath came out in puffs, and unlocked the chain. His friend at the museum, a Jeremiah Peabody ("He just sounds like a historian. I bet he wears fedoras and smokes a pipe," I had said to Luke when I first heard his name), had agreed to open the museum to us before the public so we could research the school in Bloomfield.

As Gerry pulled in front of me, I heard a roar and saw my mother's rosy cheeks behind me, her ruddy complexion a deeper shade of red than usual. Gerry motioned for us to follow him into a door on the side of the building marked *Employees,* a piece of paper with a key code in his hand. My mother and I waited behind him as he punched the numbers in, the keypad beeping with a warning sound.

"Oh, shoot," he said as he tried it again, to no avail. I noticed that his eyes seemed bloodshot and that he looked more rumpled than usual, with his glasses dusty and his cheeks drawn.

"My turn," my mother said, snatching the paper from his hand, after we exchanged a glance upon his third failed try. She squinted at the keypad, punched in the numbers, and it beeped triumphantly. A small green light turned on, and we heard it unclick.

"Are you feeling okay?" I asked Gerry as we walked inside.

He rubbed his chin quickly. "Oh yes. I was just up late doing some research. For work. With my friend."

My mother smiled broadly as she patted him on the shoulder. "Good for you. I bet she's a real catch." I hid a laugh as I wondered if it was Haley, the pretty librarian from Lake Geneva.

I hope it was, Gerry. You deserve some fun, too, I thought.

His face flushed and he adjusted his glasses. "Oh. No, it wasn't . . ."

"Sure it wasn't," my mother said as she winked at him.

I smiled as Gerry blushed harder and pointed down the hallway. As we followed behind him, my mother nudged my arm and I nodded. It warmed my heart to think of lonely Gerry, with only his historical artifacts to keep him company at night, finding love with someone else who loved something just as much as he did. I wondered what Luke and I loved like that anymore. Sure, our children. But what else did we have in common, that we both loved? Going out to dinner, cooking, going to concerts, all had been things we loved but hardly did anymore. Now sometimes it seemed like we were trapped in the prison of everyday chaos and special needs, rather than choosing to spend our lives together. I once read a statistic that nearly 80 percent of parents who have a child with autism end up divorced, their marriages cracking and buckling under the enormous weight of special needs. I thought of the night before, at the weighted silence and different beds.

Gerry led us to a dark wood-paneled office, comfortably

decorated with a sagging brown corduroy couch against one wall and a black and metal modern-looking desk against the other. On top of the desk were haphazard stacks of paper decorated with numerous coffee rings. Nothing seemed to be in any sort of order, but I felt that it likely made sense to the inhabitant, like peeking into someone's mind, mid-thought.

"Dr. Peabody isn't the tidiest of curators, but he's an amazing researcher," Gerry said after seeing my face.

"No doubt," my mother said with a nod. "When I was still teaching, my office was the same. Students would come in, survey the hot mess inside, and then slowly back away. It worked like a charm and I spent most of my office hours in peace." She sat down on the corduroy couch. "So where do we start?" She looked at me. "We have dinner reservations at The Edgewater on Lake Mendota tonight."

I eased into the couch next to her as Gerry began to check the piles of paper on the desk.

"Where are you, where are you," he muttered to himself. He turned to a stack of binders on the corner of the desk. "A-ha! The Bloomfield School for the Deaf and Dumb. Here we are." He left one on the table and handed one to my mother and one to me.

I opened mine, which was filled with pictures in plastic pages. The first page was pictures of classrooms, or what I assumed were classrooms. The children all sat on the floor, without seemingly any organization. They had books in front of them, also placed on the floor, with a teacher up front, staring unsmiling into the camera. A date on the bottom left read: *1907*.

"He wasn't even born yet. He wouldn't have been here then," I whispered to myself. I tried to turn the page, but my hand faltered, and I again looked at the children. If Will had been born a hundred years earlier, would he have been sent to this place? Would I, if I lived back then, have let him go? Would I have had a choice?

I swallowed hard, my throat wanting to close as my nose grew tingly with the tears beginning to form. I had so many choices for him, it sometimes felt like an impasse, like too many cars going down a narrow highway, a bottleneck forming. And the cars were all escaping a hurricane that threatened to decimate everything. But I had choices. *We* had choices, although they never felt like good ones. Yet as I finally turned the page on the children, I thought, *At least he will always have us.*

The next two pages were images of the outside of the building, a tall redbrick structure with what looked like a bell tower in the middle. It actually somewhat resembled my high school, an innocuous-looking building that housed rowdy teenagers and tired teachers. The third page was a picture of the sleeping quarters. Rows upon rows of metal beds with sterile white sheets and white pillows lined the room. The beds were pristine, each one made with the sheet tightly covering the mattress. There were no stuffed animals, or well-loved blankets tucked away. It looked like a hospital.

My mother murmured next to me, and I leaned over and peered at her binder. She ran a finger down a list of names, the top of the page reading: *Discharge List.* There were five columns: *Name, Age, Name of Guardian, Admission Date,* and *Discharge Date.* The first line read: *Peter McKilip, 7, Daniel McKilip, 9/01/09, 5/3/20.*

"So that kid was there for eleven years?" I said. My mother looked at me grimly and nodded. I thought of sleeping in those sterile beds, of sitting on the floor of the "classroom," for eleven years. "What happened to him after? Maybe he went back to his family?" I said hopefully.

Gerry made a noise from Dr. Peabody's chair and sat back, the chair creaking. "Not likely. The home was for children. Once they became adults, they probably moved somewhere else."

"Okay, but then why do some of these kiddos not have discharge dates?" my mother said. She held the binder up, splayed out, like a chorus singer. "Here's one: Dorothea Tobias, age ten, admission date of October 25, 1915. Discharge date: blank." She lifted her eyes to Gerry.

He cleared his throat. "From what I understand—granted, I only know about these places from what my colleagues have told me—is if there is no discharge date listed, the child"—he looked nervously at me and set his binder down on the desk in front of him—"was never discharged."

"And that means?" I sat back slowly, the realization coming over me like water filling up a vase. "That they died there?"

Gerry's silence confirmed my thought.

"Awful," my mother murmured. I could see her scanning the list, looking for those missing dates.

"Of course, that doesn't mean anything nefarious happened. This was a long time ago, when, unfortunately, children died from all sorts of preventable things. Tuberculosis, pneumonia, tetanus, the flu, scarlet fever." He lifted his hands. "Times were different."

"In many ways," I said as I shook my head, thinking of Will. "What's in your binder, Gerry?"

He lifted it back onto his lap. "Staff reports, mostly, nothing that would be useful to us—at least not at this point." He paused. "Josepha, now there's a name you don't see every day," he said with a laugh. He looked up. "I went to school with a girl named Cola, so I suppose there's no telling when parents choose a name. Try growing up as a kid with the name Gerry." He looked up over his glasses at us.

My mother laughed. " 'Mary Ellen' sounds like I should be in the convent, so I hear ya."

"And I have a name that could be a boy or a girl." I turned to my mom. "Remember senile Mrs. Steadman in fourth grade kept spelling my name 'A-a-r-o-n'?"

She didn't answer and stared down at the binder in front of her.

"Mom?"

Her eyes were wide, and I leaned over and peered down. It looked like the same handwritten scrawl of admission records until my mother tapped the page. About three quarters of the way down, there was a name: *John Cartwright*. A jolt ran through my body and I lunged closer to my mom, my own binder spilling out onto the floor. Gerry yelped, but I ignored him.

"John Cartwright, age five, admission date July 1, 1923, discharge date . . ." My voice shook. I slowly looked up and met my mother's wide eyes.

"When? What does it say?" Gerry said. He stood up and walked over. When neither of us moved or spoke, he took the binder out of my mom's hands. "Discharge date is: blank." He slowly lowered the binder, placing it back onto my mom's lap.

My mom's expression turned from shock to sympathy as she looked down at the binder and back to me. "I'm sorry, hon."

"That can't be true," I said. "So this means he was really here, and he . . . died here?" My words cracked and bumped together.

Neither Gerry nor my mother said anything in response. I stared down at the page, trying to will a discharge date to appear or for the name to come into focus and for us to realize it said something other than John Cartwright. But, of course, it didn't.

"If that's true, then why do the reports say that both of them drowned? That he was never seen again?" I said. My voice came out in desperate gasps, as I hoped to land on anything that would say it wasn't true.

Gerry cleared his throat. "Historical reports are, unfortunately, only ever as good as the people who write them down. Things like this, word-of-mouth incidents, can be notoriously unreliable. Maybe the boy—"

"John," I interrupted with an edge to my voice.

He gave me a sympathetic look. "Of course, maybe John wasn't seen after he was rescued, maybe the other guests on the yacht had too much to drink, or it was too dark, and they never saw him be rescued later. Remember, it was dark, it was after a long party, and it was raining. Not to mention, the family might not have wanted anyone to know that John had been sent away."

I slowly closed the binder in my lap. I couldn't turn the pages, looking for John anymore, knowing he lived his whole life at the school. Sleeping in the sterile beds, sitting on the floor of the classrooms.

And I knew if he was sent there, Amelia must have died in the water, John slipping from her grasp as she went under, lost forever. She died just as most people had assumed: that night, in the water. If she did jump, in the hopes that they would die together, she delivered him to such a fate. She was the one who doomed him to a life of living there. Accident or not, the register meant that there was no happy ending, no hidden wonderful secrets.

In the office, on the sagging brown corduroy couch, I put my head in my hands and pressed my fists into my eyes, desperately wishing I had never seen the register.

CHAPTER 27

AMELIA

A month after Henry had died, Amelia spent the afternoon with her mother and sisters, in wedding preparation. Mary and Jane had spent most of the time arguing over the exact shape of the floral arrangements.

"They should be ovals, reaching toward the heavens, like a prayer for your marriage," Mary said, her hand fluttering in the air.

"Mother"—Jane's face darkened, and her eyebrows hooded her lids—"no one has floral arrangements like that anymore. They need to be cascading down, like waterfalls, against each vase. Things are different from when you got married."

"Really," Mary had said dryly. "Then why were all the centerpieces at the Thomas wedding last season as tall as can be? They nearly reached the chandeliers of the ballroom in the Palmer House hotel."

The florist's head snapped back and forth like the pendulum on the large grandfather clock in the foyer, shipped all the way from Ireland, as he listened to their conversation.

"If I may—" he had tried to say several times, to no avail.

All Amelia could think was that Jane needed to finish up and choose—for the Lord's sake, *choose*—the flower arrangements so she could talk to their mother in private. She hadn't been able to speak to her alone since their conversation in her father's study after Henry's funeral luncheon.

The conversation between them continued on the ride home and as they walked into the large glass and oak doors to the house. Amelia walked into the parlor, only half-listening to the conversation.

On the opposite side of the parlor sat Eleanor, who stared out of the window overlooking Lake Shore Drive, not even pretending to pay attention to the conversation. Amelia could see her looking out below, at the children following their nannies like ducklings up and down the street, bundled in hats and gloves and heavy wool coats. On the trees outside, Christmas lights were strung, twinkling in the light snow that had begun to fall. The city came alive each holiday, with the smells of roasted meats and candied chestnuts permeating the air. From every pub, the cheers were a little brighter, a little louder, a little more joyful.

But this year was different. It would be Amelia and John's first Christmas without Henry. She had the staff put up the Christmas tree and hang the evergreen garlands on the staircase as they always did, but it felt impossibly empty, and the air held a chill even with the brightest of lights or the most roaring of fires. In fact, two nights before, she sat in front of the fireplace, on the marble carved hearth, staring into the flames, putting her palms as close to the fire as she dared, wondering how much it would hurt if she just touched them for a moment. Certainly, nothing could hurt more than Henry's death and the threat of John being sent away.

"Is this almost finished? I have an appointment for tea with Emily," Eleanor said as she snapped her head back toward the room.

Jane and Mary looked at her in surprise. Jane looked from her mother to Eleanor. "Sorry to inconvenience you. I know how busy you are."

Eleanor sighed wearily as she stood, wrapping her shawl around her shoulders. "Oh, Jane. No need for that. I am happy to visit and see your plans." She stepped forward and pulled her youngest sister toward her. "It's going to be the most beautiful wedding in the world."

Jane smiled and allowed the hug. "It is, isn't it?"

Eleanor turned to Amelia. "Care to join me for some tea at The Drake?"

Amelia looked back at her mother, who didn't meet her gaze, and a pang of fear rose in her stomach. *What if she has decided against helping me?* After all, shortly after her mother made the promise her father had walked back in and the conversation had ended. Neither of them had spoken of it since.

"Yes," she finally said, and turned to Eleanor. She would have to find another time. *But there might not be much time,* a voice whispered in her head. *Who knows how long until Margaret tries to take him away?*

"Is everything all right? You look a little pale," Eleanor said as they walked through the foyer, stopping to put on their mink and wool coats handed to them by the maid.

Amelia opened her mouth and wished she could tell her sister everything. She wished she could unyoke the burden of her secrets, the thoughts that kept her up at night, and let her sister share in her pain. But she couldn't. She glanced at the no fewer than five servants within earshot trying to blend into the surroundings. Although she trusted Eleanor, it was too risky to mention anything that went against Margaret. She seemed to have eyes and ears all over the city and could be everywhere and nowhere at the same time.

"A story for another time," she finally said with a weak smile. "I forgot I have a stop to make, so I should go straight home."

Eleanor frowned slightly, and Amelia started toward the waiting motorcar. Eleanor put a hand on her arm. "After the wedding is over, please come visit me in New York. I miss you, and I miss our summers together. Please, it would mean everything."

Amelia gave her a slight nod and then turned and hurried outside.

When she arrived home, she saw a large white envelope on the railing next to the front door. On the front was her name, *Mrs. Amelia Cartwright,* scrawled in a pointy, sharp penmanship.

"What is this? Where is this from?" she demanded, her voice echoing through the foyer. No one responded, and she realized she had dismissed all but John's nanny for the evening to save on cost. The allowances from Margaret had been severely cut after their confrontation, and she could no longer afford to have full-time help. She had even sold some of her jewelry to keep on Eloise, John's nanny.

She tore open the package, her heart racing. When she read the first few lines, her knees buckled and she fell to the floor, her legs hitting the marble with a crack. She scanned the letter, her entire body aching in pain and shock.

> *Mrs. Cartwright,* it read, *we are pleased to announce the admission of your son, John Cartwright, into the Bloomfield School for the Deaf and the Dumb. His stay will formally begin on June 15th, 1923. We will be in touch soon to schedule an orientation visit, and to go over what he will need for his housing here.*

Margaret had finally won.

She let out a scream, crumpling the paper up in her hands and throwing it as far as she could. It floated to the floor, not even giving her the satisfaction of so much as a thump. She put her head down on the marble floor as sobs racked through her body. Just the thought of him leaving made her feel like her soul was being torn out of her body. Without him, there was nothing. Without him, she was an empty shell.

"Mrs. Cartwright!" Eloise called from upstairs, and Amelia heard her rush down the stairs. She weakly lifted her head, her face slick, and saw John following behind her.

"What happened? Did you fall?" Eloise said, and she hurriedly knelt beside her.

Amelia shook her head and shakily pushed up to a seated position. She saw John standing at the base of the staircase, wearing his green woolen jumper that she had picked out last year. The light from outside illuminated his blond hair and made him look like an angel. Her face crumpled again and she held out her arms weakly, beckoning him to come.

He slowly walked forward and knelt down, touching her face with one finger, tracing a line on her cheek through the tears. Then he leaned into her, his tiny body fitting against her. She grasped him so tightly, she nearly felt his breath stop. She closed her eyes and rocked him, humming, the tears never stopping.

Now, six months after she received the letter, with John's hand in hers on the yacht, she thought of that place, that school, with the antiseptic smells permeating the air, and the children in one room together, with one single white cot each. Wearing matching uniforms, like in prison. Some of the children couldn't walk, some couldn't hear, and some didn't even know their own names. But it was all the same: They were there because either no one knew how to care for them or they didn't want to.

This is a place for unwanted children, she kept thinking when she visited. She wanted to cry out and hold each of them, tell them that surely, someone wanted them, but she couldn't. And with each child, she saw John's face, and his terror once he would realize that he was meant to stay there. Meant to be forgotten.

CHAPTER 28

ERIN

It was a bit of a rough day. . . .

I sat at my computer in the corner of our cluttered bedroom and read the latest e-mail from Will's teacher again. He had grabbed another kid on the playground, seemingly wanting to play with him, but wound up pulling the kid's hair and looked like he was going to bite him to get a response. Thankfully, an aide saw and was able to redirect him, but everyone was concerned for his and the other children's safety.

I slumped back in the old office chair that I had bought off someone on craigslist that still kind of smelled like cat urine. I heard the front door open, and I sat up straighter in my chair. I hadn't broached the subject of Lakewood with Luke since our dinner a few days before, mostly because I didn't know how to apologize and not apologize all at the same time without sounding like a jerk.

I'm sorry we had a fight, but I'm not sorry for what I said.

I turned slowly as I heard Luke walk up the stairs, through the bathroom, and into our bedroom. He had worked late, again, and gone to some networking event at a local sushi restaurant. His tie was askew and I could smell beer as he kissed me hello on the cheek. He walked over to the bed and sat down, his body slumped forward.

"Long day?" I said as I tucked a foot up on the chair and wrapped my arms around my leg. I tried to keep my voice light, but my shoulders were rigid as I waited for whatever bad news he had in his pocket.

"You could say that," he said as he splayed his arms across the bed, crucifixion-style.

"Sorry. Anything you want to talk about?"

"Not really," he said.

I swallowed hard. I knew it likely was something having to do with an account not sold or something related to his commission, which would mean another lean month of grocery shopping and watching our pennies. I looked back at my computer screen. "I got another e-mail from school. Another day, another e-mail," I said quietly. I waited for him to say something, even the weakest of platitudes, but he remained silent, staring up at the ceiling fan.

He took a long breath and then slowly sat up, balling his fists under him and then crossing his arms over his chest. "So what do we do?"

I turned away from the computer screen. He wanted me to say it. "Lakewood," I said, my voice barely above a whisper.

After a long pause in which the only sound was the thud of my heart, he said, "I guess it's something we really have to consider." He shook his head and a pained expression moved across his face. A look of failure. He lifted his chin and looked around our bedroom, at the beadboard ceiling that I loved, at the sky blue walls that I painted not long after we moved in, at the wood floors with the tongue-and-groove boards. "We would have to sell the house."

My eyes widened, and I looked down at my hands. "But we love this house. Sell it? I was thinking a loan of some sort."

He stood up and walked over to me and put a hand on my arm. "I love this house, too." He didn't say anything else, and what he left unsaid hung in the air like a half-deflated balloon. "But even if we could take another mortgage out on the house, then what? It would barely cover a year of tuition."

He was right; we didn't have enough equity. Selling the house would be a solution. When we bought the house, we got a great deal due to the fact that the previous owners had retired and were moving to Florida. They had no interest in maintaining two houses, or in the upkeep required in such an old place. The price was still close to the top end of our budget, but I justified it by saying that I loved the house enough to sacrifice other things. Of course, that was before things changed at Luke's job and before we really knew what was going on with Will and how much money we would need to funnel toward his therapies.

But it was a house that when I pulled into the driveway I still couldn't believe was mine. A house where I could swear I felt the whispers of the people who had lived here before. A house that would protect us, like it had protected others for over a hundred years.

"I understand." My voice cracked and I swallowed hard. I turned back toward my computer, scanning the e-mail from Will's teacher again, as I felt tears begin to form. "I'm okay," I said to the computer. "You're right. I just need to think through and process everything."

He put a hand on my shoulder. I leaned into him, closing my eyes. There were so many firsts with twins, but this was something different.

It was the last moment in which I believed things would work out the way I so desperately wanted them to. And it was the first moment in which I truly understood what I would have to let go in order to take the next step. It meant releasing everything I had clung to, so my arms would now be free to embrace the future.

Luke stood next to me for a few more moments, before he

squeezed my shoulder and walked out into the hallway, to kiss the kids good night.

I knew selling the house would be the right thing to do, but oh, how it hurt. I thought of packing up the kids' playroom, and all of their toys, of saying good-bye to the built-in cabinets in the dining room, of running my hand along the wood trim, with its thick grain and soft grooves, before walking away. Of saying good-bye to my crooked front porch and to the swing where I used to sit with Will when he was two and refusing to nap, when he would only be calmed by motion. Of closing the three-over-one original windows in the family room for the last time and pulling the heavy front door shut.

I felt the tears begin to fall, and before I allowed them to pull me to an even darker place I stood up and wiped at my cheeks. I went downstairs, the stairs creaking at every shift, and poured myself the largest glass of red wine I could stand from a bottle that was left over from a month ago. My mother-in-law had brought it when we had her and my father-in-law over for dinner. It was a red apple spiced wine, and at the time I had taken one sniff of it and recoiled in terror.

But now beggars couldn't be choosers, so I took two quick gulps of the too-sweet red wine, the liquid burning my throat and the alcohol filling my mouth. I ignored the aching in my molars, like the sugar was boring straight into the enamel. I walked back upstairs and read the e-mail from Will's teacher again, before I minimized the screen.

I spun in my chair a couple of times, feeling the wine kick in, softening the edges. I clicked around on social media, looking at the latest pictures Katie had posted of a bachelorette party weekend in Austin, Texas. She and five other friends wore short skirts and wedge heels and dangly earrings, their highlighted hair cascading in waves down their backs. *Best night ever,* read one of the captions. I zoomed in and studied Katie's face, un-lined and unblemished. A quick glance in the mirror above my dresser told me that even though we were only three years apart, I looked at least a decade older.

Sufficiently depressed, I clicked off social media and glanced back at my in-box, and Gerry's e-mail about the letter from Louisa to her sister caught my eye. I opened it back up and scanned it, my gaze landing on the line about visiting relatives in Adare Village.

I took another long sip of wine. "Ireland, huh? Well, Louisa, that's always been on my list, too."

Luke and I had talked about going to Ireland for our honeymoon, what felt like a million years ago. He wanted Spain, I wanted Ireland. I tried to pull the heritage card out, saying I was sure that I had relatives still living over there and it was a kind of birthright trip, but he didn't buy it. We compromised and went to Greece, touring the islands, stuffing ourselves with baklava, and washing it down with the most incredible wines. We promised each other that we would make it to Ireland and Spain at a different time. But then, of course, life happened. The last vacation we took was a weekend trip to an indoor waterpark two years ago, when I think we both slept four hours over two days and vowed to never leave our house again.

I went back to social media, liking pictures of distant cousins' birthday parties and commenting on baby announcements. I stopped on a picture of one of my mother's cousins wearing green and drinking a Guinness. The caption read: *It's St. Patrick's Day every day around here!!*

I thought again about Louisa's letter and did some quick calculations. If Emily, my great-grandmother, visited her cousins, then surely some would still be living there. I knew that the cousins in Ireland had the last name of Diamond, and I remembered my mother talking about how they owned a hardware store in Adare Village, or at least someone did at some point.

I clicked over to Google and entered *Diamond Hardware Store in Adare, Ireland,* and a list of results popped up. The first couple were for jewelry stores, but then one halfway down was a review of Diamond Hardware in Adare.

Great service, Denny and Therese always treat their customers like family.

Back on Facebook, I looked them up. One click away and jackpot. Therese Diamond of Adare, Ireland. I studied her profile picture. She had long dark hair with streaks of gray swept to the side, and the same too-round cheeks that I was cursed with. Her eyes were a bright blue and in the picture she had her arm around what I assumed was her husband, Denny.

"How neat," I said as I reached for my wine again. After a quick sip, my finger hovered over the keyboard. "What the hell, right? They're family." I typed a message introducing myself and briefly explained my quest to find Amelia and John and mentioned the letter from Louisa to Emily. At least, I intended for it to be brief, but when I looked up it was ten paragraphs long. Before I could stop myself, I hit Send.

I walked back over to my bed and collapsed onto it. I fell asleep with my clothes on, lying on top of the blanket. When I woke up the next morning, my head was pounding before I even opened my eyes. I slowly sat up, pressing the heel of my hand to my right eye, desperate to stop the pain. I could still taste the syrupy wine in my mouth as I put my head in both hands. I took some slow, deep breaths, and as the headache subsided only then did I remember my discussion with Luke.

We were going to have to sell the house. Then, another kind of pain moved through my body and wouldn't let go.

CHAPTER 29

AMELIA

"Help me with this, Rose," Georgina Lindemann said as she tried to wriggle out of her life jacket from her seat on the yacht. She still held a glass of champagne in one hand, the sticky sweet liquid sloshing over her beaded gown.

"Leave this on, Georgina. For goodness' sakes, we all know you can't swim!" Rose said with a laugh. Yet she still held one hand out and helped her friend take off her life jacket.

Amelia heard Captain Scott's protests from behind her and could see that he was shouting, although his words were whisked away by the winds whipping across the water, churning up waves and blowing the sweat from her face. John shivered, and Amelia pulled him toward her, pressing her hand against his side.

"No one here can swim!" Amelia heard the captain shout.

And as far as he knew, that was true.

A year earlier, when John first put his face in the water, Amelia thought her heart would burst in the seconds between when he submerged and when he reappeared. It was at the YMCA, when he was four years old, his tiny body bobbing up and down in the water next to his swim instructor. Amelia sat on the side of the pool, perched in an uncomfortable metal chair, as she watched John's every movement and flutter in the cold water. Her hat was pulled down low over her brow, shielding her face from anyone who might recognize her, even though it was after hours and she had paid the staff to let her and John in. If any of her society friends wanted their kids to learn how to swim, they hired a private instructor to come to their personal swimming pool or to take their child out onto the lake for lessons.

That was exactly what she had counted on when she had paid for the lessons, and for the use of the pool after hours, six months before, right before his fourth birthday.

The first time he saw the water, his eyes went wide with fear and he tried to turn on his heel and run out of the building, away from the water. Of course, he had seen deep water in Lake Geneva, at Monarch Manor, but this was different somehow. This was more terrifying. That was also something Amelia had expected and the reason why she chose a pool rather than the lake. She needed him to learn how to stay calm in scary situations in the water and to learn survival skills.

She needed him to learn how to swim to save his own life.

So each week, on Tuesday evenings when he didn't have lessons with his tutors scheduled, she had her coachman drop them off three blocks away from the YMCA building, under the guise of going for an evening stroll with her son. He would always look them up and down, meet her eyes with curiosity, and then nod. She doubled his salary, even though she couldn't afford it with the small allowance from Margaret, and the curious looks stopped.

She had coaxed John into the water for the first time by hiking up her skirt and putting her feet in, shoes and all. She could feel the instructor staring at her, and she pulled her hat lower down on her brow.

"Look! Look at me!" she signed to John as she splashed

around, water beading off of her black shoes. The water was freezing, but she smiled and threw her hands up in the air like the silliest mom in the world.

John had looked from her shoes to her, a grin spreading across his face, and he took a tiny step closer to her, wanting to see how far down her legs went.

"Put your feet in the water," she signed to him, gesturing encouragingly and patting the wet tile next to her. She could feel the cold seeping through her skirt, and for a moment she wondered how she was going to get home without everyone noticing she looked like one of the otters that lived under the pier at Monarch Manor.

John shook his head but crept closer to the edge, and she saw his thin shoulders relax as he studied the water. He was always like that, observing everything and everyone. She often wished she could close her eyes, put a hand on his head, and see what he was thinking. She felt as though nothing escaped him, and she often felt like he shared only an iceberg's tip of what he felt and thought.

His swim instructor, Michael, tried to bring him into the water also, lightly splashing at the surface and gesturing how to pick the water up with his hands, letting it fall through his fingers in mock surprise. But John remained in place, watching the water lap against the side of the pool.

The next week was more successful, and he dipped a toe into the water. He quickly pulled it out, but still, Amelia knew this was a success. The following week, it was both feet, and then after that, his legs. It took two months before he would stand in the water, and each week she sat on the side of the pool, water soaking through her skirts. After the first session, she wised up and brought a change of clothes so she wouldn't have to lie about unexpected puddles or rainstorms to the staff.

Then, finally, he was ready to put his face in. Amelia knew this was an important moment. If Michael could get him to hold his breath and blow bubbles under the water, then he could survive. They could teach him to tread water, but the breathing would come first.

He had looked at her with fear and uncertainty right before he did it, and she gave him the biggest smile she could muster and nodded her head.

It's all right. I am right here. I will never let anything happen to you, she whispered in her head.

His face went under, and Amelia didn't breathe until she saw tiny bubbles come up from under him as he exhaled. Then, his face popped back up, water streaming down, and Michael hugged him tight, patting him on the back in triumph. She had told him that she would give him a hefty bonus once John was able to take the first step, and for his continued discretion.

Amelia started clapping and cheering, frantically signing in between to John.

And so the lessons continued, in secret, until he was able to jump from the side of the pool, kick to the surface, and tread water until he was rescued.

Then, she knew he was ready.

On the yacht, in the distance, across the shore from Monarch Manor, Amelia saw a flickering light. From her vantage point in the water, even though the rain splashed on the surface of the lake, she could see three distinct flickers: flash, flash, flash. Then a pause, and it repeated itself over and over again.

It was just two weeks ago that she had told John of the plan: "We are going to go on a boat ride after Aunt Jane's wedding. And then, we are going to go for a swim, and we will swim, swim, swim to the other side of the lake. Doesn't that sound like fun?"

"Will it be scary?" he had signed back.

She pressed him to her chest for a moment, kissing the bridge of his nose as she had since he was an infant, and then looked in his eyes. "It might be, for a moment, but I will be right there. I will make sure you are safe. You are a good swimmer, and you are ready," she had signed back.

He had cautiously nodded, mulling over the possibility in his mind. Each day after that, she reminded him of the plan and stressed that it was their secret—that it was the most important secret they would ever have between them. She was for once thankful that his world was small, without many people in it, and she could more easily make sure he didn't tell someone their secret.

"Remember, do not go in the water before the boat ride," she had reminded him after the ceremony.

But now it was time.

CHAPTER 30

ERIN

"Well, you'll have to paint the stucco on top, that's for sure."
Jeannine Grant, a realtor married to one of Luke's coworkers,
squinted up at my house from the front porch. She was blond
and thin and looked like she spray tanned once a week. Her
tiny nose wrinkled for a moment before she turned to me and
smiled. "Let's see the rest of it."

Luke held an arm out and let Jeannine and me go first. I
heard her grumble about the steep pitch of the concrete stairs
leading up to the front porch, and then she did an exaggerated
half pitch as she walked across the slanted porch, her wedge
heels creaking against the old wood. Luke and I exchanged a
glance, eyebrows raised, as we trailed behind her.

"So you never painted the wood inside. Interesting," she
said as her neck craned around the foyer, taking in the original
oak staircase and the wide baseboards and hand-carved crown
molding. "I'm sure some buyers—those with a hobby in preser-
vation—will be interested in such a thing."

I thought about the article I had read the night before, when
I was doing research on what the market was like for historic
homes and came across an interview in the *Chicago Tribune*

about a woman whose life passion was preserving old houses. Alex Proctor was her name, and although she lived up in Wisconsin, she had become something of a local midwestern celebrity with her dedication to preserving the past. She had said in the article, "Old houses are a treasure, and should be treated as such."

"Some people think old houses are a treasure," I repeated to Jeannine.

She made a noise and nodded as she continued through the house, her gold dangly earrings softly clinking together as she swished her head back and forth. "Oh, hello!" She stopped when she saw Will and Charlotte sitting on the couch, iPads in hand.

"Say hi, kids," I said automatically. Charlotte looked up and quickly waved, but Will's gaze remained on his screen.

Jeannine frowned and walked over, bending down and putting her face near Will's. "Hi there!" she said brightly.

I saw him jump, and then instinctively his hand went out and unfortunately made contact with her long sparkly earring, catching it. She yelped in pain, holding her ear. She reeled back, pulling her hand from her ear and checking for blood. There was a tiny drop on her fingertip.

"I'm so sorry! Will! That was terrible. We don't hit; you know that," I said as I rushed forward. When he didn't look up, I took the iPad from him, which got his attention. He started flailing on the couch, his arms moving like propellers as he reached for it.

My face burning, I grabbed him, ducking from his arms. I looked at Luke and hissed, "I'll take him outside; you handle inside." I didn't even look at Jeannine.

I hauled Will across the front porch, and down the steps, and to my car in the driveway. I managed to get the door open and pin him down in his car seat as I strapped him in, his hands hitting my face and head. Finally, I got him inside. I turned the car's air-conditioning on and sat in the driver's seat, listening to his wails and screams of frustration as I reminded him to stay calm. I pulled the laminated visual card out of my purse, the one that said: *Take a deep breath. Calm body,* and pointed to it several times, trying to desperately hand it to him, but he was too far gone in his meltdown to come back.

As he screamed, I watched Luke and Jeannine walk through the upstairs of the house. First, they went into Charlotte's room and she opened the drapes, peering out onto the front yard. Then, I saw her in the bathroom, and even from the driveway I could see a look of concern on her face. Next up was Will's room, which we had tried to straighten the best possible, but he moved everything around immediately. The blue LEGOs were supposed to be lined up on the windowsill, and the Thomas the Train figures had to be on the floor, in a line, all their faces perfectly matched, without any space in between.

I saw Jeannine pitch forward, and I could only imagine that she tripped over the train figures. I glanced back at Will in the mirror, and he was starting to sob rather than scream, a sign that his meltdown had peaked. I unbuckled my seat belt and got into the backseat. I held his sweaty hand, his body on fire. I slowly took him out of the seat and pulled him onto my lap in the back. His body scrunched up into a tiny ball like an infant's, and I rocked him back and forth.

"It's my fault. I made a mistake. You're safe. You're calm. I'm here. We love you," I whispered over and over, my eyes closed. When I felt his body relax and his breathing go steady, I opened my eyes, and I saw Luke and Jeannine walking out of the side door, down the rickety steps that we were told had been put in by an owner in the 1920s. The basement was once a cellar with an outside door, and a previous owner had walled in the side door and the entrance to the cellar in a very homemade way, and the staircase was terrifying even on a good day.

We had talked about not taking Jeannine that way, at least on her first visit, and I could see the look on her face as she and Luke stopped in the driveway and spoke. She seemed to be talking very fast, her head bobbing back and forth, with her

216 / *Maureen Leurck*

dangly earrings swinging, as she rocked on the heels of her wedges. Luke nodded several times, his hands in his jeans, his head down. Finally, she turned and walked toward her car. She gave me a bright smile as she walked past the car and then an exaggerated sad frown when she saw Will in my lap, his body huddled against me. Luke walked over to the car and got into the passenger seat.

"Well?" I said. The air in the car suddenly felt heavy, despite the constant flow of cold air from the vents.

He didn't turn around and I saw his shoulders sag forward.

"That bad, huh?" I tried to keep my words light, but they caught in my throat like a lump of dough that had too much water in it. Sticky, immobile, unyielding. Will whimpered and I kissed the top of his head, even as he leaned away from the touch. "How can it be bad news? We've done so much to the house since we moved in."

It was true; besides painting every room, turning it over from blinding shades of yellow, green, and burgundy, we had replaced the carpeting in the family room that smelled like dog urine. (And, truthfully, occasionally still did on hot summer days. Soaked into the subfloor, is what the contractors had told us. Whichever dog had lived there before was like a urine ghost, haunting us evermore.) We had also pulled down wallpaper, re-finished the floors in the living room, repaired the fence, and done dozens more projects that slowly ate away at our savings each year.

"Market isn't the best," he said. "A few houses some blocks away were short sales, and drove the price down for everyone. Not to mention, it's going to be the holidays soon, and no one wants to buy then. If we list now, we have to list for an aggres-sive price, according to Jeannine, if we have any hope of selling and getting Will into Lakewood for the rest of the school year."

"Aggressive price? So you're saying we have to basically give the house away." I looked up at the giant maple tree in the front yard, the orange and yellow leaves still clinging to the branches. I loved the way it shaded the yard and seemed to be even older than the house. The first year we lived here, we watched in dismay as the leaves seemed to regenerate the moment we had them all raked up and in yard waste bags. More than once, Luke had threatened to chop it down as we sweated and raked and bagged. He always said it directly to the tree, too, as though it were listening. Last year, I was pretty sure it heard him, since right after he whispered, "Enjoy your last season," it dropped a pile of leaves on his head.

"Jeannine said that you usually list a house for about ten percent higher than what you want to sell it for, and then agree on a ten percent price drop. If it sells for what she thinks it will, we can send Will to Lakewood," he said.

I leaned forward. "That's wonderful! I—"

"But," he said quickly, "I don't think we can buy another house and send him to the school. There just won't be anything left for a down payment. So we would have to rent for a few years until we saved more."

"Rent?" I let the word float around the car as I absentmindedly rubbed Will's foot. Even as a baby, he loved to have his feet rubbed and touched. It always calmed him down. "But . . ." All of my protests died before I could say them. *Is that wise? How long will it take us to save? Is this a good idea?*

I knew that our path with Will would be filled with turns and twists, with surprises and setbacks, and all we could do was make each decision as it came. And I knew that this was the next, best step. For all of us. If we had to rent somewhere, but it meant that he would be happier, it would make all of us happier and be worth the sacrifice.

I took a long, slow, deep breath and leaned forward. "If that's what we have to do, then let's do it."

He stared straight ahead. "Erin, I'm not going to lie when I say this still feels like a step back. One for him, and one for us."

He held a hand in the air when I made a strangled sound. "But I trust you, and you know that I would do anything for Will. So if you really believe this is the right thing to do, I will do it."

The next day, the FOR SALE sign was in the front yard, next to my beloved maple tree. Jeannine's face stared out at it, and I swore her eyes followed me around the yard like one of those creepy haunted-house paintings. While Will was inside working with his behavior therapist, Kendra, I sat on the porch swing, my legs kicking back and forth as I stared at the sign.

"Mommy?" Charlotte appeared on the porch, one of her pigtails askew. She had fallen asleep on the drive home from school, and I had carefully transferred her to her bed.

I patted the swing next to me and she climbed up, her body fitting underneath my arm in a nook like a puzzle piece.

"I couldn't sleep. Will woke me up. He's crying about something," she said in an exaggerated, exasperated, five-year-old way.

"I know." It was the reason I came outside in the first place. Kendra had warned me the session wouldn't be pretty. They were working on his coping strategies, and trying to get him to the point where he could come out of a meltdown on his own, without needing so much adult intervention. Unfortunately, that meant the behavior would increase at first for a while.

"Why does he get so mad all of the time?" she said quietly.

I opened my mouth, the words escaping me. I knew that she could tell he was different, but we had never said the word *autism* to her, and I didn't know when we would. I pulled her closer to me, wishing I could shrink her and put her in my pocket and shield her from the outside world. "Well, his brain works a little different from yours. Things upset him more, and that's why he needs extra help in school, and at home with Kendra."

She nodded against my side. We had talked about this before; she had heard this already. And that day, thankfully, it was enough. "He still loves us, though, right?"

My eyes pricked with tears. "Of course he does, honey. He loves all of us—and especially you—very much."

She sighed contentedly and put an arm around my waist. "Oh, that's good."

I leaned down and kissed the top of her head, which smelled like the lavender shampoo she had insisted I buy at Walgreens because it had pretty purple flowers on the front. "You're his angel," I said. I closed my eyes and let the tears drip on her head, mixing with her braids and rubber bands.

What did her future look like? Would she have to care for Will for the rest of her life? Would she think of him as her burden? Would she have to fall in love with someone in the most discerning of ways—someone who would love not only her but him as well? And not just love him, but be willing to share the responsibility of his care. For the rest of their lives.

When I found out I was having twins, I remember thinking, *They will always have each other.* A built-in best friend for life. I never imagined that would become a necessary fact, rather than a joyous one. No matter how many different ways I could color the situation, to try to find the silver lining, the fact remained that he might someday have to rely on her the way he relied on us.

I sniffled into her hair. She was so small and so young—too young—to understand what her life might hold and what she would be asked to do. *I'm so sorry,* I thought. *My baby girl, Will's angel.*

She looked up from my lap and wiped away a tear from my cheek. "Don't be sad, Mommy. I love Will so much. He's so funny, and he always wants to give me hugs. Rachel says her brother puts sand in her hair and pulls the legs off her Barbies." She frowned and shook her head in horror.

I laughed and nodded. "Well, that's not very nice."

She solemnly narrowed her eyes. "Not at all. I'm glad he's not my brother."

It was so simplistic, yet so profound. I kissed her again and she scampered off inside, ready to raid the pantry for her favorite cheese crackers. I swung a few times on the swing, trying to forget that soon, I hoped, another family would live there.

I looked down at my phone and saw I had a message on Facebook. It was from Therese Diamond.

My pulse quickened as I read through the message.

> Erin—
> How wonderful to hear from you! We, too, have always wondered about our relatives on the other side of the Atlantic. Yet, despite our best intentions, we never looked into it very much. So we are so glad that you sent us this message! We own a hardware store in the village, and live in an apartment above it. We would absolutely welcome you if you choose to visit our small corner of the world.
>
> Your other query, about the mother and the child, is very interesting. We had not heard that story before. Yet, if my genealogy serves correctly, they would have been first cousins with my grandmother. While my grandmother died when I was a child, and did not know much about her life growing up, she did talk to my mother about having American relatives, and how they were a fancy lot, and had parties like no one had ever seen. (Neither had she—as she had never traveled there!) And while my mother is also gone, I did speak to my sister, and she seems to remember our mother talking about an American cousin who came to live here, and needed a fresh start.
>
> So I went through some of the old boxes of photographs stuck in our attic (which is why it took me so long to get back to you—I apologise!), and

found a few black-and-whites. One was marked
with a caption as being of the "American cousin." I
wonder if this might help you in your search? I do
not know if it is the same woman, but I wanted to
share. I had my husband scan the photo and have
attached it to this e-mail. I hope it helps.

    Again, it was so good to hear from you, and
please, keep in touch.

    Best,

    Therese

I had tunnel vision as I clicked on the attachment and waited
for it to download. The only thing I could hear was the blood
rushing in my ears. Finally, the pie circle turned dark and the
photo was downloaded.

I opened it up, and it was a picture of five people, standing in
front of a fence, with a large, hilly field behind them. There
were three women and two men. In the center was a woman
with wide eyes and beautiful curls. I zoomed in with two fingers,
and my heart stopped. Although she looked slightly older than
the last photograph, it was Amelia. She was dressed in a simple
light-colored dress, with a white apron around her waist. Her hair
was loose around her shoulders. No one in the photo smiled, just
stared grimly into the camera lens.

The second photo was the inscription, written by someone
who had perfect handwriting, like calligraphy: *Welcome for the
American cousin. Adare Village. August 1, 1923.*

I clicked back to the first photo, hoping I had missed something. Or rather, hoping I had missed him. That maybe he was
in the background, hiding somewhere, or was camouflaged by
a tree. But John was nowhere in the photo.

My phone fell from my hand as I added everything together.
The accident happened in May. John had been sent to the
school in June. Amelia went to live in Ireland by August. It
seemed I had my answer as to what had happened to them.

I felt frozen in place on my front porch. I could hear Will still crying upstairs and the rustling of Charlotte raiding the pantry. I couldn't move from the front porch. My insides felt hollow as I pictured John staring out the window of the school, alone for the rest of his life, while Amelia was halfway across the world.

CHAPTER 31

AMELIA

Rose Savington and Georgina Lindemann had successfully taken their life jackets off, despite the rain that had begun to fall around them. The captain left his vantage point and ran to them, urging them to put their vests back on. To remain safe.

With the captain busy and the rain falling around them, Amelia rose and took John's hand. Her vision went almost black, except for the image in her mind of her and John, together.

She looked down at John and nodded, seeing the rain fall from his blond hair down onto his cheeks, and led him to the edge of the boat. Before anyone could stop them or clearly saw what happened, she jumped over the edge, pulling him with her. Except once she hit the water, his hand fell from hers.

She screamed and yelled for him, before she started swimming in a panic, toward the three blinking lights on the shore, praying with each stroke that John remembered the plan. He was wearing a life jacket but could swim through the water with ease. She had made him practice it with Michael over and over before they left for Lake Geneva.

She swam until the boat grew farther from her, and Monarch Manor was a blurry illumination against the water.

With each stroke, her gown grew heavier and heavier, and her arms burned with the weight of keeping her body moving against the choppy waves. She stopped for a moment, water dripping down her face and into her mouth, ears, and eyes, and screamed his name again, into the darkness, even though she knew he wouldn't hear it.

She wiped her face and then began swimming again, cupping large handfuls of water as she did each stroke, each movement bringing her closer to the shore, closer to being with John, and away from everyone who wished to take him from her.

Finally, she was close enough for her feet to lightly touch the bottom, her bare toes brushing against the rocks on the bottom. She struggled to stand and then took two more strokes forward until she could lift her head above the water, her feet wrapped around two smooth rocks on the bottom of the lake. She wiped the water from her face and peered at the shoreline, where she saw Alfred standing with the light, flashing it off and on. Next to him was Eleanor, soaked through in her bridesmaid dress, one hand shielding her face and the other lifted in the air.

She had told Alfred of her plan when she last made a trip to the house, the first weekend the estate opened for the summer. He was the only one she could trust, and she needed someone who could move around town and make arrangements easily, without suspicion. He didn't bother to try to talk her out of it but simply listened and nodded. She and John would jump off the yacht and swim to shore, take a train first to Chicago, and then disappear.

"I will do anything you ask. Anything for you and John," he had said quietly as he continued to stir the lemon cream sauce for the chicken dish to be served at dinner.

She had wanted to tell Eleanor and have her in on the plan from the very beginning, but she couldn't risk it. She knew Eleanor would try to dissuade her from leaving, tell her that she would shelter them from the Cartwrights, but Amelia didn't want to live a life of constant worry that John would be swept away, like the sand on the shoreline that is swept to the center of the lake each autumn.

So, instead, she had Alfred tell her sister after she was already on the boat. "Feed the bunnies," she had told her, which was Alfred's code to fill anyone else in about the plan should they say the words.

She ran through the water, to the edge, her feet slipping and aching in pain as she stepped on the irregular, sharp rocks. Eleanor rushed forward, her slippers splashing in the water, and held her arms out, grasping at her sister and pulling her out of the water. Amelia slipped and fell to her knees, a sharp pain running through her body. Alfred came to her other side, the lantern in his other hand.

Amelia took a deep breath and stood, her legs shaking. Eleanor tried to pull her in for an embrace, but she inched away. Her gaze was on the tree line just beyond the water, searching for him.

"Where's John? Where is he?" she said.

Her body froze and her blood turned to ice when neither of them said anything.

"Where is he?" she repeated, her voice rising. She asked again, her scream cutting through the air. "Tell me he reached the shore before I did." When they didn't answer again, she whirled around, her eyes scanning the water for his figure. But it was too dark to see anything other than the distant lights of the various estates on the south shore of the lake.

She started to run back into the lake, water splashing around, but Alfred and Eleanor grabbed her arms.

"It's too dangerous, Amelia," Eleanor said. "You can't swim back out there."

"Too dangerous? Then I *have* to go. It's John! He's terrified, alone, somewhere out there." She whirled around to Alfred. "Keep doing the lights! He knows to swim to the lights! Why did you stop?" her voice screeched out, nearly shearing the leaves off the nearby trees.

Alfred fumbled around with the lantern, nearly dropping it into the water.

"Give it to me," Amelia said. She snatched it from his hands. *Click, click, click, pause.* Her eyes scanned the surface, trying to will his figure to appear, swimming or bobbing in the water, within reach.

Click, click, click, pause.

Over and over again, as the precious minutes ticked by. The three of them were silent, the only sound among them the clicking of the lantern. They saw the *Monarch Princesses* turn around and head back to the estate, surrendering its passengers to their fate.

Amelia stood there for hours, waiting for John. But he never came.

CHAPTER 32

ERIN

"Mom, no! Press the doorbell!" Charlotte shrieked as I reached for the handle of my parents' house. On either side of the doorway were fake spiderwebs with small black spiders dotting the netting, and bats hung from the ceiling of the porch. Halloween was only a week away, but my mother had surely had the decorations up for at least a month.

I relaxed my grip on the brass handle of the front door, a rubber skeleton head hanging from it, and smiled. "Sorry. I forgot." I carefully pressed one finger on the doorbell as Luke shifted behind me, his hands full of a chocolate chip cheesecake that I had spent the better part of the morning cursing at. Will was still asleep in the car, after a long morning of building an intricate train track.

A horror scream came from inside, and a spooky voice said, "Go away!" and Charlotte laughed and clapped her hands in delight.

"Again!" she said.

I was about to press it one more time when the door flew open and my mom, dressed as a witch, complete with black pointy hat and a green face, appeared. "Welcome to my house!"

She bent forward and peered at Charlotte. "I think I would like to use you in one of my spells. My cauldron needs a little girl, and you would fit right in."

"Grandma, you're not even scary!" Charlotte said as she threw open the door and buried her face in my mom's waist.

"Oh man. And here I thought the Wicked Witch had nothing on me," my mom said with a cackle.

I set down the bags I had brought, carefully packed with snacks, a change of clothes for Will, several games, and an iPad, and took the cheesecake from Luke. "Go ahead and wait with him. He'll be a nightmare if we try to wake him up now."

His face brightened for a moment and then he nodded seriously. "Yes, someone should stay with him." He retreated to the car, a little too willingly.

"I have some of your favorite treats in the kitchen: popcorn balls and candy corn," my mom whispered to Charlotte, and she ran away so fast that she nearly knocked my mother over.

My father's birthday was three days before Halloween, and every year he insisted we celebrate in a fashion fitting of the holiday. Growing up, it meant watching scary movies and dressing up in costumes to sing "Happy Birthday." Unfortunately, one year, the year after Luke and I started dating, my parents decided we should go to a haunted house together. I've never heard Luke scream as loud as he did when Freddy Krueger chased him around the Jaycees haunted house with a chainsaw. My parents called him Mr. Krueger the next few times they saw him.

I followed Charlotte into the kitchen, marveling at the way my parents' house could still feel so comfortable to me, even after moving out so many years ago. It was all the same: The painting from Hawaii that my parents had bought on their honeymoon and carefully packed in their red hard-shelled suitcase, the framed embroidery piece from a little girl in 1850 that my mom had found in a garage sale, the bulletin board that had invitations to parties that happened two years ago. The carpeted bathrooms and dining room, going against every ounce of logic that existed. Yet in the corner of the (also carpeted) family room I saw something new. In my mother's old china cabinet were a few of the Precious Moments figurines from my grandmother's house.

"I thought you said you were going to sell those to one of your friends from your bridge club," I said with a smile.

She shrugged, smiling a crooked smile outlined with black lipstick. "What can I say? I guess the hoarding tendencies didn't filter out completely through the genes. Besides, she loved those damn things so much, it seemed wrong to just give them away."

"Well, are you going to come and say hello or do I have to track you through the whole house?" My father's voice wafted through the house from the kitchen. "You'd better get in here before I let my granddaughter eat an elephant's weight in sugar."

In the kitchen, I found Charlotte sitting at the bleached-wood island with a forest green Corian countertop, all the rage back in 1993, her hands already sticky from the popcorn balls.

"Nice costume," I said as I gave my dad a hug. He had black ears on, with black whiskers drawn on his face.

"I'm your mother's familiar, as I have resigned myself to being every day," he said with his palms in the air.

"Well, we are here for your birthday; shouldn't you get to be in charge for once?" I said as my mother walked into the kitchen, her black robes billowing behind her.

"I know my lot in life, and it's to let Mary Ellen lead the way." He leaned over and kissed my mother on the cheek, whispers of green paint remaining on his lips. He whispered to me, "No telling what would happen should she get some eye of newt, anyway. Best to just go along with her plans." He looked around and frowned. "Where's my favorite boy?"

"Sleeping in the car. If we wake him, we'll need more than a magic spell to fix things," I said. I set the cheesecake down on the island and slapped my father's hand away. "Not until we sing." The chocolate chip cheesecake was a family recipe, passed down from my dad's mother, who apparently didn't believe in any shortcuts in cooking. It was a wonder she found time to do anything other than watch the oven and make frosting from scratch.

"So what's new, Erin-go-bragh?" my dad said.

I shrugged and I felt my face grow warm. "Not much. Well, we've put the house on the market." I tried to keep my voice light, but it came out like a strangled scream.

My mother's hand stopped in midair, and she stared at me. My dad moved closer, his hand running along the green kitchen island, his wedding ring scratching along the surface.

"It's not a big deal," I said quickly, and took a step backward, resting my hands on the countertop behind me. "It's time." I heard my voice come out foreign, belonging to someone else.

"What are you talking about?" my mother said with a frown. "You love that house. You said you never want to live anywhere else."

"Well." I glanced down at Charlotte, who was watching me with big, round eyes. I walked over and put my arm around her shoulders. "Honey, why don't you go and find some of those peanut butter M&M'S that Grandma always has in the TV room?" She looked up at me, and then slowly around the kitchen, before she nodded and walked away.

"Sorry," my dad said. "We don't want to upset you. It's just so shocking. What's going on?" He leaned forward, his cat whiskers pointing down on his cheeks, his eyes serious behind his glasses.

"We need money to pay for Will's school. We really loved the private school, but as I've said, it's insanely expensive. We don't have any other way to pay for it. Can't get blood from a stone," I said with a thin laugh. "The only way to make it happen is to pay for it ourselves." I looked down. "And it's an arm and a leg."

My parents exchanged a glance, the same worried look that I

saw when I first told them we had gotten Will's official diagnosis. I recognized it in a personal way, as Luke and I had shared it more than once in an IEP meeting or when we would meet with Will's speech therapist to get the results of his latest assessment. It was a look of helpless despair, of knowing your child was struggling and having no way to help him. And apparently, it never faded.

"I'm so sorry," my dad said quietly. "I can't imagine how hard that is for you."

My mother cleared her throat and took off her pointy hat. "Where are you going to live?" She rubbed her chin, green paint migrating to her palm.

I laughed quietly. "Always right to the point, Mom. I'm not sure. It depends on what we get for the house. We will have to rent, since we won't really have a down payment after closing costs. After a few years, we can hopefully buy a house again." I didn't add that I had looked at the financials and didn't see how even that would be possible without winning the lottery, or a sudden windfall of cash from a rich, unknown relative.

"Well, that house has a bunch of problems, anyway. You guys are always having to fix this or repair that. Better off to let it be someone else's problem," my mom said. She nodded firmly, as though she had thought of the plan all along and was happy we were finally listening to her. This was always her playbook for "helping" me through things: minimize the problem, no matter how big, and move on. More than half of the time, it worked.

But not this time.

"Mom, I love that house." I released my hands from behind me and leaned back with all of my weight. My feet slid forward in my flats, until they met the edge of the kitchen island. "It's my home." Tears filled my eyes and threatened to spill over.

"Hey, Mom, can I go outside and see the Halloween decorations?" I heard Charlotte call from the other room.

"Of course." I shook my head and sniffled, tucking my hair behind my ears.

My dad stood up and put a hand on my shoulder. He gave me a sympathetic look, and I managed a smile, before he followed Charlotte outside. I heard the ghoul on the side of the house—the one that had been there since I was in high school—go off in a dying, staccato way.

My mom, hands on the island in front of her, slid over until her hip was resting on mine.

"Mom, I feel like I'm drowning. I feel like I'm doing this all on my own, and that I'm failing in the worst possible way. That I'm failing him, that I'm failing myself, Luke, Charlotte. I feel like things will never get better, and I just keep waiting for the next problem to appear." I covered my face with my hands.

"I'm sorry, hon," she said as she lightly tapped her hip against mine. "But you have to realize all the good things you do have, and stop staring at all the bad. What you have may not be what you pictured, but if you don't stop thinking about everything you don't have, you're going to miss what you do."

I opened my eyes and inhaled a ragged breath that burned my nose. "It's not that easy." I looked at her, and she put an arm around my shoulders.

"Sure it is," she said.

"Yeah, right." I snorted and looked out the kitchen window, toward the back of the yard, by the fence where I once built a tree fort with Katie that was specifically designed to catch fairies and trolls and where, a few years later, I kissed the boy who lived next door—Johnny—before he ran off and screamed in horror. "Guess the troll traps do work after all," Katie had said when I told her about the kiss.

Luke ran in front of the window, looking over his shoulder. Will, who had apparently woken up in the car, chased after him. His smile could have lit up the entire backyard, as he ran with his curls blowing in the wind. In his hand, he had a branch with a few stray autumn-hued leaves still attached. My first instinct was to tell him to put it down, that he could get hurt. But I just watched.

Luke stopped and spun around, his arm outstretched, waiting to be captured. Will stopped suddenly, a few feet from his father, paused, and then dropped the branch and ran toward him. He ran straight into Luke's body, hands at his sides, accepting the embrace. Luke did a mock stumble backward and then crumpled to the ground, Will on top of him.

I heard Will's laugh float through the kitchen window, to my left. To my right, I could hear Charlotte's shrieks of delight from the front yard. They met just above my head and swirled together like food coloring on a plate, red and blue making purple. A beautiful, deep purple.

Look and see what you have, not what you don't.

"Everything will be just fine. You are so lucky. You have everything you need," my mother whispered into my ear. Her arm was still around my shoulders, and her hip touching mine.

I reflexively wanted to argue with her or at least roll my eyes at her false optimism. Instead, I closed my eyes and waited. I waited for the What If moment to hit me, to imagine we were here in their kitchen discussing a family vacation or the restaurant we ate at the night before. Not crying about selling our house, not worrying about risking our financial future to help Will.

It felt as though each time I had a moment of happiness the What If was waiting in the shadows, ready to snatch my ankle as I walked by. But this time, it didn't come.

All I heard was Will's giggles, Charlotte's screams of delight, and Luke's joy. I was the only one holding on to the pain.

I slowly opened my eyes and looked outside again. Luke and Will stood in the back of the yard. Luke had his finger outstretched, pointing at a woodpecker halfway up the tree. Will's back was to me, so I couldn't see his face, but I could tell by his body language that he was listening.

And I knew that this was what really mattered. Not the

house, not the school, not anything else. Our family. And everything else could be sacrificed and changed.

In that moment, I finally understood. That there was beauty in protecting and loving a child who needed us more than anything and that maybe he wouldn't be *fine,* but he would be Will. He needed me to be the mom he deserved, and maybe that was a mom who would meet him on the floor and line up trains with him, rather than encouraging him to put them on the track.

And I realized: It was us who needed to be taught, not him. This was our lesson to learn, not his.

For the first time in a long time, I felt it wash over me, ever so slightly like a gold-spun netting, spooling around and around until I couldn't help but notice.

It was peace.

On the way home, after a dinner of lasagna and garlic bread (to scare away the vampires, of course), Luke drove us home through the darkness. For the first time in a long time, my body felt light, like I had set down a heavy backpack I didn't know I was wearing.

The last thing my mother said to me when we left, as she hugged me good-bye, was, "Don't you give up, kiddo. I won't allow it."

I looked out the windows at the cornfields that passed our car, and the exit that approached read: LAKE GENEVA. In the distance, somewhere off the highway, was the lake where everything began for Amelia and John. I traced my finger on the window and again tried to imagine Amelia leaving John while she started a new life. Despite all the evidence to the contrary, I still couldn't fully accept that she had done such a thing. It didn't ring true in my heart; I felt it, deep inside my bones: There was no way she would have left him behind. Just as I would never leave Will.

"Don't give up." My mother's words came to me again, as I searched the far horizon for any sign of the lake.

"I never did send Gerry that photo of Amelia in Ireland," I said. The words felt foreign, like I wasn't the one saying them.

"You didn't? I guess I had assumed that you did. It seemed like the logical next step. I didn't ask you about it, because of everything with the house," Luke said carefully.

"I know. I'm sorry. I haven't made this any easier on you. None of this is your fault," I said.

His eyes flickered to me, and he took one hand from the steering wheel and covered mine. "Thanks." He sighed. "So are you going to send it to him? The picture, I mean."

I folded my fingers around his palm and squeezed. I looked out into the darkness, Lake Geneva far behind us now. "Yes. I'm going to try again. One more time."

We rode home the rest of the way in silence, holding hands. I rested my head against the window and looked up at the brilliant spray of stars in the sky, waiting for a shooting star.

CHAPTER 33

AMELIA

Amelia looked out over the water, at the stillness of the lake. The stars reflected on the water's surface, and it was hard to imagine that there had been an accident, or any rain or disruption at all, just a few hours before. The sun was beginning to peek over the horizon, showing the first streaks of yellow and orange over the heavy tree line.

She had slept on a blanket by the dock, refusing Alfred's offer to sneak her into the servants' quarters, in case John somehow found his way to her. Long after Eleanor said she had to return to the party to avoid suspicion and to play the part of the concerned aunt and sister, Amelia sat in the same spot, scanning the water for John.

The only thing she saw was the ripples made by turtles sticking their heads above the surface, and the only sound was the crickets and bullfrogs that guarded the night. She didn't allow herself to cry; there was no reason. He was somewhere, with someone, and that thought kept her awake through the night, waiting for him. She whispered prayers to every saint she could think of and begged Henry to keep him safe.

As the morning sky illuminated with the sunlight, triumphing over the stars and the night, she heard a sound in the woods behind her. Sticks cracking and leaves rustling. She quickly stood, her heart pounding.

"John?" she said weakly, even though she knew he couldn't hear her. She clenched her fists as she tried to will his tiny figure to appear from the woods, somehow. Someway.

Yet the only person who appeared was Alfred, dressed in his dark shirt and pants that he wore beneath his white service coat. His cheeks were drawn with exhaustion, but his hands waved in the air.

"They have him," he sputtered out as he stumbled toward her, his feet catching on the thick roots that crisscrossed the ground. "John. They have him."

A jolt of electricity ran through Amelia's body, like she had been struck by lightning. She ran toward Alfred and grabbed onto his arms. "Where is he?" She scanned the woods behind him, searching for any sign of her son.

Alfred panted, and she wondered how he had gotten around to her side of the lake. He inhaled sharply and adjusted his glasses. "At the house, at Monarch Manor."

She turned sharply toward the house, in the distance. She could see the *Monarch Princesses* docked on the water and the remnants of the party still scattered on the lawn. Soon the servants would begin to dismantle everything and the house would look as though nothing had happened.

"He somehow found his way back to the dock of the house, and your mother pulled him out. Actually, Miss Emily was the first one to see him, and alerted your mother. From what I understand, from what your sister said, your mother tried to bring him inside with little fanfare. But Mrs. Cartwright saw them, and now she knows that John is well," he said quietly.

"Should—should I go to him?" She dropped Alfred's arms and rubbed her face. If she returned, she could easily say that she swam to shore and survived the accident, and they, too, could go on as though nothing had happened.

Until, of course, Margaret continued with her plan to send him away.

Alfred understood her expression. "It's up to you." He folded his arms across his thick waist.

"I can't imagine what he's thinking. Has anyone told him that I'm alive, that I'm waiting for him?" she asked.

"I'm sorry, but I don't know," he said.

Amelia pressed a hand to her heart, trying to choke back the sobs as she thought of John grieving, alone, in the house. She hoped that Emily and Eleanor and her mother were with him, and held him as he slept. She couldn't imagine how scared and shocked he must have been. It was the first night that he had ever spent away from her.

"I'm sorry, but I must return to the house. Things are going on as planned, with the breakfast this morning," he said.

"Even though I'm missing?" Amelia turned in surprise.

Alfred nodded slightly. "Your mother knows you are here, and she is insisting everything continue, to keep the guests' minds off what happened. The guests are being told that everything is being taken care of, and there are crews searching the lake to rescue you and John. Your father and Jane have been told not to worry, by your mother. Thankfully, they seem to be listening. She thinks it is best to close out the weekend, and have people leave quickly after." He leaned in closely. "For everyone's sake," he said.

She nodded, thinking of all those people, gossiping and expressing mock horror at it all. Except for one.

"And Matthew?" she said, her voice barely above a whisper. "What does he believe?"

Alfred's expression shot a pain through her heart. "He's devastated, of course. I don't believe he slept at all last night. He has been trying to arrange for more yachts to keep searching the water. He tried to climb aboard one on his own, to find you. I think he was ready to start swimming before your mother stopped him."

Oh, Matthew. I'm so sorry. I never once thought of how this might hurt you. All I ever wanted for you was to be happy. The last thing I wanted was to make you worry, to involve you in this. She put her head in her hands and tried to steady her breath.

"I need to go back to the house now. I'm already late," Alfred said. He turned to leave, and she followed.

"I'm coming with you," she said. "I need to see John. I'll stay hidden, and find Eleanor and my mother and figure out a plan," she added when she saw his expression of protest.

She glanced back at the house from the distance one more time, preparing to walk back into her past.

"Nora, I have told you at least a dozen times that you must serve the guests from the left side. You cannot keep making that mistake, or I will be the one to pay for it." Alfred's voice wafted through the thick oak door of the butler's pantry. Amelia crouched behind the icebox, her body aching from the sleepless night. More than once, she had to press herself against the plaster wall behind her when a maid opened the door, before Alfred could yelp in protest that no one was to enter the pantry except him.

He had brought her into the house, through the service kitchen, when he dispatched the servers to begin pouring coffee and juice for the brunch guests. He had thrown a blanket over her head, with the plan to explain that she was a guest still drunk from the wedding, embarrassed to be seen by anyone.

She waited there, the stifling heat of the pantry building as the morning went on. She didn't dare open the small window above the shelves and let the lake air circulate and cool her skin. Her bridesmaid's dress was torn and dirty, and her hair clung to her head like a bonnet. Finally, the commotion in the prep kitchen ended and the door creaked open.

"Quickly," Alfred said as he waved his hand.

Amelia hurried out of the closet, just in time to see her mother walk into the pantry. She froze, her hand in the air, still holding her skirt. Mary wore a pale gray sundress with a tea-length skirt.

"Mo—" She didn't finish as Mary rushed forward and threw her arms around her daughter. The weight of her mother's arms around her made her collapse forward, and sobs racked her body.

"Please, you need to be quiet," Alfred hissed as he peeked out of the kitchen doorway, around the corner toward the living quarters.

Mary grabbed Amelia's shoulders and looked her square in the eye. "John has been rescued, but Margaret saw him as he came offshore."

Amelia stepped back, her ankle wobbling, and Mary reached forward to steady her. "It was all for nothing," she said.

Mary dug her fingernails into Amelia's forearms. "She does not know you were rescued. And will never know. Thus, I am sure that the expectation is that he will be sent to the school, quietly."

"You can't send him there," Amelia whispered, her heart pounding in her chest.

Mary pulled her face closer, and Amelia could see the flecks of gold in her mother's blue eyes—the same gold as the monarch butterflies she so loved—and lowered her chin. "We won't. For all the Cartwrights know, he will be sent there next month, and they won't have to worry about it any longer."

"They'll know," Amelia said as she bit the side of her lip. "They'll know if he's not there. The staff will easily tell them that he never arrived."

Mary turned her head slowly toward Alfred, who cleared his throat.

"Yes, well, that is my part to play. An old schoolmate of mine, Josepha, is a nurse at the facility. Terrible place, she says, but there isn't work anywhere else. She says—"

"Alfred?" Mary interrupted as she dropped her arms from Amelia's shoulders.

"Yes. Sorry." He adjusted his glasses. "She is going to help us and record that he was admitted. She says the headmaster doesn't know any of the children, and only uses the admission log to determine who stays there. She is going to write his name down, with the proper date of admission, and then if the Cartwrights look for proof, they will have it."

"Why would she do that?" Amelia said.

Alfred gave her a thin smile. "She has four children of her own, and doesn't make very much money."

Amelia raised her eyebrows and looked at her mother. "You're paying her off?" Mary didn't say anything, her silence her admission. "But what if the Cartwrights come to visit him, or what if someone wants to see him?"

Alfred and Mary remained silent, looking at her, her naïveté bursting like a bubble in the warm kitchen air. "Of course," she said finally, "no one will ever come looking for him." She grabbed a fistful of her skirt and twisted it, taking a deep breath.

"But we still have to be very careful, Amelia," Mary said. "I am making arrangements with Eleanor right now, so you need to stay here, hidden."

"Can I see him?" Amelia said quietly.

Mary shook her head and gave her a sympathetic look. "Not yet. But he's safe, and is with Emily. The last I saw, he was looking through *The Velveteen Rabbit* again, and Emily was playing with her puppets." Mary put her hands on both sides of Amelia's face. "Trust me." She kissed the top of her head before she turned and left, her skirt swishing behind her.

"What now?" Amelia asked Alfred.

He turned and pulled a biscuit out of the bread box on the counter of the kitchen. He handed it to her. With a small smile, he said, "You are now a ghost."

CHAPTER 34

ERIN

I waited outside of the Geneva Lake Museum at closing time, shivering in the November air. We had our first snow flurries that morning. Even though the meteorologists had accurately predicted the snowfall, it still seemed like a shock when I woke up and saw a dusting on the lawn, like someone had spilled a bag of confectioners' sugar on the grass.

The twins' eyes had lit up when they saw the flakes falling from the sky, and I let them run outside in their pajamas and try to catch the snow on their tongues. After a few minutes, their cheeks were ruddy and their noses runny, so I bundled them inside and plied them with guilt doughnuts, promising them that I would be home from Wisconsin as soon as possible.

I kicked the gravel rocks in the parking lot of the museum around as I checked my phone. Five-oh-four pm. Gerry should be coming out any minute.

It was the weekend after we had visited my parents. When we arrived home that night, after I put the twins in their beds, I left Gerry a message and forwarded him the picture of who I thought was Amelia in Adare Village. He responded with a polite thank-you and said he would look into it. Two days ago, he responded that he might have a lead. And then, nothing. I hadn't heard a word despite responding to the e-mail and sending him a text.

"Gerry!" I said when I saw him walk out of the museum, a box of manila file folders under his arm.

He startled and dropped the box, papers spilling all over the sidewalk.

"Oh, shoot. My fault," I said as I jogged over to him. I bent down, the knees of my jeans resting against the cold pavement.

"No, no. Please. Let me," he said quickly, and held up a hand. He wore a brown suit, as he always did, but that day he had on a pink-and-blue-striped tie, and I realized it was the first time I had seen him wearing any kind of bright color. He carefully stacked each folder on top of another and then lifted the whole stack as he stood. His knees wobbled under the weight of the papers, and I held a hand out to catch him as he steadied himself.

"I'm so sorry to barge in on you like this. I just wanted to follow up on the lead that you found," I said quickly. I looked down at the stack of folders in his hand, and shame washed over me. This wasn't his quest; it was mine. Who was I to demand he give my project his full attention? "I just haven't slept much since you said you might have found something."

He adjusted his glasses and studied me for a moment, shifting the folders from one hip to another, before giving me a small smile. "I appreciate your passion." He laughed. "I felt the same way when I worked on a restoration and research project for Black Point Estate a few years ago. It consumed me."

"That's a great way to describe it." I held my palms in the air. "Well, anything you can share?"

"Well, yes, in fact." He glanced at the papers in his hands. "Would you like to come back inside, so we can talk?"

* * *

Gerry's office looked like a TV show about hoarders. Featuring a very, very meticulous and smart hoarder. There were stacks of similar manila folders everywhere, in neat piles with perfect ninety-degree angles. Some stacks had to be nearly one hundred folders high, resting precariously on the floor in strange patterns, looking like the pillars from the ruins of an ancient city.

I carefully walked around the stacks, holding my breath, not wanting to upend his life any more than I already had. On the chair opposite his desk was another stack, so I stood next to it, as still as possible.

He sat down in his desk chair with a creak and turned on his computer.

"Again, I'm so sorry. I'm sure you had somewhere to go, or something to do, and I showed up like some stalker," I said.

He didn't look up from the screen. "It's quite all right. I do have plans, but they aren't until later."

I again wondered if his plans were with Haley, the librarian. I eyed his brightly colored tie and wondered if maybe she had bought it for him.

"All right, so, I contacted my counterpart in Adare Village, and sent her the photograph that you received from your relatives." He gave his computer one final tap and then looked up. He sat back in his chair and crossed one leg over the other. "A woman by the name of Marguerite Brown. Wonderful lady, and very knowledgeable of the town's peccadillos."

I nodded and wanted to lean forward, to pull the information out from him like a string on a doll.

"Now, she was able to compare your photograph of Amelia to a few others that they have in the town. And you know, that town really is fascinating. It is home to Adare Manor, which was once the estate of Lord and Lady Dunraven. It's a big Gothic building that's been turned into a hotel. And in fact, on the grounds, there are ogam stones, and the ruins of an abbey, and—" He stopped and shook his head. "Sorry."

"Don't be sorry. I love it," I said with a laugh.

"Anyway, she was able to find a few other photographs that you might be interested in." He clicked around on his computer while I waited, a line of sweat running down my back. "I apologize for not telling you this earlier, but I've been lecturing every night in local venues, and my schedule has become almost unmanageable." He swiveled the computer screen toward me.

I leaned in closer. I set my palms carefully down on his desk, in between two stacks of papers. My breath caught in my chest as I looked at a black-and-white photograph of a woman in front of a thatched-roof house. She wore a dress, with black boots. Her hair was braided in a crown around her head, and she had an easy smile on her face. A smile that was unmistakably Amelia.

"That's her," I whispered. I pointed to her. "I can't believe it. It's Amelia."

"No," Gerry said. I looked up in surprise. "This woman's name isn't Amelia. It's Bridget Regan."

"Bridget? No, I'm sure it's Amelia," I said slowly, the realization dawning on me. "She changed her name?"

He blinked in confirmation. "That's my assumption, and the assumption of Marguerite as well."

"She changed her name," I repeated, crossing my arms over my chest. "Why would she do that, unless she was running away from something?"

"Ah, yes." Gerry stabbed the air with a finger. "This might help to explain that further." He clicked again on his computer, and my heart started to pound so fast, my hands tingled and shook.

Another picture came up on the screen. It was the same woman—Amelia, Bridget—standing in front of what looked like a rosebush. This time, her dress was more formal, like she was attending an important event, and she wore heels.

And her arms were in front of her, placed on a child's shoulders.

He was blond, with large eyes and round cheeks. He, too, smiled for the camera, with his hands clasped in front of him. He was dressed in a dark suit, with black shoes.

His hair was longer and he seemed older, but I knew it was him. It was John.

I put a shaking hand to my mouth, my stomach churning. "It's him," I whispered. I turned to Gerry, tears filling my eyes. "It's John."

Gerry nodded, smiling broadly. "I believe so. Actually, Brendan. Brendan Regan, Bridget's son," he said.

"Bridget and Brendan," I said carefully. I shook my head and leaned in again, my finger tracing John's face. "He lived. He was alive." My voice cracked. "How? What happened? How did they end up in Ireland, without anyone ever knowing?"

"Well, that we may never know. But I do think we can fill in at least a few of those blanks," Gerry said. He turned off his computer, and the image of John and Amelia faded from view. "Now that I had the name from Marguerite—Regan—I was able to do a bit of genealogy and trace them properly. It seems as though Amelia really did love this town, and her ancestral home."

"What do you mean?" I said. The blood was rushing so loudly in my ears, they started to ring.

"Well, at some point, they came back," Gerry said. "Or at least, one of them did. There are Regans in the area, who at least appear to be related to them." He cleared his throat. "And you, in a distant way, I suppose."

"Wow," I said. I took a quick step back and brushed against one of Gerry's piles, sending one wobbling back and forth. I inhaled sharply as it leaned to one side but didn't fall. I started to reach for it, to straighten it back, but he made a strangling sound.

"No. No. Please leave it," he said. When I stood up, my hands away from the folders, he continued, "I took the liberty of contacting them, since they're locals. And . . ."—he paused, his eyes glittering—"they have some things I think you might be interested in seeing."

CHAPTER 35

AMELIA

The first moment that Amelia saw John after he was born, she felt as though it was the first day she had ever truly lived. His tiny body, wrapped in a white swaddle blanket, was placed in her arms, and she saw how perfectly he fit into the crook of her elbow, like it had been waiting for his sweet head all along.

"There you are. I've been waiting to meet you," she had whispered to him. He opened his eyes briefly at the feel of her breath on his face and looked at her. She felt as though he could see right through her, something so primal and perfect, as though she had known all along that moment would happen, somewhere deep inside her soul. He was another piece to her puzzle—the most important, largest piece in the landscape.

He was meant for her. And she, for him.

Henry fell in love with him, too, and barely wanted to allow the nannies to care for him as Amelia healed from the birth. She would often catch him staring at John, studying his face, trying to memorize each soft line and gentle curve. She would pretend to still be asleep, or tiptoe back around the corner, to let them have their moments together.

But she knew in her heart that he was hers. He had been there all along, waiting to be born.

She never thought that she would feel that same sense of wonder again as the first moment she held him. And yet she was wrong.

In the kitchen of Monarch Manor, after Eleanor quietly whisked him downstairs under the cover of a cloak, Amelia held him again and felt as though he had been born all over again.

When Eleanor walked in with him, Amelia had been hiding in the butler's pantry again, counting the bags of flour and sugar to pass the time without losing her mind. As each minute ticked by and John was somewhere else in the house, she felt her sanity slip away. When the floorboards in the kitchen would creak, she would hold her breath, hoping it was John and praying she wouldn't be discovered.

But then, when she heard her sister whisper, "Here," she slowly creaked open the door and saw John's face peeking out from a long dark rain cloak, his eyes round with fear and his mouth trembling.

She pushed open the door with a reckless thud and reached for his shoulders as she pulled him close, nearly suffocating him against her chest.

"John. Oh, John. You're here." Her words fell out in a messy tumble, mixed together with tears and relief. He tried to pull away slightly, and she pressed him tighter to her body, wanting to absorb him back inside and for them to become one.

When she finally released him, she put her hands on his cheeks and held his face close, kissing his nose and his forehead. She held his gaze for a moment, the same look that they had given each other right after he was born.

The look that told him nothing would stop her from protecting him.

"I'm so sorry," she signed to him. "You are safe now."

"Em." Eleanor's voice broke the spell. "We have to move quickly."

Amelia lifted John up and held him like a toddler, his head dropping on her shoulder and his body limp against her. She hoisted him up, tucking an arm underneath his bottom.

"What's our plan?" she said.

Eleanor wore a beautiful white lace sundress and a straw sun hat. With surprise, Amelia glanced outside and saw a brilliantly blue sky, not a cloud anywhere. For some reason, she had pictured the outside to mirror her feelings of gloom and anxiety, as though she couldn't imagine the sun to dare shine when John wasn't with her.

Eleanor reached into a small bag on her shoulder that Amelia hadn't noticed before. From it she pulled out a yellow-and-white sundress and a white sun hat, both for a child. "Put these on John." She held them out and Amelia shifted John to one hip as she slowly took them.

Eleanor nodded. "I'm going to give you and John the tickets meant for me and Emily. You will go to New York, and I will meet you both there the following day, to figure out the rest of the plan." She pulled out an outfit of hers for Amelia, and another sun hat. "Hopefully no one will question you and they'll just think you were another wedding guest with your child."

"What about my things? Originally, Alfred was supposed to have a trunk waiting for me on the shore, with some money and clothes." She swallowed hard, wondering why she ever thought the plan would be so simple. How could she have ever believed she and John could simply slip away forever, with only a modest trunk?

Eleanor nodded. "He told me. He will have it for you when he drops you and John—Emily," she said emphatically, "off at the train station in Williams Bay."

"And the Cartwrights? What will you tell them? She knows John is alive—and they must think I drowned," Amelia said as she rocked John back and forth. The weight of his body was pressing on her lower back, causing jolts of pain to run up to her shoulders.

"Mother and I will smooth things over with them. We are going to tell them that I will take him to the school next week, and that's why we are staying back from New York for a few days. When you get to the city, go straight to my apartment. There is only a skeleton staff right now, and I can make sure they stay quiet about the arrangement. But, Em, we will need to get you and John out quickly, since the regular staff isn't as discreet." She pressed her mouth into a line and slowly shook her head.

"I don't know what to say. I can't thank you enough for all of this. For putting yourself—" Amelia's voice broke and tears ran down her face.

"Stop," Eleanor said. She leaned forward and squeezed her arm. "Just be safe. Your safety and John's safety is payment enough."

They heard a creak in the hallway leading up to the kitchen and she widened her eyes. "Get ready. Alfred will be here soon to take you to the station." She kissed her sister on the cheek quickly before slipping out the door.

As the train left the Williams Bay station, Amelia stared out the window, watching the town she had loved go farther and farther from her view. She held her gaze on the lake for as long as she could, the water sparkling in the brilliant sunlight until it faded like the spark off a match going out in the rain.

She took several deep breaths, her body still shaking from seeing Georgina Lindemann on the train platform. Thankfully, she had seen her from behind and was able to quickly rush herself and John onto the train car before Georgina turned around.

When Amelia could no longer see the water, she leaned back in her seat, John draped against her lap while clutching his toy horse, and closed her eyes. At her feet was the trunk of things Alfred had collected—a brown leather case that held her entire past and, she hoped, enough money to buy them a new future. She didn't know what that future would look like, but she knew that she and John would be together in it, yet so much farther from home than she had ever imagined.

She thought of how much Matthew wanted them to travel together, to explore new lands and different cities, and she couldn't imagine leaving her home and family behind. And now, of course, she was the one slipping away into the unknown.

She drifted off to sleep quickly. The rhythmic sounds of the tracks clicking underneath her and the white noise of the conversations of the passengers seated around her sounded like a lullaby. Even in her sleep, her arm never left John, her palm moving up and down with his breath.

CHAPTER 36

ERIN

"This is it," Gerry said as he pulled his Prius into the gravel driveway of a small brown cottage just outside of Lake Geneva. He put the car in Park and I studied the house. It was a story and a half, dark brown, with a small front porch. On the front porch lush pots spilled over with mums, and in a corner of the lawn were tall sunflowers, gently waving in the breeze.

"The Hoppe gardening gene lives on," I whispered to myself with a smile. Through a heavy line of trees, I could see the faintest glimmer of Lake Como. The sunlight filtered through what was left of the leaves, illuminating the yard in a kaleidoscope pattern. I didn't doubt that the beloved monarch butterflies always found their way to the yard.

I followed Gerry up the wooden steps to the front door, the sounds of wind chimes on the eaves tinkling with each breeze off the lake. I wrapped my cardigan sweater around my waist as a chill of anticipation ran through my body. The front door slowly opened, and a tall woman with striking red hair and a dusting of freckles across her nose gave us a wide smile.

"There you are. We've been waiting for you," she said as she held open the screen door.

* * *

The inside of the house smelled like chocolate chip cookies, although I didn't see any in the kitchen, where Gerry and I sat around a small butcher-block island, cups of steaming coffee in front of us, as Susan and Greg Regan pulled black-and-white pictures out of a crumbling cardboard box marked *Photos*.

"And this one here, this is a photo of my mother and father at their wedding," Greg said as he carefully placed the photo on the table. I leaned over and smiled at the photo. The groom wore an early-1970s-style leisure suit and the bride a white dress that resembled a nightgown.

"So, just to be clear, this is Kathy and Mike, correct?" Gerry said as he looked down at the picture. Greg nodded. "And Mike's father—your grandfather—was . . ."

"Brendan Regan," Greg finished.

Gerry and I exchanged a small smile. I leaned in closer and studied the groom's face, John's son. Even though he smiled, I recognized the downturned lips, and although his face was leaner than the pictures I had seen of John, I could make out the familiar roundness that dominated the family genes.

"Or, from what you've told me, John . . ." Greg trailed off.

"John Cartwright," I said quietly.

"It's just such an unbelievable story. I'm having a hard time wrapping my mind around it," Greg said as he shook his head. He glanced at Susan, who smiled.

"I think it's just the most wonderful thing I've ever heard. Who would have guessed that there was so much intrigue, and so much love, and so much sacrifice in their past?" she said with a smile. She leaned forward and looked at me. "How incredible that you discovered all of this."

I looked down at the back of the electric bill that Gerry had used to map out the family tree, using the Regans to fill in the blanks. From what we knew, at some point Bridget and Brendan had returned to the United States. Brendan—John—married and had twins, Michael and Maelissa. Michael eventually had two children of his own: Greg and a daughter named Amelia. *Amelia,* my heart whispered when I heard the name. I wondered if he knew about Amelia or if the name was somehow in his subconscious, woven into the invisible strands of DNA.

"I'm not sure who this is in the picture with Brendan, but they appear to be great friends," Greg said as he slid a photo toward us.

I looked at the face of the woman who had her arm around John's shoulders, and recognized the sparkle in her eye and the upturned nose. "That's my great-grandmother Emily." I smiled at Greg. "Well, I guess it's good to finally meet my distant cousins."

"I repeat: 'This is the most exciting thing I've ever heard,' " Susan said with a sigh. She stood up and pulled the coffeepot out from the machine. "More? We have a lot to cover, it seems like." She held the pot in the air, ready to pour. "Greg, did you grab that chest from your mom's house? The one from the attic?"

Greg shook his head and stood, the legs of his kitchen stool scraping against the linoleum floor. "I forgot. Let me go dig it out."

I accepted another cup of coffee and looked around the kitchen as I brought it to my nose. The house was adorable, with wood paneling in every room, and walking distance to Lake Como. I could smell the crisp lake air through the open windows. I thought of the distance to Monarch Manor, and I realized that Lake Como was the closest lake to the estate, other than Lake Geneva. I wondered if Amelia chose to live here so she could be as near as possible to her childhood home. To be as close as she ever could to the girl she once was. To the Before.

"Found it!" Greg said as he walked into the kitchen, the linoleum squeaking under his feet. He placed a small leather-bound chest on the kitchen island, on top of the hastily drawn family tree. "This is one of those things we kind of moved around from house to house, without anyone really claiming it or taking special notice of it. But my father always told me it was a family heirloom, and that my great-grandmother had brought it over from Ireland with her."

Susan chuckled and placed her hands on the island, clasping them together. "Greg's dad treated nearly everything as an heirloom, though. Ahem, Lake Delavan Fishing Derby trophy from 1987."

Greg nodded. "Sure did. If we revered everything he did, we would be out of a home."

I laughed. "Well, in addition to physical characteristics, it certainly sounds like the family tradition of never throwing anything away remained in the DNA," I said as I thought of my grandmother's Powers Lake house.

"And for that, we preservationists thank you," Gerry said.

"May I?" I said as I gestured toward the chest. I ran a finger along the top of it, carefully avoiding the cracked places on the chest. It was old, probably more than a hundred years old, and so I carefully lifted the rusted metal latch and slowly opened it with a squeak. It released a cloud of dust from inside, as though it sighed in relief at finally breathing fresh air.

Inside were only two items. The first was a small wooden toy rocking horse. The paint was worn around the edges, where it looked like tiny hands had loved it and gripped it close. I carefully placed it on the kitchen island, watching it rock back and forth for a moment before I turned back to the chest.

The second item was a book. I lifted it, running a finger along the familiar title.

The Velveteen Rabbit. The pages were worn and yellowed with age, and the binding crackled as I opened to the first page and read the first few familiar lines. Tears began to prick at the corners of my eyes, and my nose tingled as I looked from the book to the toy horse.

"This was John's horse, and his book," I said with a whisper.

I ran a finger along the horse, watching it rock back and forth on the island. "Welcome home," I said.

Long after I said good-bye to the Regans and Gerry headed back to his house, and to his life, I sat on the public beach in Williams Bay. The beach had long closed at the end of the summer season, so I was alone. The wind whipped across the lake and through my cardigan. I hugged my knees to my chest and stared out at the water, and at the empty space where Monarch Manor once stood.

Amelia had given everything up for John: her family, her childhood, her home. Even her name. The power of love changed everything.

I let a handful of coarse sand run through my fingers, the cold, damp grains chilling my fingers. I realized it was often how I felt about being a mother. Grasping at things, never quite reaching them. Sand between my fingers, the days escaping my palm. I set my hand back down into the sand and looked back out at the water.

My children had transformed me, too. Not just in the obvious physical and mental changes that parenthood brings, but something deeper. Something more powerful. The things I was most proud of: my dedication to Will and Charlotte, my willingness to keep going, my tenacity . . . those were things I had gathered on our sometimes-challenging path, like a twisted scavenger hunt. And it was a journey that led me to become an even better version of myself. A better mother. A better person.

Like the butterflies of Monarch Manor, and the Velveteen Rabbit, I had transformed.

Into something Real.

CHAPTER 37

AMELIA

"Is this really good-bye?" Eleanor said as she pulled Amelia tightly to her.

"For now. Just for now," Amelia said.

They stood in the entryway of Eleanor's apartment in New York City, Amelia's trunks scattered around them. John sat on the smallest one, the leather-bound one that held his books and his toys.

Amelia breathed in deeply, inhaling the scent of her sister's lilac perfume, and tried not to think of when she might smell it again. She hadn't slept much the night before and had lain awake next to a sleeping John as she tried to calm her fears about leaving everything she knew behind. There was no other choice; that much she knew. Yet the thought of traveling to a country she'd seen only once before kept her awake as the moon rose high in the sky and then fell back down below the horizon. When she heard the birds outside begin to chirp, it was time to rise and prepare for the long journey ahead.

"And you have all of the papers I gave you, yes?" Eleanor said as she clasped her hands in front of her stomach and pressed them inward.

Amelia nodded. "Of course." Eleanor had arranged for Amelia and John to travel to Ireland via a steamship. It would take them weeks to arrive there, and Eleanor had secretly sold some of her jewelry to pay for the best accommodations available for them. Once Amelia was there, her mother's relatives from Adare would meet them at the dock and help them settle into their new lives. Far away from home. But together, forever.

It had been one week since the wedding, a week since the boat accident. Mary, of course, knew of the plan, but their father did not. Mary thought it was best for Amelia and John to land in Ireland before she told him, because he would have tried to stop her. And it was best to let the Cartwrights believe the story they had concocted.

Jane didn't know the truth, either, but Eleanor also promised she would tell her when the time was right. She had vacillated between happiness at her new marriage and dramatic displays of grief for her sister, another performance that helped the Cartwrights believe that Amelia had drowned.

Eleanor bent down and brushed John's hair from his eyes. She cupped a hand under his chin and let the tears spill down her cheeks before she pulled him close. "Sweet angel," she whispered to herself, and she swayed back and forth in the embrace. When they parted, she looked in his eyes and smiled, tweaking his nose.

He laughed and signed, "More."

Eleanor was about to do it again when there was a knock on the door. She turned her head in surprise and looked at the grandfather clock against the wall. "He's early," she said as she slowly stood.

"Who?" Amelia said. She took a step toward John in alarm, putting a hand on his shoulder.

Eleanor gave her a small smile and then walked toward the large wood and glass front door and opened it herself, her staff still on vacation. And there, on the front step of the apartment, was Matthew.

The early-morning light behind him illuminated his figure, making him look like he emerged from a sunbeam. He stepped inside, and took off his hat, and held it nervously in front of him. He didn't say anything as he looked from Amelia to Eleanor to John.

Amelia's head felt light, and she blinked twice, expecting Matthew's figure to fade away and go back to the past where she had said good-bye. But he stood there, flesh and blood. She took a step toward him and lifted her palms.

"How?" she said.

"I told him," Eleanor said from behind her. "After the accident, he commissioned his own boat to search for you, all night long. He said he would never give up looking for you."

Amelia didn't turn around and took another step toward Matthew. He looked at her, the fear and uncertainty in his eyes reflecting back to her, and she realized he was worried she would reject him. Again.

"I'm sorry, Em," Matthew said. He put his hands to his sides. "I just had to see you. I couldn't imagine you traveling so far away without saying good-bye."

Her hands shaking, she took two more steps until she was right in front of him. She could see her dress vibrating against her chest, her heart ready to explode. She put one hand on his chest, and he slowly covered it with his. He took his other hand and placed it on the small of her back, and drew her near. She closed her eyes and rested against his chest, the first moment of true respite that she had in months.

"He said he would travel anywhere to see you," Eleanor said.

Amelia opened her eyes and smiled, and pulled away from Matthew. "You always did say you wanted to explore the world."

Matthew looked down, still holding her hand. His thumb brushed against the top of her hand. "I still would. Go anywhere, I mean. With you." He looked over her shoulder. "And with John."

She shook her head. "I would never let you. You have choices, a life to live; we don't anymore." She turned and walked over to John and put an arm around his shoulders.

"I've made my choice," he said. Eleanor walked over and handed him a piece of paper. Amelia recognized it as a steamer ticket. He held it in the air. "If you'll have me."

She let her hand drop from John's shoulder and again crossed the foyer over to Matthew. For a moment, she paused. She was prepared to go overseas on her own with John, and it had never crossed her mind that anyone would come with them. It had always been that way: She and John. A team. A unit.

She walked over, stood on her tiptoes, and kissed Matthew, and her entire body woke up as though out of a coma. She wanted more than anything to take him with her, to sail across the ocean and start a life together. But she had done the unthinkable and walked away from her life, and she knew that she would forever feel the pain of that choice and question it every day. She couldn't let him suffer in the same way, not when he still had a chance to do everything he wanted in life.

So she said, "Good-bye, Matthew."

CHAPTER 38

ERIN

"Another year gone. The time flies so fast, doesn't it?" my mother asked as she leaned back in her chair. On my dining room table in front of us were the remnants of the twins' birthday cake, the 6 still barely showing on top. My mother had brought it to my house, strapped to the back of her motorcycle, from a bakery in East Troy. A princess cake, she called it. A Danish dessert of green marzipan, custard, raspberry, and chocolate chips. My father followed behind in their car, just in case the snow got heavy and they would need to ferry the dessert away to safety in the backseat.

I ran a finger through the whipped cream border on the plate, the tiny amount left after Will and Charlotte slashed their fingers across it before we even had a chance to sing "Happy Birthday." "Strange, I guess. Every day is so long, but I don't know how they all add up so quickly. How on earth are they six?"

I craned my neck around the corner of the dining room for a view of the family room, where Luke and my dad sat sleepily staring at the television, with Charlotte and Will bookending them. Charlotte had a new doll on her lap, a present from my parents, and Will held fiercely on to his new Thomas the Train figure. In the big picture window behind the couch, snow lightly fell, adding another couple of inches to the already-tall snowpack on the ground. We had a blizzard two weeks earlier, just after Christmas, and each day Mother Nature had decided to add a few more sprinkles from her snow shaker.

"Oh, kiddo, when you get to be my age, you stop wondering where the time went and start worrying about how you're going to spend what's left of it." My mother ran a hand through her gray hair.

"Speaking of the passage of time, Gerry said the preview party will likely be next month," I said as I tapped the worn wooden table.

"Perfect. Send me the date when you have it. That's going to be the neatest thing, to see all of that in one place," she said.

After we had unraveled the mystery of what happened to Amelia and John, I donated everything to the Geneva Lake Museum, so that Gerry could make a special exhibit on them. Well, I donated almost everything. I kept the antique copy of *The Velveteen Rabbit,* as a reminder that it is the messiest, worn things in life that are truly special.

My mother leaned forward and glanced around my shoulder before she whispered, "I have to tell you, I didn't want to jinx anything, but I can already see a difference in Will."

I glanced back at him, his eyes sleepy from the long day of opening gifts and consuming sugar. The house was still on the market, but we didn't want to wait to enroll him in Lakewood Academy. So we scraped together enough to enroll him for the rest of the year, from liquidating some of Luke's 401(k). He had only been there for about six weeks, but from the first week he already seemed happier. I had texted Traci a picture of him walking into the building on the first day, a hint of a smile on his face, and her response was: *Told you. Go get 'em, Will!*

We continued to measure things according to Will's own scale. Usually, on birthdays he would scream and cry if we tried to sing to him. It resulted in one of us having to console him while everyone else sang to Charlotte. This year, after much prep and help from his new teachers, he sat for the whole song and almost smiled. Twice.

I picked up my phone and swiped to the picture I snapped of the two of them behind the cake, candles blazing, as we sang. It was what I had wanted for so many years, just a photo of them as children on their birthday. Of course, I had one from their first birthday, all chubby arms and cake-covered cheeks, but nothing after that. Until now. It felt as though the missing years of photos represented me, what I missed. How I was lost. And now, finally, I had returned. Once I let go of what I wanted for me, I was able to remember what was really important: Them. Their happiness. Their smiles.

"I see it, too," I said to my mom. I set my phone back down and crossed my arms over my chest. I looked around the dining room, at the popcorn ceiling we never got around to scraping, at the notched molding along the walls. "This time next year, we will be in a new house." I rolled my eyes. "God willing."

My mom leaned forward and put her arms on the table. "Well, that's actually something I wanted to talk to you about." She looked at me, her mouth pressed in a line and her cheeks soft. "Your father and I have decided we want to help you. Help you and Luke. All of you," she said. Her voice broke off at the end and she looked down.

"What do you mean?" I said, and cocked my head to the side. "With money? If so, no way. We aren't taking anything. We will figure it out on our own."

She held her hands up, palms in the air. "Just listen." She put her palms down on the table. "We finally got an offer on Grandma's house in Powers Lake," she said with a smile. "It's for . . . a lot of money. From a builder who wants the lot to build some state-of-the-art smart house on the hill. Anyway, the owners want the privacy of Powers Lake, and hers is one of the biggest lots available. So, they made us an offer we couldn't refuse."

I took a deep breath. "They're going to tear her house down?"

She nodded. "I know. Bummer. But I'm only okay with it if the money goes toward something good, something she would want. And what's more important than what's right here? What's more important than our family?"

"Mom, still. You and Dad should take that money, and buy a condo in Florida with it. Or take a cruise around the world. It's your inheritance," I said. I wrapped my black sweater around my waist and tucked my legs up on the dining room chair, which protested with a squeak.

"It's already been decided. Don't try and talk me out of it. You know it's pointless to argue with me when I've made up my mind. It's just a house, Erin. A house that had a whole lot of junk inside." She chuckled. "But just a house. The stuff we leave behind—just that: stuff. You guys—Luke, Charlotte, Will—are what's important."

"Oh, Mom. I don't know what to say," I said. I put my hands over my face and tried to hold back tears.

"Now stop that," she said. "Or else I'm going to start hoarding stuff of my own that you'll have to clean out after I die. Deal?"

I laughed and dropped my hands from my face. "Deal," I said.

My mom reached her hand across the table, and I shook it. She held on to my hand and smiled. As she did, Will wandered into the dining room and climbed onto my lap. I closed my eyes and listened to the chatter of Charlotte in the next room with Luke and my dad, with Will's humming as the background.

Everything was as it should be. Not perfect by most standards, but by my own.

There wouldn't be any more What Ifs.

Only What Is. Because that was more than enough.

CHAPTER 39

AMELIA

Amelia sat on the grass, the blades sharp beneath her dress, her blue-veined legs in front of her.

She rested a hand on the grass and looked at it. Her hand looked like it belonged to someone else, surprising her with the purple veins and age spots running across the top. "I've earned them," she always said to herself, although it never really made her feel any better. Looking in the mirror made her feel even worse. So instead, she looked ahead. This time, toward the edge of the water, where the grass met the rocks.

At the edge stood John with his wife, Paige. His hair was just as blond as she had always known, but it was flecked with dark streaks of brown. She had only seen one small strand of gray, despite his forty years. They held hands and looked out at the water, their gazes somewhere off in the distance. Occasionally, she saw him drop her hand and sign something; from what she could tell from farther away, it was usually him repeating a story about the lake that she had told him or some memory of growing up on that very grass.

Farther away, with their feet in the water, were his and Paige's children, twins Michael and Maelissa. John and Paige had met back in Adare, and the three of them immigrated to New York City to be with Eleanor and her family ten years prior. But they hadn't been back to Lake Geneva before then.

Amelia looked over her right shoulder, at what was left of Monarch Manor. It had fallen into disrepair in the years since she had last seen it, so many years ago. When Paige pulled the car up the gravel driveway, Amelia had gasped and grabbed the back of the driver's seat. Although she had been warned that it wasn't as she remembered, it was still difficult to see it drooping toward the ground like it was in pain.

She turned her head to the left, toward the gardens of milkweed, still in bloom, and spotted a monarch butterfly flitting along the stems. Still, they remained. Her mother, father, and sisters were long gone, but the butterflies still came. And Matthew, too, was gone.

Six months after she arrived in Ireland, she was in her cottage, peeling carrots at her worn wooden table while John played with his wooden toy horse on his bed. It was January, and a winter wind whipped around the cottage, across the meadows, and through the wood fence that surrounded the property.

The green door blew open, and she had slowly stood before turning and sighing. It was the third time that had happened that morning, and another reminder to fix the latch.

"Amelia," said a voice at the door.

She had frozen in her spot, her hands at her sides. She saw John look up, his eyes wide, before his face broke out into a brilliant smile as he signed back, "Hello."

"Amelia," said the voice again. "Hello?"

She had kept her eyes closed as she turned, afraid to look, afraid that what she believed was, in fact, there. Afraid that the things she had only allowed herself to think about, to wish for, to dream about, had happened. Because if they had happened, if he was really there, she wouldn't be able to say no this time.

Yet Matthew was there, in her cottage, standing in the threshold with the door open behind him, so that the winter sunshine created a blinding outline behind him. His hat was in his hands, and a suitcase was at his feet.

"I had to see you. Your sister told me how to find you," he had said. When she didn't say anything or move at all, he dropped his head. "I've made a mistake. Eleanor was so sure you would be happy to see me."

John had slowly walked forward, the smile still on his face. He stood next to his mother and glanced up at her, a questioning look moving across his face when he saw she didn't hold the same smile. She had put a hand on his shoulder and looked up again at Matthew.

"Why are you here?" she had asked, without realizing how harsh it sounded. She took a step toward him. Her feet felt heavy underneath her, but her head felt light, like she had just woken up from a long night's sleep and stood up too quickly.

She had run toward him and kissed him before he could say another word. Her body fit into his arms like it always had, like two puzzle pieces that were made side by side. When she had slowly opened her eyes and looked into his, she didn't have to ask *why* again. She could see what she always did but never allowed herself to understand: He loved her. More than anything else. More than traveling, more than the future. And she loved him the same.

He had held an arm out and pulled John into their embrace, the final missing piece.

She had closed her eyes and rested her head on his chest, one arm around him, one arm around John, and felt as though she had been brought back to life, like the first signs of spring after a long, harsh winter.

She held him and didn't let go until his final moments years later, when she held his hand as he drifted away.

Once, she had a choice. Only it wasn't really a choice, because John was everything.

And as she watched him and his wife walk along the shore of the lake she loved as a child, with their children splashing their feet in the same water, she could see Monarch Manor in its glory, and everything that it held, and she knew that her past and future finally fit together like two hands clasped in prayer.

She was home.

AUTHOR'S NOTE

From the moment I began writing *Monarch Manor*, I knew the book would be different. The dual narrators, historical setting, and family mystery were all new story elements for me, but the largest difference is how many personal connections I have to the story. The most significant of which is that, like Erin and Amelia, I have a child with special needs. I identified with their emotional journeys and wanted to explore the enormous amount of choices that mothers are faced with and the varied opportunities for sacrifice: physical, emotional, mental. Yet, sacrifices aside, I most importantly wanted to write about the beauty in parenting a child with special needs, and the gift of the way it changes a family—for the better.

In my previous book, *Cicada Summer*, I wrote about a woman who loves old houses, and that is also a passion of mine, as seen through Erin's love for her own house and Amelia's attachment to Monarch Manor. I've always been fascinated with the idea that every person who lives in a house leaves a piece of themselves behind—the true magic of a home. I've also always been interested in the historical era of Lake Geneva, with all of the storied estates and glamorous parties. I took a tour of Black Point Estate on the lake, a preserved treasure from a bygone era, and gleaned a lot of inspiration from my time there. It was such a delight to hear about the drama of the wealthy families, intermingling and intermarrying, with huge family complexes on the lakefront. To this day, when I am out on the lake I can almost see the white tablecloths on the lawn, and glasses of champagne next to fine china.

In addition to Lake Geneva, another place in the book that is special to me is Amelia's adopted home of Adare Village in Ireland. A few years ago, I was fortunate enough to travel there, and from the moment I stepped foot on the cobblestone streets and laid eyes on the thatched-roof shops I fell in love. And once I saw the incomparable Adare Manor, I was sold. I felt an undercurrent of magic when I was there, and I knew I wanted to have it make a cameo in my writing. When it came time to choose where Amelia would make her new home, there was no question that it would be Adare Village.

Monarch Manor is peppered with many personal connections, and writing about each of them truly brought together many things that I love. It is my tribute to the special places and people that I hold close to my heart, and I feel so fortunate to share it with readers.

ACKNOWLEDGMENTS

Monarch Manor is a book that evolved throughout the years, both on the page and in my head, before coming to this final incarnation. And for that, I have many people to thank. First and foremost, to my agent, Holly Root, who never once told me to stop rewriting this story over and over. (And over and over.) To my editor, Esi, who understood exactly what I was trying to do, and pushed me to take the book to the next level. A huge thank-you to everyone over at Kensington, who astound me daily with their hard work and dedication to the book.

A big thank-you to everyone at Black Point Estate in Lake Geneva, for all of the information and inspiration. There are pieces of the estate and the stories I heard sprinkled throughout the book, and into the very foundation of Monarch Manor. And also to Mary Burns Gage and Ann Wolfmeyer, authors of *Lake Geneva: Newport of the West*, which was an invaluable resource while I was researching the history of the estates around Lake Geneva.

To everyone who e-mailed or contacted me after the publication of *Cicada Summer:* It truly made my day every time I heard from each and every one of you. Lake Geneva and the surrounding area hold a very special place in my heart, and it was wonderful to know that so many others feel the same way.

To the Kilmer-Lipinski crew: Thank you for always making me laugh, and especially for always forcing me to watch terrible movies. (The year 2018 was truly the year of *Birdemic*.) And to the Leurck family, for all of your support and love throughout the years. To my friends, both old and new (Wheaton tribe represent!): Thank you for all of the offers of child care, words of encouragement, and for showing up every time I needed you guys, without question and usually with a glass of wine. And I would be remiss if I didn't mention Jill Cantor, author friend extraordinaire and fabulous writer—I'm sorry for all the neurotic e-mails!

And finally, to Kevin, Ryan, Paige, and Jake: Thank you for being the reason I do everything, and for always reminding me that the best is yet to come.

MONARCH MANOR

Maureen Leurck

ABOUT THIS GUIDE

The suggested questions are included to enhance
your group's reading of Maureen Leurck's
Monarch Manor.

DISCUSSION QUESTIONS

1. A major theme in the book explores the sacrifices (emotional, physical, financial) that parents make for their children. Who do you feel had to give up more in her journey, Erin or Amelia?

2. How would you describe Erin and Luke's marriage? How does it change by the end of the book?

3. Throughout her life, Amelia was unable to let go of her feelings for Matthew. Do you think she made the right decision in pushing him away throughout the story, or should she have accepted the relationship sooner?

4. What does Monarch Manor symbolize and represent in the story?

5. Who did you connect with more in the story, Erin or Amelia? Why?

6. How do Will's needs affect and change the way that Erin parents Charlotte? In what ways do these needs affect Erin's relationship with Luke? How do John's challenges affect the way that Amelia sees the world? In what ways does it affect her relationships?

7. Do you feel that Erin and Luke made the right decision in sending Will to a therapeutic school?

8. How does Erin's relationship with Traci affect her thoughts on Will's future?

9. Amelia has a very strong connection to Monarch Manor. How does this affect her decisions and plans for the future?

10. Erin and Amelia both have complicated relationships with their parents. In what ways are their relationships similar? In what ways are they different?

11. Throughout the book, Erin comes to terms with the idea that what she wants for Will might not be what's best for Will. Have you ever had to let go of an expectation for your or someone else's future?